THE FREAK SHOW CASE
A Pegasus Investigations Mystery

Brian D. Eyre
Lezlie K. King

Swinging Cats and Blinking Hats Press
Dallas, Texas

This is a work of fiction. All of the characters, organizations, and events portrayed in this novel are either products of the authors' imaginations or are used fictitiously.

THE FREAK SHOW CASE: A Pegasus Investigation Mystery

Swinging Cats and Blinking Hats Press
www.swingingcatsandblinkinghats.com

Prologue

It's hard to love somebody who totally doesn't love you. It's even harder to love somebody who loves you totally. The pretty young lady sprawled out on the hardwood floor has spent most of her life thinking about love and learning this.

For years, she's thought about how much she loves her family. They don't always make it easy, but she loves them always. They always love her, even when she's not easy to love.

For months, she's thought about how much she and her boyfriend love each other. She would do anything for him, and she knows he would do anything for her.

For weeks, she's thought about how much they love their baby. She wishes their loved ones could be happy for them. They're young, but life's too short to wait forever for what you want.

For days, she's thought about how badly she misses him when he's away, and how glad she'll be once they get married and never have to be apart. She even loves missing him a little bit, because she knows he misses her just as much.

For hours, she's thought about what to wear tonight. She loves choosing outfits to dress to impress. She's already impressed the one man she wants to impress, but she enjoys the process too much now to skip it.

For minutes, she's thought about why she's so tired. The thought that she's been drugged never crosses her mind. When her head hits the hardwood floor, she wakes up realizing that she has been drugged.

For seconds, she thinks she should make somebody pay for doing this to her. She never gets the chance, but she's right.

Somebody should most definitely pay for doing this to her!

01   Old Acquaintance

"Hey, Lance Armstrong, aren't you going to greet an old friend?"

"I don't have any friends who call me Lance Armstrong." I answered before I turned around to look at the homeless looking guy at the bottom of the stairs leading to my office. I hadn't even glanced at him as I passed. It's not that I'm not affected by the problems of the homeless; it's just that I'm barely keeping Pegasus Investigations afloat with the help of part-time work as a bicycle courier. I can't afford to help every homeless person I see in downtown Dallas.

When I finally looked at him, I recognized him as a local 'entertainer' who actually helped me solve a missing person case a few years ago. I also remembered how reluctantly he helped me. On most people, his spiked black and yellow hair would have drawn notice.

However, the piercings in his ears, nose, tongue, and around his eyes rendered the hair almost unnoticeable. Additionally, the black long-sleeved spider web design shirt ripped open to reveal his left nipple also drew more notice. It also drew attention to the nipple ring with a handcuff key dangling from it. I'm no expert on handcuff keys, but it appeared to be genuine police issue.

He followed me up the stairs, and I wordlessly opened the door and nodded for him to follow me in. When we were seated, I said, "Why are you, of all people, hanging around outside my office? Hoping to take another swing, thinking you've gotten faster?'

"No, Dude, it's not like that at all. I thought we got all that worked out. I mean, Hell, you found the chick, sent her home to momma, got paid and all that, right? It's not like I did anything wrong in any of that."

"Maybe not, Freak, but she was 17."

"Hey, it's not like she was wearing a 'Hey I'm underage' badge when she came on to me. Hell, if it hadn't been for her wanting to dedicate her life to me, you might have never found her, no telling where she might have ended up."

1

"Okay, so now you're going to change your name to Mother Theresa. Why are you sitting in my office?"

He stood up quickly, and for a moment, I thought he might try his right hook again. I doubted it, but just in case, I also stood up. At 6'9", I had a half a foot on him, but he probably didn't weigh much less than my 210.

It didn't matter since I already knew he had one of the slowest punches in Dallas. We looked at each for a few minutes, before he finally sat back down. As I sat down, he spoke. "I need help, Man."

"I think we've both known that for some time, but I just do investigations. The Parkland psych ward is over on Harry Hines."

"Okay, I see now why you live in this rat hole. If that's how you treat customers, I don't see how you even afford this joint."

I didn't know what to say to that, so I said nothing. I'd learned a long time ago that not saying anything is usually a good idea. While I said nothing, I thought about the office he'd just insulted. Maybe it didn't compare favorably to his place, but I like it.

It's conveniently located on the second floor of a two story building just on the southeastern edge of downtown Dallas. That puts it within walking distance of almost everything a busy private investigator would need.

From here, I can walk to City Hall, the Jack Evans Police Headquarters Building, the Dallas County Sheriff's department, most of the associated jail facilities and the central public library. Most importantly, I can easily walk to Stefan's sandwich shop.

Stefan is a nice old man who generally lets me have a sandwich and a bag of chips on a promise to pay when I can. His only stipulation is that I don't ask when he's busy. Since Stefan quit having busy times before the Cowboys left the Cotton Bowl for Texas Stadium three decades ago, this works well for me.

—

2

Also, since the office is on the second floor, the homeless people that can be found in any downtown area generally aren't much of a bother. I guess the same bad fortune or lack of ambition that causes them to be homeless also tends to keep them attached to the street or the ground floor of buildings.

So, all in all, I hoped the city wouldn't decide to put a park here and force me to relocate again anytime soon. Whoever decided that downtown areas need to have parks on every corner should be prosecuted to the fullest extent of the law.

What downtown areas need are thriving businesses. Forcing a business to move in order to accommodate a park can't be the best way to accomplish this. But since Dallas has been doing this for at least four decades now, I doubt it will stop until all that's left around here are skyscrapers, parking lots and parks.

In addition to being in a great location, the office's layout is also perfect for me. It's large enough that I can live and work out of one location and small enough that I can afford it. There's no way I could afford any of its special features, but fortunately those had been paid for before I got there.

The previous tenant was a commodities importer named Salvatore Perlini who made several changes to the place before leaving town, and most likely the country. I know more about Mr. Perlini than I care to know mostly because Federal agents representing four different agencies have inquired about him and the office. It's a little scary how chatty some people in the Department of Homeland Security can be.

Regardless, I can't complain about living and working in a place that's been converted into a virtual fortress. The windows on the north and west walls are all bulletproof glass. The south and east walls don't have windows. Even the interior doors are bulletproof steel doors similar to those used in banks.

The small waiting room at the entrance has a built-in bench and table that are both indestructible and impossible to steal. This allows me to leave the door unlocked for clients when I'm out, while my worldly possessions, such as they are, stay safe. The only loose items in the waiting room are framed copies of my license and the certificate of occupancy. Nobody has ever tried to steal either one.

My favorite feature is the window which covers most of the wall separating the waiting room from the main office. Like the others, it is bulletproof. It is also one-way see-through and impossible to detect from the waiting area. On the side in the office, there's a sliding panel.

The panel is controlled by a remote control that I keep locked in my desk drawer. In addition to hiding the window, it adds a touch of class to the place, since it looks like a large and expensive framed painting. Technically, it is an expensive work of art.

I'm not sure exactly what commodities Perlini imported when he was here. I am sure that anybody who spends the money he spent converting a 600 square foot office in this part of Dallas should be investigated by every law enforcement agency in the country.

I'm glad he converted the place into the perfect office for a busy private investigator. I'm also glad a friend of mine knows the landlord and convinced her to let me take it 'as is' instead of undoing the conversions. I just wish I knew how to become a busy private investigator.

Thinking about the office's security reminded me that I was sitting opposite the type of person an office might need protection from. I thought about asking him to leave, but decided against it. If he thought about saying anything, it didn't show in his passive expression. It took me years to master the art of silent negotiation, and this kid came by it naturally.

Either that or he was just too stoned to speak. I'd been his age once, but I'd never been too stoned to speak. When I was his age, Pegasus Investigations was a thriving enterprise. Back then, I was just a tall, skinny kid working as a downtown bicycle courier. Then the old man who ran the agency took me under his wing and taught me how to use my eyes and my ears when out on my bike to learn things he needed to know.

He also paid me, which was nice. After helping him out on a handful of cases, he offered to hire me full time. Since I figured being a private investigator would be almost as glamorous as riding a bike for a living and might allow me to spend more time in the air conditioning, I gladly accepted. That was almost two decades and at least four moves ago, and the old man retired after the first move and left it all to me.

Now, Pegasus Investigations is a sole proprietorship with no employees, and the bike couriers make more every day than I make on my best day, so I don't often pay them to help me. Fortunately, I still get some work on the bike, which helps me pay Stefan back occasionally.

Riding the bike also helps when I do have investigating to do, since that's how I learned the trade in the first place. Even in this paranoid, post 9/11 culture, companies that wouldn't let the Queen of England loiter outside their office, will let a bike courier waltz around like a principal through a high school and not think twice. Since most bike couriers are less dangerous and look better than the queen, that's probably not a bad policy.

The first thing the old man taught me about running the business was that no matter how small-time I might be, it's important not to look small-time. It's not easy to make a three room loft look like a big time office, but I did the best I could.

The main room is set up to look like a reception area complete with a desk and two client chairs. It also has a conference table and a little kitchenette, which wouldn't look out of place in the reception area of any major detective agency.

Since mine isn't a major agency, the two doors behind my desk don't actually lead to a labyrinth of offices. One leads to my bedroom and one leads to a second bedroom which I use as a living room.

However, from the client chairs, each one appears to lead to an office. I also put one of those unisex restroom signs with the pitiful

—

silhouette of both a girl and a boy on the bathroom door. If that doesn't look big-time, I don't know what would.

In the waiting area, I'd hung the plaque the old man gave me when he retired. I've brought it to the new office each time I've had to move. It's solid brass and reads:

Pegasus Investigations

Est. 1959

Carlisle Jennings, Proprietor

Nobody calls me Carlisle, but it is my name, so I guess it belongs on the plaque. Shortly before I was born, my parents sat in the Cotton Bowl and watched Duke Carlisle lead the Longhorns to the national championship by beating Roger Staubach's Navy team. Dad wanted to name me Duke, but Mom did not! They compromised; I became Carlisle.

As soon as I was old enough to tell people what to call me, I shortened it to Carl. If I'd been born ten years later, Dad probably would have named his only son after Roger Staubach and I'd have a normal first name. I don't guess it matters, though. Nobody calls me Carl, either.

The way things were going, I doubted I would need the plaque much longer. Soon, I'd either have to go back to riding the bike full time or find a real job. My girlfriend, Emily, loves the fact that I run a detective agency, but eventually she'll be less excited than she is disappointed that it doesn't turn a profit. For that matter, I probably will, too.

Finally, my guest broke the silence. "If I promise to quit calling you Lance Armstrong, will you take my case? You should, you know. I do have the money to pay you. Besides, you're the one person I can trust."

Career advice from a kid who makes his living sticking needles through himself onstage, I can generally do without. However, I knew from our previous encounters that he made more money in one run with his 'Absolutely Incredible Completely Unbelievable Freak Show and Burlesque Revue' than I typically make in a month.

—

6

With that thought in mind, I asked, "What do you need help with?"

"I can't find a girl."

"You mean suddenly there's a shortage of girls who are turned on by guys with needles sticking through every extremity?"

"No, Dude, there's always plenty of chicks that dig that. I mean I can't find a certain girl. You know, a missing person, your specialty. I mean, unless you've decided not to be Sherlock Holmes and gone back to riding the bike all the time to make a living."

As I thought about an appropriate comeback to his second attempt to insult me because I ride a bike more profitably than I run a detective agency, it occurred to me that the best way not to go back to riding the bike full time, was to accept a client who got on my nerves every time I talked to him and investigate his problem like detectives do.

I decided to give it a try. Of course, I didn't know at the time that taking the case would lead directly to me no longer needing the plaque the old man gave me. "My friends don't call me Sherlock Holmes, either, Freak, but tell me about the girl."

Calling the potential client 'Freak' wouldn't negatively impact our business relationship. It was, in fact, a way to make it a contractually legal client discussion, since Freak Show is, or anyway was, his documented legal name. For the next hour and a half, I pumped Freak for information. He gave me an amazing amount of information about the missing girl.

He described her as 5'7", with hair that was blue the night they met, but was naturally brown. She also wore it blonde, auburn, pink, green or any combination that suited her mood. He said she had hazel eyes, but would occasionally wear designer contacts to change their color to go better with her hair or outfit.

He knew her shoe size, 6 or 6½, depending on the height of the heel, and the style and brand of the shoe. He talked about her favorite bands, Toadies and Big Head Todd. He also told me what he thought of her choice of bands. He said her favorite hangouts were The Gypsy Tea Room,

7

Darkside Lounge, Club Dada and Reno's. He liked her favorite hangouts much better than her favorite bands.

She usually hung out somewhere in Deep Ellum four to six nights a week, sometimes as late as 4 a.m., more often until around two, but she always left before midnight on Saturdays. She went to church every Sunday and didn't want to oversleep.

He told me more things about the missing girl than I know about Emily. He also gave me two pictures he said were of her even though they didn't even look like the same girl.

The girl in one picture wore Goth makeup, with jet black hair and a black choker. She looked like she either was playing a role in a theatre production of Beetle Juice or was planning on joining a cult. Even though it was a color picture, it looked more like a mug shot than a snapshot.

The other picture showed a girl with pink hair with bright blue streaks that made it appropriate for Deep Ellum or being in a performance of The Rocky Horror Picture Show. However, the blissful, yet reserved smile in the second picture looked like a prep school yearbook picture.

Freak swore that both pictures were the same girl, but the only similarity I saw was a necklace with a heart-shaped pendant wrapped around the chain. Before he left, he told me the last time he had seen her was at Reno's in late May, just before he took his act to Vegas.

I felt like my client had given me enough information to accept the case. I wasn't thrilled about the idea of working another case in Deep Ellum, nor was I excited about working for this client. However, I needed to work to make a living, and it seemed like the type of case I could solve.

Although Freak seemed reserved at first, he eventually gave me the most detailed information I've ever received when starting a missing person case. There was one thing about her that he didn't tell me. He either didn't know - or just wouldn't tell me - her name.

02   New Case

After he left, I reflected on the situation. I had a case, not just a case, but a case I might be able to solve. Freak may have been trying to insult me, but the truth is that missing person's cases have been my specialty for quite some time now.

The case that Freak helped me solve may have been my most lucrative case. After all, rich suburban parents are usually generous when their prodigal daughters are returned to the fold. However, my track record for finding missing persons of all types has been pretty good.

I don't know the business plan for all detective agencies, but for me the best plan is to get simple cases that can be solved and solve them simply. Regardless of what the journalists at the Dallas Observer or the muckrakers at the Morning News might want you to believe, most crimes are solved by the law enforcement officers that the taxpayers' money keeps employed.

They have both the skills and the resources to solve most cases. My niche in life is to help people with problems that don't fit this category. This is not to imply that the police don't search for missing persons; it's just that sometimes having one private detective looking for a specific missing person can help where the understaffed missing persons departments can't.

Of course, my spiel on why a potential client should hire me wasn't needed now. The client had already hired me and left a generous cash retainer for my services.

I guess I went over the spiel to convince myself that I should earn the cash money that my undeniably strange client had left me. I had a hard time convincing myself that a girl Freak couldn't find and wouldn't name was really a missing person, but I finally decided that a case is a case and a client is a client.

Missing person cases generally end up falling into one of two categories. Some missing persons are crime victims; some are runaways.

Both types can be of any age. Finding runaways is easiest if you can empathize a little. We tend to think of kids when we think of runaways, but adults of all types have also been known to run away.

The concept of the 'runaway bride' is not just the source for bad movies that Emily and I can waste time watching. It is something that really happens. For adults or children, the trick to finding a runaway is to understand enough about what they were running away from to predict where they might have gone.

Freak had assured me that the missing girl I was seeking was an adult. Of course, since he had a history of not completely grasping the concept of adult, I was keeping an open mind regarding the subject of how old a girl I was seeking.

I decided that before I started searching for a runaway girl with no name, whose age was uncertain, and whose hair color would change with her mood, it might be a good idea to make sure I was looking for a girl who was missing, waiting to be found and not a girl who was dead, waiting to be identified. So I decided that tomorrow morning, I should go talk with my friend at the county sheriff's department.

Since I didn't really have a plan, I didn't set my alarm, so it was just after 10 am when I left my office and started walking. It was a pleasant morning, which in June in Dallas means it wasn't quite 100 degrees, and the walk gave me time to think about how to approach the case.

It also sent me under twenty-nine sets of banners touting the local teams' trips to the playoffs. Since the Stars had flamed out early, and the Mavericks had just finished a disastrous collapse in the Finals by losing game six, 95-92, I would have gladly pulled them all down personally.

On the way, I stopped in and used some of the retainer to settle my account with Stefan, who was so happy to have a reason to open his cash register that he insisted on giving me a sandwich on the house. I didn't normally eat that early, but it would have been rude to refuse.

——

10

I still had no idea how to go about finding a nameless missing person, but I had a full stomach which proved beneficial as I waited to talk to my friend. Although I know and am known by many law officers, both with the city and the county, only a few of them do I truly call friends. Blake Harrison is one of the best.

The Sheriff's department doesn't officially have a missing person's department, but Blake was promoted a few years ago from Juvenile to a position that would be head of missing persons if such a position existed. This had happened because he had demonstrated his ability to find missing people.

It also helped that the County Commissioner's Court had realized that missing people, especially kids, from suburbs that weren't within Dallas city limits and thus in the Dallas Police Department's jurisdiction often turned up in the downtown Dallas area. It was obviously better for public relations and tourism in the area, if the missing people turned up alive.

I've known Blake for years. A few years ago, I filled in on his hoop-it-up team for Dallas' annual three on three basketball tournament, and we had finished a very respectable 5th in the open division. He played guard for the Southern University team that upset Georgia Tech in the '93 tourney, and he still had the stroke, if not the hops.

I, on the other hand, played one year at a local junior college before realizing that I wasn't particularly good at basketball or college. My height somewhat makes up for my nearly total lack of basketball skills.

More recently, Blake's promotion a few years ago and my contribution to it has definitely served to strengthen our bond. We cooperated on a case which resulted in the rescue of a ten-year old boy, whose recently paroled father had kidnapped him.

We found the boy at a crack house in Cedar Hill and got the boy out without incident. Well, I did get shot, but other than that, it was mostly without incident. We returned the boy to his mother in Richardson who was my client. I got paid; Blake got promoted. As they say in the movies, it was the beginning of a beautiful friendship.

Most of the Sheriff's Department offices are at Lew Sterrett, but for some reason, Blake's isn't. He is now in an office on the fifth floor of the new wing of the George L. Allen, Senior Courts Building at Commerce and Houston Street on the western edge of the downtown area.

His office comes with a nice view of the JFK Memorial which is little more than another park with a small monument in it. He also has a staff which consists of an administrative assistant and two investigators.

I arrived at his office at 11:35, expecting him to be available as he usually is around that time. His administrative assistant, Ana Marie, told me to expect a long wait or come back later, but I had already made the trek, so I decided to just wait until he could see me.

I waited for a couple of hours, thinking how glad I was that Stefan had given me the sandwich. Finally, Blake came out and ushered me into his office asking, "How much money do you need to borrow?"

I couldn't believe the question, so I just stared at him, waiting for an explanation. Eventually it came.

"I've known you more than 10 years; I've never seen you wait more than 30 minutes for anything. When Ana Marie told me you'd been in the lobby for over two hours, I assumed you needed money."

Since we're friends, I let that assumption slide, and explained that I was working and wanted to chat about my case. However, I did wonder why I had waited for hours to get help on a case I didn't care about.

What I wanted to know was if any recent crime victims met the description of my missing person. In the process, I didn't want to admit that I was working for a client who had not supplied me with the name of the missing person, or for that matter that I was working for one of Deep Ellum's less respectable entertainers.

While there aren't any specific laws against going onstage and sticking needles in yourself for a living, it isn't the type of occupation the

12

sheriff's department generally endorses. As I was thinking about that, another thought occurred to me, "What's the big idea behind making me wait three hours anyway? I thought we were friends."

"Not my fault, my friend. Everybody and all their brothers have their panties in a wad over that suburban mayor's missing daughter. I spent the last four hours getting reamed because he called everybody on the County Commissioner's court complaining that our department is not providing them with adequate assistance."

"Are you?"

"What! Now you want to start in on me?"

"Not me, I'm just making conversation."

"Well, conversation is another thing I don't have time for. I have three people on this staff and forty cases in progress. We're trying to help them, but what the hell do they expect? Let's talk about your case."

"I'm searching for a missing girl who used to be a Deep Ellum regular, but hasn't been seen since the end of May. My client insists on confidentiality, so I can't give you names. My assumption is she's just playing games, but I'd like to make sure she's not in the morgue with a Jane Doe toe tag, before I start searching Deep Ellum for her."

I didn't much like misleading Blake, but I didn't technically lie to him. If he chose to assume that my client had confided in me; that was a reasonable assumption, but not a certainty. Having known me as long as he has, he should know by now that I don't always attract that type of client.

"So you're searching for a girl that you hope is playing a game by running away from the Deep Ellum scene? That's a twist. We've both found kids in Deep Ellum that ran away from their suburban parents, but you are trying to find a girl who disappeared from Deep Ellum, and I wouldn't bet much on your chances."

"I wouldn't either, Blake."

"But I wouldn't bet against you either. You've shown me in the past that you can get information from those Deep Ellum lunatics that I could never unearth, so maybe you have a chance. I'd offer to help, but I've got my hands full here."

He then tried to get me to share the name of my client or the missing girl. For obvious reasons, I chose to be stubborn on both subjects, but I admired the professionalism of his repeated and varied attempts.

Finally, he sighed, and looked at his watch, "It's almost 4 o'clock; I've got to go to a meeting with the District Attorney that will take at least an hour. Why don't you lock up behind me, and I'll meet you for a beer over at Walt's around 5:30. Just don't let me find out that you used my computer while you were in here."

I just grinned as he hustled out the door. We both knew that he didn't technically tell me not to use his computer; he just wanted it on record that he didn't authorize me to do so.

Since he had let me know he wouldn't mind if I used his PC to search the Sheriff's Department database, he must have been really floored by the fact that I waited so long. Either that or he was really preoccupied by the pressure on him to focus on his case.

After he left, I locked the door and made myself comfortable in his ergonomically designed chair and went to work. I placed both pictures of the missing girl on the board he kept by his desk for that purpose.

He placed pictures of the missing persons on the cases he was working on it to make sure he never forgot that his job was to find people, not close cases for the Sheriff's department. He had explained the board's purpose to me years ago.

Now, I had a board just like it back at my office. It wasn't the only great idea I had borrowed from him. I found room for my pictures on the board between two other pictures and went to work.

He had a Dell Latitude laptop that put the computer at my office to shame. He also had pretty much every peripheral and accessory that could ever be needed.

It certainly made obvious one advantage of 'working for the man' instead of being an independent investigator. Most of this setup hadn't been here the last time that Blake had allowed me to use his system.

My plan was to check the morgue database for anybody whose description matched the girl I was seeking. Typically, searching the morgue files for a missing girl is a pretty straight-forward process. Just enter the missing person's name and any known aliases, then if you don't get a match, you compare her description and pictures to the descriptions and pictures of any Jane Doe.

Of course, in this case, my search would not be limited to Jane Doe; since I had a Jane Doe of my own that I was seeking. I had just opened up the database to start my search, when I heard the door lock turning and looked up and saw Ana Marie open the door and walk in.

"Does Blake know you're using his computer?" The way she asked it, it was obvious that she had already formed an opinion.

I didn't want her to throw me out, but I didn't want to throw Blake under the proverbial bus, either. Blake's wife, Jade, had told me that she was sure Ana Marie had a crush on her husband, and it was somewhat obvious to everybody but Blake. Still, she is a county employee, so I answered evasively, "He knows I'm here."

That satisfied her. If Blake knew I was there, then it had to be okay for me to be there. In her eyes, Blake could do no wrong. Any friend of Blake's is a friend of hers; any enemy of Blake's is in big trouble because she is fiercely loyal and as feisty as she needs to be.

I wasn't there when it allegedly happened, but according to local legend, she once tossed one of Dallas' most famous and infamous County Commissioners out of their office. She then told him to never come back without her express permission, simply because he made a rude comment about Blake while in the waiting area.

The commissioner had tried (and failed) to get them both fired. According to the legend, he hasn't set foot in this building since.

She had walked into the office far enough to see what I was doing on the computer and saw that I had the morgue database open, "So, who are we looking for?"

With me sitting in Blake's chair and her standing, we were almost eye to eye. I pointed at the pictures I had added to the post-it board, and she studied them intently before asking, "Are they related?"

"What?'

"The girls you're looking for, are they related? They're so different, but it looks like they could be sisters. They have the same high cheekbones, and both have perfect teeth."

"Actually, it's the same girl, I think."

Her brown eyes squinted and her forehead wrinkled a little as she looked past me at the pictures. "I guess it could be. It wouldn't be that hard to be sure." She hesitated a few seconds before she continued.

"Our computers have become a lot more sophisticated since the last time Blake risked his career by letting you use his computer. I hope you understand and appreciate the chances that man takes to help you out."

I did and I did, so I didn't say a word as she ushered me out of Blake's chair and took over the search. First she took the pictures off the post-it board and scanned them into the system.

After she scanned each one, she placed it back on the board where it had been. I tried to follow what she was doing, but apparently, both she and the computer were faster than I am. I hate people staring over my shoulder when I work on a computer, so I didn't. Instead I just paced.

Pacing contributes very little to the solving of cases, but I have a great deal of practice at it, and it does help pass the time. I was still pacing, not pacing urgently, when Ana Marie called me over, "Come look at this."

I went over and looked at the computer where the two pictures were displayed side by side above a tool bar of icons that I knew nothing about. "Okay, you scanned in the pictures, what am I looking for?"

She clicked on one of the icons, and the picture on the left began to change. It only took about 45 seconds for it to morph into an exact replica of the picture on the right. Then she clicked another icon and the picture snapped back to its original form.

"Now, watch this," she said sounding not unlike a child trying to make sure her parents see her first high dive into a swimming pool. I watched as she cropped both images, so that only the face was visible.

This left two faces on the screen, not showing the black hair or the blue and pink hair, not showing the choker or even the identical necklaces. When the images were reduced to just faces, she clicked on the same icon she had used earlier to morph the image. It took about two seconds for the images to match completely, and when she snapped it back, it was obvious that the pictures were of the same girl.

Ana Marie pointed out a dialog box at the bottom of the screen that read 98%, "That's the chance these two pictures are of the same person. Anything higher than 85% is considered worthy of further investigation. When we first got the software, we all scanned in lots of pictures of ourselves and other people we knew. None of us had two pictures that rated higher than 96%. You are looking for only one girl."

"Well, thanks for confirming about the only thing I already knew about my case."

"What's her name?"

It was a logical question, and I was tired of deceiving people who were going out of their way to help me. "I don't know, and I don't think my client knows either. Can you show me how to use that program?"

She looked at me sadly for several seconds; then shook her head, "Only you, Amigo, only you."

The comment didn't seem to need a response, so I just pointed to the computer screen. She spent about fifteen minutes showing me how to use the new software. As soon as she decided I had grasped the basic concepts, she left without another word. After that, it took another forty-five minutes for me to compare my missing girl with every girl in the morgue database who had died in the last month.

There were forty-seven young girls who had died in that period, only seventeen of whom even remotely matched the description of my Jane Doe. Of those, only two were even rated as at least an eighty percent match. Neither girl seemed to fit the profile of the girl I was seeking, but I printed a few pictures of each to show to Freak, just in case.

I hated using photo paper and ink that was paid for by taxpayers on my case, but I couldn't exactly write a check to the County to reimburse it. Instead, I just decided to buy Blake's beer at Walt's. That really wouldn't reimburse the county, but it might ease my conscience a little.

I now felt certain the girl I was seeking wasn't currently in the morgue database. I knew all too well, though, that this didn't mean she was still alive. Still, it made me feel much better. I felt better, but I was also tired of being in Blake's office, tired of staring at a computer screen, and very ready for a beer and a chance to relax and talk with Blake.

I decided to wait for another day to check out the needle in a haystack hope that I could match an unnamed missing person with an actual missing person with a name. Plus, I still held out hope that with the pictures I had of the girl, I might be able to get her name using old time pavement pounding, instead of technology. With that decided, I gathered up all the pictures, locked up Blake's office and headed over to Walt Garrison's Rodeo Bar.

03   Rodeo Bar

Blake always refers to Walt Garrison's Rodeo Bar as Walt's. I've never heard anybody else call it that. My guess is that he does it because even though he grew up in New Orleans, he's always been a huge Dallas Cowboys' fan. He apparently believes that being on a first name basis with one of the team's early icons somehow connects him more closely with his beloved football team. Somehow, I don't think it really does, but to each his own.

I was on a first name basis with former Cowboy Everson 'Cubby' Walls before he walked on at Grambling State. Sure, Walt won more Super Bowls with the Pokes than Everson did, but Cubby went to more pro bowls. Maybe if Joe Montana's attempted throwaway had cleared Dwight Clark's fingertips, I'd feel more connected, but I doubt it.

Legend has it that in the 70's, Cowboys president Tex Schramm used to underpay players and tell them they could make it up later in life by trading in on their association with the team. I don't know if that's true or not, but many former players have indeed made good money by doing so. Walt Garrison doesn't seem to be one of them.

In fact, if you didn't know that he was a former player, you wouldn't figure it out from the décor. The walls are adorned with hundreds of photos of real rodeo cowboys, as well as wagon wheels of varying sizes and more cow skulls than I care to count. There is also a life size wooden Indian at the front door, and a few smaller ones scattered about.

In short, the place is touristy in a stereotypical fashion that would be insulting if wasn't obvious that the love of the rodeo and the old west was real. It is actually the guest bar and lounge for the Hotel Adolphus, so it can be excused for being touristy.

One thing Blake definitely likes about it is that it is not on the list of places that county employees frequent. That makes it a reasonably safe place to discuss business without worrying that one evening's discussion will become the next morning's gossip.

When I passed through the revolving door entrance, I saw Blake sitting at his usual table in the corner under the television. That table has a great view of the entire bar, as well as the pedestrian traffic on Commerce and Akard Streets and the Starbucks across the street in the Magnolia Hotel.

When the bar isn't busy, April, the bartender, also waits on tables. Blake motioned her over as I was approaching the table. He had been there long enough to already have a good start on a Michelob Ultra. I sat down and ordered a Shiner, and Blake signaled for another.

April is a vivacious, svelte blonde with the high cheekbones that typically grace magazine covers. She almost certainly would have been a fashion model if she were 5'9", instead of 5'6". She knows she looks like a model, but she thinks she should be a detective.

She may be right; she hears and remembers everything that goes on at the Rodeo Bar, and has helped Blake and me both on previous investigations. Sometimes I forget how exciting working on a case seems when you're not really a detective.

For me, it's just a way to make a living, or at least try to make one. That makes it easy to forget how much I loved this stuff when I was a bike courier full-time. Maybe one day, April will be a full-time detective and miss how much fun it had seemed when she was a bartender.

Blake and I admired April in silence as she went back behind the bar to get our beer. I was still discreetly enjoying the view, when Blake spoke, "You do take on the challenging cases, don't you?"

"Well, if they aren't challenging, you guys in the Sheriff's department or someone at DPD usually has them solved before I get a chance at them. Besides, I do like to have enough money to eat every day and take Emily some place nice occasionally."

"Maybe so, but our clients always tell us the name of the person we are looking for before we start the search."

I wasn't surprised that Ana Marie had told Blake that I didn't know the name of the girl I was seeking. I was, however, impressed with how quickly she had let him know. It didn't matter much. Like I said, I had grown tired of deceiving my friends almost as soon as I had first started.

That might explain why I'm not rich. Still, I had to say something, "True, but at least my clients don't make me spend all day in meetings explaining why I haven't solved the case. I get the impression that your 'client' would rather find someone else to blame than actually find the girl."

"You sound like you were there. If I didn't already know you were illegally using my computer during the hearing, I'd swear you were there. The council was busy trying to make sure everybody else knew it wasn't their fault. Nobody actually listened to anything about the progress of the investigation."

"I don't need to find anybody to blame. Why don't you tell me about your progress?" I wasn't that interested in the case, but Blake and I always liked to talk about our tough cases. It sometimes helped us see things we had missed.

"Katherine Elizabeth Hightower is the daughter of Robert Montgomery Hightower and Bunny Emerson Hightower. She graduated in May with a perfect GPA from Ursuline Academy, where she was alternately known as Kate, Kathy, Kitty, Liz, Beth and Betty. She lives with her parents in Mesquite. Her daddy is the mayor, and her mother is the first person everybody calls when they need a fundraiser organized."

"Ursuline isn't exactly around the corner from Mesquite, is it?"

"No, but it is prestigious and expensive which is what the mayor likes. Plus, her GPA there led her to an academic scholarship at Southern Methodist University. While waiting to start college, she volunteers several days a week at the North Texas Food Bank. The lady who runs the food bank first noticed her missing. She says Katherine was one of her most reliable volunteers, so she was shocked when she didn't show up for her shift several days in a row."

I had to ask, "Her parents didn't notice she was missing."

"The girl's room has its own entrance at their house. They say they often don't see her for weeks at a time. Also, her dad was busy with his reelection campaign, and her mother had been in Boston for an Emerson family reunion."

"The perfect family," I said trying not to sound overly sarcastic, "as long as family doesn't include anything involving love or togetherness."

"You tend to judge people quickly, my friend, but in this case I agree. The father is one world class jerk, and the mother isn't much better. However, they do have a missing daughter, and the girl does need to be found. It's not her fault that her parents have too much money and mixed up priorities."

"That's true, plus they can't be doing too terrible a job as parents if Katherine is a food bank volunteer. Not that many kids devote time to charity, and there aren't too many charities that are more worthy of time. I met Emily while volunteering there, you know."

"I had forgotten that. Maybe one of you can help me out if the investigation leads there."

"We'll both be happy to if we can," I told him honestly.

"Even so, don't be too quick to credit their parenting success. One out of two isn't that great when it comes to child rearing, and Bobby Junior is a complete pain. I've never met a more churlish kid. I'm amazed he's not at Lew Sterett or in jail someplace."

"Maybe he's just out on parole."

"No, he's only seventeen, and I checked his record. Somehow, he's never even been formally charged with anything, although that might change in a hurry if I have to spend much time with him."

"Other than a bratty kid, where is the investigation heading?"

"So far, the investigation isn't really leading anywhere, which may be why I waste time every day getting reamed by county commissioners who wouldn't know how to conduct an investigation if their lives depended on it."

Our conversation was interrupted by April delivering each of us a beer. It wasn't that we thought she would share our conversation with anybody, but April has a certain presence about her that causes even happily married men like Blake and happily involved, but not married, men like me to need a reset before continuing a conversation. Emily and Jade never fail to comment about this on those occasions when the four of us meet here.

For a change, I spoke first, "So let me see if I understand the situation. You are looking for an intelligent, wealthy girl of legal age whose parents and brother are jerks. Probably, she has decided to not be around them for awhile."

I continued, "Just track her credit cards, ask her friends where she would have gone and find her. Then you tell her that she has every right to go as far away from her dear daddy, her sweet mommy and her baby brother as she wishes to go. Then ask her to leave a note next time."

"You have summarized the situation exactly the way that the County Commissioners see it. Maybe, one day you'll be a Commissioner. But there are problems with your plan. She hasn't used her credit cards lately, and she apparently has no friends."

"Oh! So she is a chip off the old block, huh?"

"No, both her parents have plenty of friends, and her father seems to have his share of enemies, as well. Politics will do that. Our department has talked to every student and teacher at Ursuline, and not one has had a single bad word to say about her. Nor have they said a single good word about her. They all say the same thing: she went to class, worked hard and never connected with anybody in any way."

"So what's your plan?" I asked.

"I plan to keep getting chewed out in meetings every day and concentrate my staff's resources on finding people who want to be found, or at least aren't as capable of not being found. For heaven's sake, I asked the father how much cash money the girl might have to get a handle on how long she could go without using a credit card. You want to know his answer?"

"Probably not," I answered honestly, "but tell me, anyway."

"He said he had no way of knowing for certain, but that it probably wasn't more than ten or fifteen thousand dollars."

"And you say my case is challenging? I may not know her name, but I think it's safe to presume she doesn't have fifteen thousand dollars in cash money to spend to keep me from finding her. At least if she's got that kind of money, you don't need to look on Harry Hines or Industrial. Nobody could go through that kind of money and need to be hooking this quickly."

Blake had signaled earlier for another round, and he didn't say anything as April delivered two more bottles of beer. After she left, he asked, "That, such as it is, is my plan. Do you have one?"

"I'm just going to do what I do. I have the two pictures of her, so I'll go down to Deep Ellum this weekend and ask around. Surely, somebody down there can tell me her name. Nobody can hang out down there as much as she apparently does, without somebody knowing her name."

"Well, if that's the plan, it's good that it's your plan and not mine. When I go there, nobody will tell me anything. I don't know how you do it, but somehow you tend to get people to talk. Let me know if you need backup, though."

I told him I would. Then we turned the conversation to the Cowboys and Mavericks and Rangers and Stars and pretended we were simply two sports fans in a great city to be a sports fan.

It took us several more beers to adequately address the chances each team had in the current or upcoming seasons, but eventually we agreed that the Stars and Cowboys were most likely to improve soon. We also agreed that the Mavericks had just choked away the best chance for a victory parade that was in the immediate future for any of the local teams.

When April brought the check, I grabbed it and reached for my wallet. Blake protested enough to be polite, but allowed me to pay the tab out of Freak's retainer when we left. It probably wasn't the first time I'd picked up our tab at Walt's, but it was a bit unusual.

One thing I like about the Rodeo Bar is that it is only a ten minute walk from there to my place. The sun had gone down enough that the weather wasn't too hot on the walk. On the way, I spent a few minutes reflecting on Blake's case.

It didn't seem possible that a wealthy, intelligent girl could spend two years at a school whose main purpose is to create a network of wealthy, intelligent girls and not make a single connection with another wealthy, intelligent girl. I made a mental note to suggest to Blake that he try to track down any friends from before she got to Ursuline.

04   Deep Ellum

Saturday night, I walked from my place to meet Freak at a biker bar in Deep Ellum called Reno's. Normally, I don't ask or allow my clients to help me on an investigation, but this was not a normal case, and Freak was definitely not a normal client.

The last time I had tried to get answers out of someone at Reno's, I had tried several approaches which had all failed. Only after I was able to convince Blake to accompany me with a couple of Sheriff's Deputies wearing the official uniforms and carrying the guns associated with their profession had I gotten the answer that led to the solving of that case.

In spite of Blake's friendship and our previously successful collaborations, I had no reason to ask or expect to need that kind of show of force at this time. So, in the hope of loosening some lips and gaining some access that I couldn't otherwise expect, I decided to accept Freak's insistent offer that I let him help the investigation by taking me to all the places and people who might be able to help.

Reno's is on Elm Street in what is commonly referred to as the heart of Deep Ellum. In addition to bikers, it's a popular hangout for the youths that educators like to refer to as disenfranchised. Many, if not most, of the bands that play there can't be listed in the local paper with their actual name. So if the show gets listed at all in their weekly concert calendars, it is with the brackets that indicate that a euphemism is being employed.

I didn't read the concert listings that week, so I don't know if the show headlined by a band called the Kansas City Faggots was mentioned at all. What I do know is that most of the parents who grew up listening to Queen and AC/DC would be appalled if they knew that their precious, innocent children were going to a show by a band with such an offensive and politically incorrect name. Irony tends to be ironic.

I also knew that Reno's had been the last place Freak had seen the missing girl, and that she had been a regular visitor there. Of course, that was assuming that my client was being honest. I had to acknowledge that this was not necessarily a safe assumption. Freak was loitering outside when I got there, and he greeted me with a traditional handshake that would have been more appropriate at city hall. The handshake may have been appropriate for city hall, but his look most definitely was not.

He was in full 'Freak Show' regalia. His sleeveless Marilyn Manson tee shirt left his arms free to display at least a dozen oversized safety pins pierced though various parts of his arms. One of the safety pins went through the 'F' in the tattoo on his bicep which read 'Freak'. The 'F' was styled after Tony Hawk's Famous Stars and Straps logo. Like Hawk's apparel line, the tattoo looked hip and expensive; two things I can't claim to be.

Freak had also cut through the shirt so that the part of the shirt that should have displayed Mr. Manson's right ear was open to reveal his pierced right nipple with the sterling silver padlock hanging from it. The padlock probably weighed more than my watch, and its color perfectly matched the jewelry in his ears, nose and around both eyes. I tried, and mostly succeeded, to act as if his look didn't bother me at all and returned his handshake as if we were two attorneys meeting outside the main courthouse.

Before we went in, I tried again to get Freak to tell me the name of the girl we were looking for. I even tried reasoning with him.

"Freak, you have to tell me the girl's name if you expect me to find her. I'm good at finding people, but to find people, I have to ask questions. I have to beat down doors and pester people who don't want to answer questions with questions about the person I am trying to find."

Freak's answer was short, "Whatever."

I ignored him and continued, "You've seen me work; you know how I do it. Eventually I ask the right question of the right person, and it pushes the right button. Sometimes that person takes a swing at me, remember? But the only way that the right button gets pushed is if I know the name of the person I'm looking for."

Not surprisingly, reason had little impact on Freak, "Hey, Marlowe, I'm paying you good money because you're supposed to be good at this, not just because we're friends. If I thought it would be easy, I could have hired anybody."

"My friends don't call me Marlowe, either, but I am good at this. I'm just suggesting that I could do what you hired me for more efficiently if I wasn't impeded by a lack of information."

Freak gave me a look that I think was meant to be disdain, but looked more like petulance and ushered me into the club. I was wearing the most effective Deep Ellum disguise that I owned: black Wrangler jeans, a black retro Jim Morrison tee shirt I bought at Hot Topic a few years back and shoes I'd owned since I first started as a bicycle courier all those years ago.

The outfit itself wasn't really out of place if it had been on someone a few years younger. Regardless of how well Blake thought I could handle myself in Deep Ellum, I still felt about as comfortable as a snail at a frog jumping contest when I went there.

Of course, even in Deep Ellum, Freak drew more curious stares than I (or anybody else on earth) possibly could. The big difference, and the reason I somewhat welcomed his help, was that he actually had friends and a certain amount of street cred with the people here.

At Freak's suggestion, we had arrived toward the end of the opening band's set, so the club would be quiet enough that I could ask questions as needed. Tonight's opening act was called American Tarot. Like all bands that played here, they were loud enough to be heard on Elm Street, but, unlike many of the bands that played here, I could actually hear and understand some of their lyrics.

——

The bouncer was a 7 foot tall, 300 pound bald man from Nigeria who calls himself Sam The Man. His real name includes an "S", an "A" and an "M", but is three times as long and ten times as hard to pronounce, so he goes with Sam The Man. He greeted us as we entered, "Hey Freak, why you hanging around with Larry Bird? Hoping he'll teach you how to grow taller?"

My friends don't call me Larry Bird either, but Sam and I share an uneasy alliance based on mutual respect. Also, all tall guys, who don't play basketball for a living, share the common thread of being asked twenty times a day why we don't.

I decided to let the comment slide and just nodded at him, but Freak took the bait, "No dude, I heard that the bouncer here just sits on his ass, taking X, so I thought I should bring a bodyguard. Famous people like me can't be too careful."

"Yeah, you're famous, if infamy counts as fame," Sam retorted. "How was your trip to Las Vegas, Nevada?"

"It had its moments. Bobbie Jo's brother let us borrow his band's tour bus, so we rode in style the whole way out there. There was so much liquor on the bus; she and I were the only ones sober enough to drive by the time we got to New Mexico."

"You rode in style? Charlie told me that bus was nothing special."

"No man, his band may be nothing special, but that bus is the bomb."

"You didn't do any of the driving, did you?"

"Hell to the no! Driving is for ordinary people. An extraordinary gentleman such as myself deserves to be chauffeured. Raymond was reasonably sober until we got to Albuquerque. Bobbie Jo drove us the rest of the way to Vegas and all the way back."

"If Bobbie Jo is ordinary, I'm the Czar of Russia, but you shouldn't drive since you never learned how and you don't have a license."

"I've always been too busy being krunk to sweat the mundane tasks of others. By the way, do you know there are almost as many Freak groupies in Vegas as there are here?"

"Of course there are, Freak. You're down to one groupie here, so zero is almost as many."

Freak responded with a version of the same punch he'd tried on me years ago, but this one was clearly in jest. "Whatever! The best part was our last show was on Flag Day. I bought a case of those lapel pins with the American Flag and the girls stuck 50 of them into me for the show finale. It took about 20 minutes and the crowd went crazy."

"The casino owner insisted on calling the Guinness Book people and said he'll book me for any patriotic holiday any time I want to appear. He was just pissed that I didn't do the same thing on Memorial Day when our run started."

In spite of my reluctance to enter the conversation, I couldn't resist the urge to ask one question, "So, why didn't you do it on Memorial Day, Freak?"

"Dude, Flag Day is all about honoring the flag. Memorial Day is for honoring people who died in wars. I know you think I'm twisted, but even I'm not going to go onstage and have girls attach dead people to my body, at least not as part of a performance."

"Of course not, Freak," Sam chimed in. "Some thrills aren't meant for public consumption, right?"

I saw that both of them were barely suppressing a laugh, and realized that I had become their audience in a game of 'shock the audience.' Before I could decide whether to be offended or honored, two kids started fighting by the stage and Sam ambled over to get it settled.

It was obvious by watching that the fight had started over a pair of sunglasses and the kid holding them wasn't about to let them go. They looked like Oakley's and knowing that they probably cost over $100, I didn't blame the kid. As usual, Sam handled it quickly and had each participant under one arm escorting them out when I had an idea, "Freak, get Sam to take the kids somewhere we can question them."

To my client's credit, he didn't argue or delay, he hustled over and caught Sam in time to say something to Sam and get him to change directions. The questions Freak wisely chose not to ask at first came as soon as he got back to me, "What's up? Why do you want to question those losers? How are they going to help?"

"Because, you know as well as I do how hard it is to get anybody down here to talk. The most important part of asking the right question is asking the question right. And one way to ask the question right is to ask people who are too scared not to answer, and right now, those kids will answer any question I can think of to ask."

"But what if they don't know anything?"

"Then I keep finding people to ask and keep asking questions. Where is Sam taking them?"

Freak led me through the crowd to an office. For some people, it is a major ordeal to get through a crowd like this, but if you are 6'9 or have needles pierced through most of your body, it is much easier. In the office, Sam was behind a desk staring at two very frightened kids. The sunglasses were sitting on the desk in front of Sam who was smiling mirthlessly at the scared pair.

05   Scared Pair

Sam made the introductions, "These two young dirt-bags are Seth and Eric. Both of them claim the other was trying to steal this fine pair of sunglasses. The tall distinguished gentleman before you is the world-famous detective Sherlock Holmes and the handsome young man at his side, you most likely already know as the Absolutely Incredible Completely Unbelievable Freak Show."

Not surprisingly, Seth was the one who looked like a college student. He wore twill pants and a golf shirt which looked completely out of place here. Of course, before the fight started, his golf shirt had almost certainly been covered by his floor length black trench coat that matched the one worn by about twenty percent of the non-bikers here no matter how hot it got outside.

He probably hadn't been winning the fight, since what was left of the coat was loose on his body, bundled up to cover his waist, but very little else of his preppy clothes. He probably didn't expect any of his apparel other than the trench coat would be seen this evening. His black NYPD baseball cap covered hair that would have fit right in at a Young Republicans Rally.

Eric's coat had escaped unharmed, but it was open to reveal that the rest of his outfit matched the look perfectly. I suspected that Eric was not his real name, since his clothes and hair were a complete likeness of Brandon Lee's character in 'The Crow'. I surmised that he had borrowed the character's name as well as his look. Other than the matching trench coats, the only thing the kids had in common is that they were both fidgeting anxiously.

As I had expected, two scared young people sat ready to be interrogated. Some of the cops downtown would love such an opportunity. Freak had gone over and picked up the glasses and was looking them over intently.

Sam continued, "My plan was to throw them both out onto Elm Street and keep that nice pair of glasses for myself. But, I couldn't pass up this rare opportunity to watch the world's greatest detective at work."

I couldn't tell if his speech was intended as a sarcastic insult or to put pressure on the kids, but I didn't care. The kids were now looking at me with the same fear in their eyes they had been showing Sam earlier.

"So, King Solomon, do you have a plan for figuring out which of these young men is an innocent victim and which one tried to commit a crime in my fine establishment and will have to answer to me."

I didn't have any friends who called me King Solomon either, but I was saved from having to admit that I didn't have an actual plan when Freak unexpectedly spoke up, "I do."

I don't know who was more surprised, but Freak didn't say anything else. He nodded at me to follow him and started walking out the door. Given the way he had hopped lively to get Sam to bring the two kids in here, I didn't see any reason to argue and I followed him out of the office through the club that was now rocking too loud for conversation and out onto Elm Street, which was only slightly quieter.

Once we were out on the street he handed me the glasses. "Look at these things, Dude, they're not glasses."

I looked them over to see what he meant. They looked like the expensive Oakley wraparound style sunglasses, or perhaps a knockoff, but I didn't see any logo on them, just a small circle between the lenses where the Oakley logo would have been. I still wasn't sure what Freak meant, "Okay, if they aren't glasses, what are they?"

"They connect to a Digital Video Recorder that is designed to look just like an MP3 player. That circle between the lenses is a camera, these are microphones here on the earpieces. Dude, one of those guys is a bootlegger, not a thief, and he'll have the recorder on him somewhere."

I had to know, "Are you sure?"

"Trust me, Dude, I'm sure. These are bootleggers' glasses, I guarantee it."

We made our way back to the office and the door was locked. I knocked, and Sam opened the door with a big grin on his face.

"I got tired of having to physically restrain these two so I locked the door. I don't know what your plan was, but it worked. Young Seth here has admitted to trying to steal Eric's glasses and apologized to him and to me. Says that he's never done anything like this before, but they just looked so cool, he couldn't resist."

"So, did you call the police, yet?"

"I was going to, but then I realized that I hadn't gotten to watch the world's greatest detective, yet."

The sarcasm was getting old, but it was time for me to go to work. "Seth, you seem like a nice young man, you must feel terrible about having made this one mistake, don't you?"

"Yes. Sir. I don't know what I was thinking. I'll pay for any damages, but I really wish you wouldn't call the police."

"Oh, I'm sure we won't have to call them if you cooperate, and you are going to cooperate, aren't you?"

"Yes, Sir."

It was not hard to tell that he had gone from being scared to being completely compliant for one reason and one reason only. He knew that stealing was a crime in the real world, but making bootleg videos was a more serious crime in Deep Ellum.

"Look kids, we're in a private office, no reason to maintain a look, and it's way too hot in here for those trench coats. Why not take them off and then we'll continue our little chat."

Eric took his off, but Seth just looked at me. I nodded at Sam, and he walked over behind Seth. Seth looked up at Sam, over at Freak and then back at me, "You can't make me take it off."

"Actually, I can, but I don't have to. These two gentlemen would enjoy ripping it off of you and completing the process of tearing it to shreds, and I can't think of any reason to deny them the pleasure."

"I want a lawyer; you can't do this to me."

"I'm sure after you get booked into Lew Sterrett, you'll get a chance to call a lawyer. Of course, they'll take the coat off for you prior to booking you and put all your personal items in a little plastic bucket tagged with your name."

Eric had quit fidgeting, but Seth hadn't. I knew the plan was working, so I continued, "Usually, people get most of what goes in that bucket back, but it's not guaranteed. Anything you want us to keep safe for you? I don't listen to music that much, so I'm sure you can trust me with your MP3 player."

Seth reached inside his coat and set the recorder on the desk, "Fine, you caught me, I was recording the opening act. What? Is that a felony or something? Three big guys beating the crap out of a young man is more a felony to me, and if you guys try to make this more than it is, that's what I'll tell the cops."

I was just about to remind him that perjury was, in fact, a felony, when Sam spoke up, "Seth, look at that mirror behind the desk. It doesn't really go with the room design does it?"

Seth barely replied, "No I guess not, but I don't really care."

"You should care, because right behind it is the camera that not only recorded you sitting here without being assaulted, it also recorded you confessing to stealing those glasses and threatening to lie to the police."

Seth quit posturing and accepted that he was caught. Eric had given up long ago and was just waiting to see how bad things were going to get. I decided to offer them an out, "Lucky for both of you, we aren't cops; we just want some information and need some honest answers. Can either of you answer questions honestly in this comfortable environment, or do I need to have the police come get you for that?"

They both agreed to answer any question I asked, and I proceeded to ask them many questions. Since my first impression of the two pictures were that they were two different girls, I presented them that way to the kids as I asked.

After about an hour of questioning the two, the only possibly useful things I learned were that Eric had once hit on a girl who looked like the goth picture of our missing person at Club Dada and been rejected politely, and Seth thought the other version looked like a girl he had seen at Grapevine's wine festival this spring.

When I was sure I had all I was going to get from them, I looked at Sam and said in my best lawyer voice, "I have no further questions, should we remand them to custody or release them?"

Sam was holding the recorder as he said, "Typically, when we catch a bootlegger, we keep the tape and kick the crap out of the guy, but there's no tape to keep here, I guess technology has moved past that."

Freak smiled as he answered, "Bootlegging has gone digital, old man. Some of the bands carry a data scrubbing magnet to wipe the data. If Tarot is still backstage, you should get them, they might have one."

Sam made a couple of calls and pretty soon there was a knock on the door and a member of the band came in and introduced himself, "I'm Kenny, what's going on here?"

Sam explained the situation and Kenny looked at the glasses and recorder, then turned and handed Seth a business card, "Nice equipment, email me the file when you get a chance." He headed for the door, then added, "Don't get caught next time, you idiot."

I couldn't think of anything to add, so I nodded at Sam, and he ushered Seth and Eric out the door. Freak and I just looked at each other and realized it was time to leave. As we were leaving, I asked him, "How did you know about those glasses?"

"Oh, I have a pair that I used to wear to Dallas Gentleman's Club and Million Dollar Saloon before ... Anyway I have a pair I used to wear.

Maybe you should get yourself a set. They could be useful in your line of work. The whole set up only cost about three thousand dollars."

I really didn't need to be the world's greatest detective to grasp the meaning of his attempted redirection of his answer. I had never really understood the attraction some men have for strip clubs, but I did know the only thing that would cause a man who liked them to quit going.

I was certain I was carrying two pictures of the reason he didn't use those recorder glasses any longer. I was learning more about my client than I was about the missing girl, but that might eventually prove to be useful. I didn't bother to tell him that I didn't exactly have three thousand dollars to spare, even as a business expense.

Freak and I repeated the process in Deep Ellum on Sunday and Monday, but learned nothing that seemed likely to be helpful. Not learning anything was not that unusual for me, but it seemed to be bothering Freak. "Are we getting anywhere? Are you going to be able to find her?"

I didn't really have a good answer, but I knew enough about clients in general to know when a show of confidence is required, "This is what I do. I'll find her; just let me do my job. Most cases aren't solved by hanging out with the client. Let me go to work and I'll get results."

Freak looked at me for a few seconds before walking away without saying a word. I was trying to convince myself that this was a vote of confidence, when my brain started recalling a few of the famous people who had been fired within days of receiving a vote of confidence.

Maybe I would be smarter to quit looking for a vote of confidence and start looking for something that would help me find the girl. I promised myself I'd begin doing so aggressively starting Wednesday morning.

06   Personal Evening

Tuesday night is always date night for Emily and me. We figured if we always make one night for each other, it will keep our schedules sane even given the odd hours I sometimes work and the long hours she often works in the accounting department at J.C Penney's.

In the four years since we had agreed to this, we probably haven't missed more than a half-dozen Tuesdays. That's why at 6:30, I was wearing slacks and a striped shirt while sitting on the patio of Spiatza's in the West End waiting for her to arrive.

The dress code at Spiatza's didn't require the nice attire, since they don't have a dress code. I've learned though to always be ready for one of Emily's pre-planned 'whims' that might take us out to Greenville Avenue or any other nightspots in Dallas that expects men to dress like gentlemen.

Emily is a very structured person, so her pre-planned whims are her concession to my desire for spontaneity. She can plan out an entire evening, but if she doesn't tell me the plan, it's still spontaneous for me. I love that she is willing to indulge me that way.

Another little thing I love about her is that she is always late. In this inconsistent world, it's nice to have something you can always count on. Plus, since she's always late, I never have to hurry anywhere to meet her. All I have to do is be prepared for her 'spur of the moment' changes.

The West End entertainment district in downtown Dallas is physically about a mile and a half from the collection of bars and tattoo parlors known as Deep Ellum. Conceptually and spiritually, the distance is more like a million miles.

From my home office, it is less than a mile to either area. Somehow, my social life almost never takes me to Deep Ellum. In the same manner, my professional life never leads me to the West End. The only thing the two areas have in common is that both can be called euphemistically entertainment districts.

The West End crowd is mostly twenty-five and older, predominantly from the suburbs, present company excluded. It also is generally relatively affluent, again present company excluded. And it almost always takes time to ensure it is dressed to impress.

The Deep Ellum crowd is younger, sometimes too much younger. It tends to be more racially diverse and it commits or falls victim to roughly fifty times more crimes per capita. It spends time making sure it is dressed to appear as if it is not dressed to impress.

The women in the West End are likely to be wearing Capri pants and heels. Their dates often wear shorts that are as long as the Capri pants with loafers or sandals.

In Deep Ellum, the girls and their dates both wear jeans or cargo pants and gender indifferent footwear. They might spend more money on clothes than the West End crowd, but they make sure nobody can tell.

The bars in the West End are mostly national chains, like Friday's and On the Border. An occasional independent will usually survive long enough to give the place an identity, but chains dominate the landscape.

Deep Ellum has more unique places like the DarkSide Lounge and Gypsy Tea Room, as well as the Double Wide and Adair's which provide a place in Deep Ellum for rednecks to get as out of control as the stoners.

Also, the West End is a happening place bustling with activity at 6:30, and nearly a ghost town by 2 a.m. Deep Ellum is barely existent before 9 o'clock, but a hive of activity (some of it legal) well after 2 a.m.

In Deep Ellum, you can see a concert by any number of bands hoping to be the next Nine Inch Nails or Korn. You can also get a tattoo and score some cocaine or heroin, as easily as you could buy a glass of vintage California Chardonnay in the West End.

In the West End, you are more likely to hear a cover band singing Loverboy and Air Supply songs poorly. You can also get an airbrushed temporary tattoo and take your date for a ride in a horse drawn carriage.

Another thing I love about Emily is that she can appear to fit in and enjoy herself in either environment, or any other place for that matter. It is because of this, that Freak started calling her 'Chameleon Lady' when he met her a few years back.

It's also a characteristic she thinks we have in common, but I suspect I only have it when I'm with her. As I waited for her in the West End, I speculated on how few people in the West End this evening had been to Deep Ellum in the last week or ever.

I was certain that nobody I had interviewed on Saturday at Reno's Chophouse was likely to be coming here anytime soon. Only about a mile and a half physically separate the two locations, but each is a separate continent as far as atmosphere, culture and clientele is concerned.

Emily arrived at 6:57, early by her standards, and since she was wearing an olive and aqua silk dress and matching open toe slides with kitten heels, it was safe to presume she had something spontaneous planned. As she crossed the West End marketplace to Spiatza's, the sun shone on her auburn hair, and it seemed for a few minutes that the entire West End was basking in her glow.

She has a knack for walking into any environment as if she owns the place and tonight is no exception. As she got closer, I also noticed a cat that ate the canary look on her face that told me I was right to dress for more of an event than simply dinner at Spiatza's.

I rose to meet her, although reluctantly. I hated to fill any of the space between us with my ungainly strides because there was something so delectable about watching her approach. When she was about three feet away, the sun winked at me from her diamond solitaire necklace.

I had bought it for her at Neiman Marcus a couple of years ago after finishing up one of those true rarities, a lucrative case. I thought to myself once again what a great investment it had been. Emily looked up at me and said, a little out of breath, "Thank you!"

"You're welcome." I said politely, and then added, "For what?"

40

"For watching me walk over here, like you'd be happy to just skip the date and head straight back to your place." Then she reached her arms around my neck and pulled me down for a kiss, like she has done countless times. As her soft lips met mine, I realized that was exactly what I'd been thinking.

The kiss ended with a giggle from her. "Put it out of your mind! I really look forward to our Tuesday night dates. And after the week I've had, I've been looking forward to this one more than usual."

With a chuckle of my own, I told her, "I've had a bit of a week myself."

Grinning now, she segued into one of our regularly scripted lines, "What would you like to do this week?"

"We could go to a park and watch grass grow. That's always fun."

She replied as she always does in her best Gracie Allen voice, "No, that's too much excitement for me."

Okay, so we aren't exactly Burns and Allen. We are our only audience, and it always amuses us. I was not the least bit surprised to learn that she actually had a plan.

"A woman at work was talking about this great little place over in Uptown that sounds like fun, Vino 100. They're having a wine tasting tonight of Spanish wines, if that sounds like fun to you."

"Well, I'm usually more of a beer guy. But I know how much you like wine, and I do like the thought of you enjoying a delightful glass of wine or several, especially since there is the chance that it could end with me enjoying you if you enjoy enough of the wine." I said with what I hoped was a wry grin, "Let's do it."

"I do enjoy the way you enjoy me in all your creative ways," she said with the exact grin I hoped I'd been wearing.

07   Scenic Uptown

Very few cities have actual trolley cars these days, and Dallas doesn't have that many things that can't be found in almost every city. So, it wasn't hard to convince Emily to walk from the West End to St. Paul Street to catch the McKinney Avenue Trolley into uptown for the trip.

I settled the tab at Spiatza's, and we walked up Lamar to Ross and over to St. Paul to catch the trolley. The walk from the West End to the trolley normally takes me five to ten minutes, but I walk at a slower pace with Emily, so it took about fifteen.

Good things always happen when I'm with Emily, so the trolley was just pulling up as we turned the corner onto St. Paul. The trolley cars run every fifteen minutes, and when I ride one alone, I always seem to have to wait at least ten.

In 1989, Dallas bought and restored two cars which had been part of its trolley system in the 1930's. The current route goes from the northeast edge of downtown, through the uptown area and all the way to City Place on Central Expressway.

The smaller of the two cars is called 'Petunia', and the large one is called the 'Green Elephant'. They both make a great deal of noise as they rattle along creating the sense that you are bouncing around, but actually provide a fairly smooth ride.

The Green Elephant is the more comfortable of the two, and in keeping with the luck that I usually have when with Emily, the Green Elephant was the one we caught. We climbed aboard and waved a greeting to the volunteer who was running the car that evening.

As we crossed over Woodall Rogers into the Uptown area, I was again struck by the overwhelming contrast between Uptown and Downtown. Although the West End and Deep Ellum districts in downtown were as different as night and day, they both appeared to be part of the same city. If they had nothing else in common, at least there were old buildings anchoring both.

Uptown with its Crescent Hotel and Ghost Bar would look more apropos in Beverly Hills or New York City than a few miles from where I plied my trade downtown. Even the hair salons and fitness centers in Uptown don't seem to belong within walking distance of the rundown office buildings around my place.

The other thing that separates uptown from the rest of the downtown area is how proud it is to be Uptown. There are over twenty businesses in the area which use the word 'uptown' in their name. This includes three bars, two hair salons, a carwash and several restaurants. The same types of businesses that operate any place operate in Uptown. The ones here just seem to take more pride in it.

The trolley line has a stop at Howell Street, and Vino 100 is right there on McKinney Avenue, so we were almost in the place when we stepped off the trolley. Once inside, I was surprised to see a large turnout for a weeknight. Most establishments on McKinney make their money on the weekends and might as well have been closed during the week.

That obviously was not the case at Vino 100. The place was relatively small with only about twenty tables or so. Looking around I didn't see any open tables. Emily didn't even seem to hesitate as she took my hand and walked directly to a table where a couple was already seated.

"Looks really crowded tonight. Do you mind if we join you at your table?"

They looked a little startled for a second, their expression causing Emily to attempt to suppress her amusement. The woman seeing the look on Emily's face began to giggle. This broke the ice, and we were all laughing as she motioned to the two open chairs invitingly.

The man looked to be in his late thirties, while the woman appeared to be at least a decade younger. Given that Dallas trails only L.A in the number of plastic surgeons per capita, this only meant that both were somewhere between eighteen and fifty years old. I didn't notice any signs of cosmetic surgery, but I usually don't.

The woman was a trim brunette, with a small mouth and a quick smile, and the man had wavy, sandy blonde hair, with the build of someone who played linebacker in college, but was now letting age or home-cooking catch up with him.

He reached across the table and took my hand in a confident politician's grip, "I'm Jack Cannelly and this is my wife, Bethany." He glanced at his wife and they both smiled politely, showing off the perfect store-bought teeth that only the idle rich and professional models can afford.

Jack shook Emily's hand far longer than politeness required, while I wondered if the couple were models or the idle rich, or both. Emily escaped the handshake without needing my help and continued the introductions, "I'm Emily, and this is Carl."

Just then a tall, very slim, dark haired man in a blue button down shirt stood up at the front of the room and cleared his throat.

"Hi, welcome to Vino 100. If I could get everyone to settle in, we'll get started. Our servers this evening will be Jill and Stuart."

As their names were called, Jill, a petite twenty-something blonde on the left side of the room looked up and waved, and Stuart, a young guy who didn't look old enough to drink wine, much less serve it, looked up and nodded at the room from his post on the right side of the room.

Our host continued, "This evening we'll be covering some fascinating Spanish wines. Since I've done this before, I know some of you are just here to drink, but I hope you will indulge me. I studied a long time to learn this, and my wife is tired of hearing about it, so I have to share it with somebody."

As we all laughed politely, I realized that I was not interested in almost exactly the same manner that Emily would not be interested in an

---

in-depth discussion of the possible ways for the Mavericks to defend the pick and roll, but I did my best to look fascinated and not embarrass her.

Our host continued, "This first wine, which Jill and Stuart are pouring now is from the Bodegas Montecillo. 'Montecillo Rioja Crianza' is a perfect red just great for everyday consumption. It is filled with jammy red and dark fruits, medium bodied with a velvety texture on the palate and a smooth solid finish."

As I waited for the signal to take a drink, I tried hard not to think about a missing girl with no name. I quickly realized it was going to take more than wine to make that happen.

Everyone around me chuckled at something our host said. I laughed along, realizing that I was thinking about the case, instead of listening. I decided to think about something more pleasant, like just how incredible Emily looked in that dress and how the aqua accentuated her blue eyes.

Not surprisingly, this got me thinking about how much better she, and her blue eyes, would look out of that aqua dress. This naturally led to many other pleasant thoughts. Suffice it to say that I did not spend much time during the presentation thinking about missing people or Spanish wines.

After six wines and an hour and a half of my life that I'll never get back, the speaker finally concluded with what sounded very much like a sales pitch. Emily looked up at me with a radiant smile, "Let's buy a bottle."

I leaned in and kissed her on the cheek. "Okay, pick whichever one you want. Jack, Bethany, if you'll excuse me for a second. I'm just going to go make use of the facilities." After sitting through the wine tasting, it felt good to stand up and stretch my legs. Like most tables and chairs in public places, Vino 100's were designed for people shorter than my six foot nine.

When I got back to the table, I was not surprised to note that Emily and the couple were chatting as if they'd known each other forever. Emily has a knack for making others around her comfortable in any social setting.

What did surprise me was the topic of the conversation. As I got back to the table, Jack was in the middle of a discussion. I only heard the end of it, "....surprise me even slightly if she's just hiding in one of the rooms in the house. It's probably just a campaign stunt to help him get reelected."

When he finished, I inquired politely, "Who is hiding as a campaign stunt?" Even when I'm not interested in a conversation, I like to at least know what the conversation is about.

"Mayor Hightower's daughter; he's acting like something might have happened to his daughter so people will vote for him. He's been playing the family man card to win elections since she and her brother were babies."

I was suddenly interested in the conversation, but Bethany apparently wasn't. "Jack, these people don't want to hear any more about it. You don't like the mayor; everybody knows you don't. Lots of people don't like their bosses. I don't see any reason for you to ruin everybody's evening by talking about it all night."

I wasn't personally involved in the case of Mayor Hightower's missing daughter, but I thought this might be a chance to learn something to help Blake. I knew from our chat at the Rodeo Bar that nobody was telling him anything revealing about the family.

"No, go on, you aren't going to ruin our evening." I said trying not to sound too inquisitive or eager. I wanted to sell him on the idea of continuing without letting on that I knew anything about it.

I'm not sure how well I pulled it off, but Emily closed the sale for me, "Yes, do go on. I wouldn't have brought it up if I wasn't interested."

She nodded at me as she continued, "He'd rather sell houses than know what goes on inside them, but I really love interesting stories."

"Well, Bethany hates when I talk about my work in social settings, but I don't mind telling you what I know. Who knows? If I can keep him from being re-elected, maybe he'll put his house on the market." He looked at me before continuing. "Maybe you can be his seller's agent."

I had already picked up on it, but Emily had obviously given them the impression that I was in real-estate. I wasn't sure why she had, but I saw no reason to contradict her.

"Maybe I can, but tell us more about it. Like she said, Emily loves interesting stories and since I'm in real estate, I don't ever have any."

Bethany had spent the better part of the evening either looking down at her lap or straight into her glass, but now she looked at me, "Oh, but I'm sure you do. I bet real estate is a simply fascinating field. If I had to work, maybe that's what I would do."

"Well, dear, as long as the mayor doesn't get around to firing me before he finally loses an election, you won't have to work." Jack looked at Bethany reprovingly as he continued, "That is, unless you decide to divorce me and run off with a real estate agent."

It hadn't occurred to me that she might have been flirting with me, but after his comment, I realized that she probably had been. I was wondering what would cause someone to flirt in that situation. I was pretty sure I didn't want to know. I suspected it didn't bode well for the long term success of their relationship.

As I was pondering Jack and Bethany's chances for a happy, long lasting marriage, Emily interjected in her usual gracious manner, "I'm sure Bethany just meant that all stories are interesting to those who haven't heard them."

Her smile as she looked at me was dazzling. She always seemed to be in her element when she was helping me or thought she might be helping me investigate something.

Emily was at her most charming as she continued, "Since we haven't heard the story of your relationship with the mayor, we'd love to hear it. Wouldn't we, darling? I'm sure it's a simply fascinating story."

I nodded politely, "We'd both love to hear about it." I also leaned over and softly kissed Emily's lips. I wanted Jack to know I wasn't interested in his wife's flirting. I also wanted his wife to know I wasn't interested. Mostly, though, I just wanted to kiss Emily.

I suspected that once Jack got started, it would be harder to get him to stop than to get him to continue. I've never been more right in my entire life, unless you count the first time I asked Emily out on a date, but that's a story for another time.

"I've been city manager in Mesquite for nine years. I love the job, and I love my part in making Mesquite one of the best cities in Texas." Jack said the phrase 'city manager' the way a small boy would say engineer or astronaut, as if it were the most important and exciting job anybody could ever dream of having.

I could have pointed out that Mesquite isn't exactly considered the jewel of the Metroplex. I didn't, of course, in the spirit of friendly conversation.

He continued, "Hightower has been a pain in my backside the entire time. It was bad enough when he was on the council back then. But since he's been mayor, he's become completely intolerable. He only got elected to the council in the first place because he spent more money on his campaign than all the other candidates for every seat combined."

I saw no advantage in mentioning that most city elections are won that way, so I didn't. Instead I just let Jack keep talking.

"Then, he used the same outspend everybody campaign strategy to win the last mayoral election. He thinks he can buy anything or anybody he wants with his money. The scary thing is he may be right. The funny thing is it's not even his money really."

Emily was listening intently like she always does. She also picked up immediately on the question I wanted to ask. I wanted to ask it, but I didn't ask because I wasn't sure I could ask it nicely, and I wanted the chat to remain nice.

I learned early in my career as an investigator that the golden goose of a talkative person could be killed with a single question. That's one of the main reasons that I generally choose to be quiet, when in doubt.

Fortunately, Emily can ask any question tactfully, "How does he get to buy people and things with money that isn't really his? Sounds like something I'd like to learn. It could come in handy."

If the question offended Jack, it didn't show, "Oh I guess, technically it is his. After all, he earns it every day by being married to the ice queen who inherited it."

"So, he married money and used the money to get elected to public office. If that were a crime, the capitol building in Austin could be turned into a jail."

Jack and Bethany laughed at my joke. Emily had heard me tell different versions of it so many times that she simply squeezed my hand and smiled. Her smile was more gratifying than their laughter, but at least the golden goose was still talking.

"You're right about that, Buddy. If I didn't have any other problems with the guy, I wouldn't mind that he bought the elections, or that he got the money to buy it by marrying an ice queen."

Emily kept him going, "But there's more?"

"Damn straight, there's more. He thinks every employee of the city from the city manager on down to the road crews should be at his beck and call 24/7. When it ices over, the road crews have to start on his street, and I know for a fact that they do his driveway as well."

To be polite I shook my head reproachfully for him. "I'm sure that kind of special treatment isn't legal. Why doesn't one of the news outlets do an expose on him? 'Local Mayor Abuses Authority' is the kind of headline or tease they thrive on."

"You'd think so, wouldn't you? Maybe nobody cares but me, and there's nothing I can do about it. After all, since he is the mayor, he is my boss." He looked adoringly at his wife as he continued, "Since unlike him, I married for love instead of money, I do want to keep my job."

Bethany smiled back at him, but she looked more bored than adoring. I couldn't help but wonder if she too had married for money. I suspected it didn't matter very much to him, and it definitely didn't matter much to me.

I seldom find fault with people for trying to stay employed. I especially respect the importance of staying employed to support a family. Blowing the whistle on corruption is a noble thing to do, but it is almost never a good career move.

Emily broke what others would probably consider to be an uncomfortable silence, "Love is the only good reason to marry; I'm happy for both of you."

I took a shot at getting the golden goose talking again, "Why don't you tell us a little bit more about the Mayor and his family?"

What makes the talkative golden goose golden is that they talk and talk. Jack proved to be the perfect example once my question got him started.

09   Interesting Family

"The Mayor's family is nothing more than a campaign tool for him. He married for money. Once he had it, he used it to buy votes. He also used his family to get votes. They always looked like the perfect couple. But, of course, everyone knew better."

I hated to slow him down, but I wondered if what he meant was that he knew better now, "How did people know, and what did they know?"

He had a good answer, "Early on, especially after he lost the first time he ran, it was obvious because the only time they would quit fighting was when the photo was taken or the commercial was filmed. I was still working my way up the ladder then. But, we all joked about it."

He paused and looked at Bethany, but if she had anything to add, she chose to keep it to herself.

"Later on, after he first got elected to the council, nobody saw them fight much. That is mostly because the family was almost never seen together after that first election. His wife may as well have been a model hired for his television campaign."

Suddenly Bethany had something to add. "As if! She isn't pretty enough to model for a J.C. Penney's catalog let alone a real modeling job like a television campaign. Her daughter is darn lucky to have gotten her looks from her father. Now, there's a girl who could be modeling."

I'm not sure how Emily would have reacted to the veiled shot at her employer in a different situation. I probably don't want to know, but I do know that her reaction that night will always be on the list of reasons I love her. It won't be as high as the fact that she is the most beautiful and perfect woman I've ever met, but it will be on the list.

Emily just smiled, "I'm sure she's not pretty enough for either type of modeling, but if you have enough money you can start near the top in any field, even modeling. It worked for Paris Hilton, didn't it?"

Bethany agreed, "I guess you're right, although at least Paris has halfway decent legs and her body has some shape. The only thing Bunny has in common with most models is the condescending attitude."

"You know I don't follow the news that closely, especially not suburban politics. However, I've seen the mayor and he seems like a decent looking man. What does his wife look like?" I directed the question to either, but I knew it would be Bethany who answered.

"She looks like her name says she should. She's got huge rabbit-like teeth and huge ears that even a rabbit would be ashamed to have." She smiled a little at her own analogy before continuing.

"Also, her ears aren't even the same size. Oh, and don't get me started on her nose. You think Paris Hilton needs help there? A thousand plastic surgeons couldn't get Rabbit's nose to look half that acceptable."

I didn't think she was anywhere close to being through with the disparaging remarks about Mrs. Hightower. In fact, I was sure she was just getting started. Unfortunately, I couldn't think of any good way to keep the pump primed, but move it to a more helpful subject.

I glanced at Emily and she seemed content to keep listening. I was willing to listen to more if I had to, in the hopes of hearing something that Blake might want to know. Still I was happy when Jack put his hand on his wife's knee and interjected before she could continue.

"Honey, that's probably enough about her looks. We all agree Mrs. Hightower is not model material." He glanced up at Emily and me, "Don't we agree on that?"

Even having never seen the woman, Emily and I quickly nodded our heads in agreement. There's probably not much we wouldn't have agreed about to get the conversation away from that particular subject.

"Jack, you told us earlier that he's been playing the family man card to win elections forever. Tell us more about that."

"Like I said, it's like his family is nothing more than a campaign strategy. You would not believe the dishonest crap I've seen him pull. Let me give you some examples."

Emily smiled as if this were the most interesting conversation she'd ever heard, "Yes, we'd love to hear some."

"Here's one example. He based his last reelection campaign almost entirely on 'his' success in improving the city's public schools in the state rankings. It didn't matter at all that the schools were rated only slightly higher than before. It also didn't matter to him that what little improvement did occur, occurred in spite of the mayor, not because of him."

Jack paused to take a small sip from his glass and seemed to savor the moment. I doubted if it was the wine he was savoring.

"Every campaign poster and advertisement was based on how great the city's schools had become. Pictures of his daughter standing on the entrance steps of Mesquite High School and his son at the front of Agnew Middle School were on every flyer."

Jack paused, and Emily politely asked, "Isn't it common for candidates to use their family in their campaign material? I seem to recall seeing families in literature I've received leading up to this election."

Jack barely glanced at Emily before continuing, "Sure, families are often part of any political campaign. It just seems dishonest to present your family as something it obviously isn't. For God's sake, the boy had been put into Alternative Education for disciplinary reasons when Hightower started distributing those campaign flyers. A/E students attend a completely separate campus. A campus, I might add, that wouldn't look nearly as flattering on a campaign flyer."

"Sure." I agreed, "Pretending the kid is in one school when he's actually in another isn't honest. But, isn't that why honest people seldom make successful politicians? Besides, these days, I understand it doesn't take that much for a kid to land on suspension. Wasn't it in Mesquite that a Native American boy got suspended for declining to get his hair cut?"

"That was not our fair city's proudest moment, I'll admit. Hey, I thought you said you didn't follow suburban news?"

"Well, I am in real estate," I lied. "I have to follow some local current events. I'm just saying that getting suspended these days doesn't mean a kid is a future criminal."

"You're probably right, but getting suspended for breaking into a classroom means about what it always has. It may not mean he's a future criminal, but it does mean he committed a crime."

He said it the way an attorney finishes a closing argument. I hadn't been under the impression that we were arguing, but if Jack thought we were, it couldn't hurt to let him think he had won.

"Okay, you win, the kid's a delinquent. I sometimes try too hard to give people the benefit of the doubt." I may have grown tired of lying to friends, but I was more than making up for it by lying to relative strangers.

"You have no idea how right you are. He only got suspended because seven teachers and the vice principal were there when he got caught. I've heard that his Daddy has covered up far more heinous offenses."

"Such as?"

"Oh, it's all rumors and innuendoes. I'm not going to repeat any of it, even if I do believe it. And trust me; I do believe some of it."

I did trust him on that subject. I just wished he would elaborate on it. I didn't know any way to make that happen so I tried something else. "So, is the supposedly missing daughter a young troublemaker also?"

"Not that I know of, although it wouldn't shock me. But the way her daddy used her in that campaign was even less honest. I understand not wanting the voters to know about his son. But the way he used her was worse."

"How so?" Emily and I asked in unison.

"He presents her as a shining example of how efficient the public schools have become under his leadership. Then six weeks after the election, she transferred to Ursuline Academy, a private school in Dallas."

By this time, all four of us had empty glasses, and Vino 100 was starting to dim its lights. Bethany whispered something in Jack's ear which I presumed had something to do with it being time to leave.

If I had heard it, I most likely would have agreed. Jack proved me right a few seconds later. "Hey, I'd love to bore you guys with more gossip about the fine city of Mesquite, but it's getting late. And it is, as the kids used to say, a school night."

We all stood and politely said our goodbyes, and they left. As soon as they were gone, Emily leaned in tight against me and asked, "Well, did we learn anything that might help Blake?"

"Learn anything? I was just trying to make interesting conversation, so you wouldn't be embarrassed to be out on a date with a boring real estate agent."

"I'm not sure why I told them that," she sounded like she felt guilty about it, but I wasn't sure why.

"I'm glad you did, pretending to be something I'm not is sometimes part of my job. If he had known I'm a detective, he might not have wanted to discuss the mayor. And God only knows what he would have wanted to talk about."

"Oh, I'm pretty sure what he wanted to talk about would be somebody whose first name is Jack and last name is Cannelly." I was still laughing at her joke when she kissed me.

"Hey, I'm starting to enjoy being a real estate agent. And I know a cozy little property on the southeast edge of downtown that I'm just dying to show you."

This time I kissed her as she was laughing. Then we went to my place, and I showed her the property. At least I showed her as much as can be seen in the dark.

10   Reluctant Cooperation

Wednesday morning I woke up with a newfound thought that Freak's ability to get people to speak to me might not mean that he was getting people to open up to me. So, I spent the next few nights going from club to club showing pictures of the girl to anybody who would talk to me.

Percentage wise, the number of people who would talk to me unescorted in Deep Ellum was extremely low. Even so, after spending sixty hours or better at it, I had actually gotten to show the pictures to hundreds, if not thousands, of people.

Amazingly, at least fifty of them recognized the girl in one of the pictures and knew her by name. Unfortunately, it seemed every one of them recognized her by a different name. By the end of the weekend, I realized I had gone from searching for a girl with no name to searching for a girl with too many names.

Even I was able to realize that it was the same thing. I wasn't ready to give up the case or anything, but I couldn't help but wonder if I had accomplished anything at all during the time I had been on the case. Depression is an occupational hazard, but I wasn't ready to succumb to it. Not yet, anyway.

I had also shown her pictures to every bartender in Deep Ellum and not one showed any sign of recognizing her. I had hoped that a bartender might have served her and seen her driver's license, or more likely, her fake i.d. Either there was a tremendous conspiracy working to protect the girl's identity or she hadn't spent any time buying alcohol at the bars in Deep Ellum that she frequented.

Maybe she was Deep Ellum's only teetotaler. More likely, she was just one of many attractive young ladies who learned early on that attractive young ladies never have to buy drinks if they are patient enough to wait for some young, or not so young, man to offer.

Just because Deep Ellum may be an entirely different planet doesn't mean certain universal guidelines don't still apply. By the time I gave up the search on Monday night, I was tired of the search, and even more tired of Deep Ellum, but mostly I was just plain tired.

Since Tuesday was July 4th, Emily and I made date night an all day event. The highlight, for Emily, was the fireworks show in Addison. For me, the highlight was being with Emily all day, not thinking much about missing girls.

At eight o'clock Wednesday morning, my client called. Eight is an early hour for me even if I hadn't been out late the last five nights, but for Freak, it's astoundingly early. Especially when you factor in that he doesn't own a phone, so he had to leave his place and go somewhere to call me.

He got right to his point, "I'm going to come by for a progress report today. What time would be good?"

I wasn't used to clients who actually cared what time would be good, so I didn't really have an answer ready. "We can do it over the phone, right now if you want. There isn't much progress to report."

"No, if I liked handling stuff like this over the phone, I'd own one myself; just tell me a good time to drop by."

I had learned long ago that client progress reports with no real progress to report often tended to lead to ex-clients and unemployed detectives. With that in mind, I decided to put it off until I at least had time for breakfast, "How about ten?"

"All right, Monsieur Dupin, I'll see you at ten." he agreed.

He hung up before I had time to tell him that nobody calls me Monsieur Dupin, either. But I was impressed that his knowledge of crime fiction extended all the way back to the late great Edgar Allan Poe or at least to some movie version of Poe's work.

Since I was afraid this might be my last morning with a paying client, I decided to treat myself to a real breakfast, instead of relying on my toaster. After I was dressed in my best 'don't fire the detective' clothes, I walked on over to Tootsies on Ervay.

I don't know if Tootsies has the best inexpensive chicken fried steak in the area, but it is definitely in the running. However, I am certain it has the tastiest bacon, which is the most important part of an unhealthy, but delicious and affordable breakfast.

I was well fed by the time I mounted the stairs to my office at a quarter to ten. My client was already there. A potential client arriving early for a consultation is usually a good sign. A current client arriving early for a progress report usually isn't. I was glad I hadn't waited till I got back to change into my 'don't fire the detective' clothes.

When I walked in, my client asked, "Are you getting anywhere?"

"Honestly Freak, not really. I've searched the county morgue database, and there's nobody there that matches her features, so she is probably alive. But even that isn't certain. Without knowing her name, her real name, it is difficult to be certain of anything."

"I knew that. Did you learn anything in Deep Ellum over the weekend? Or were you down there on a separate case?" Again, he sounded petulant; even though I'm sure he was trying for accusatory. "Or are you investigating me instead of looking for the girl?"

"I run my investigations as I see fit. I don't need your authorization to ask questions in Deep Ellum or any place else. I appreciate the effort you took to come down there with me earlier, but I thought maybe I'd learn more without you being there."

"You're right. I was just a little surprised to hear that you had been down there all weekend. Most investigators, hell, most cops, won't go in there on a dare. I had forgotten that you aren't most investigators. Did you learn anything?"

"Not much. She seems to have been seen enough to be recognized by many people down there, but everybody knows her by a different name. She apparently introduces herself by a different name to everybody she meets. That is usually a sign of somebody trying to hide something, but I can't imagine any secret that would need to be hidden in Deep ..."

Freak interrupted, "I don't think she wants to hide anything, except maybe herself. She doesn't give different names to different people; she gives a different name each day. That's why I couldn't tell you her name. I know her as well as anybody down there, and I've never heard her use the same name twice."

"How many different names have you heard her use?"

Freak actually thought about it for a few minutes before answering, "Several hundred, but most of them really aren't names. She often just picks a word at random, like Bluebonnet or Sunset."

"Or Sparkle or Paisley," I interjected with a couple of the names I had heard her called while I was canvassing Deep Ellum.

"Exactly," he concurred. "If she has any pattern to her choices, I've no idea what it is. You aren't quitting on me, are you?"

"No, Freak, I'll keep looking and asking questions as long as you want to keep paying me, but I may be wasting my time and your money unless we find a way to get her real name."

"If I knew her real name, I'd tell you, but I don't." He sounded more depressed than I'd felt when I thought he was planning to fire me. "Even if I did know one, how would you know it was her given name?" he continued.

"I don't know. The best way to be sure would be to run her fingerprints, but somehow I doubt she gave you a nice clean set of fingerprints to identify her with while she's been yanking your chain by giving you hundreds of different names."

Freak screamed, "She isn't yanking my chain!"

It may not have been the loudest, highest pitched scream I'd ever heard from a man, but it was in the top three. I was trying to decide how best to soothe the client (and my eardrums) when he continued in a more normal voice.

"Look, I don't expect you to understand. Hell, I don't really understand it myself. The thing is she never pretends her name of the day is the one her parents gave her, at least not with me. It's just her way of deciding what to be called each day. Besides, it's not like the name I use is the one my parents gave me, either. The only difference I see is that she is creative enough to come up with a new one daily, and I stick with this one. She's not yanking my chain!"

"I'm sorry, Freak. I can't take the comment back, but I apologize for it. It was out of line."

"Forget it. You're a good man, you wouldn't have said it if you understood. Someday, maybe you will. Where do you find fingerprints?"

"Any smooth clean surface will have them. What works best is a surface like glass or tile that nobody else has touched. If you had a glass only she drank from, for instance."

He thought about that for several minutes, then asked, "How are fingerprints run, and can you do it?"

"Well I'm no expert, but you need a sample of the person you are running and then it's just a question of matching them to prints on file in the police database," I explained. "I can't do that, but if you think you have a sample, I have a friend at the Sheriff's department who might run it for us."

"Confidentially?" he asked.

"I don't know. There are rules that he has to follow to access the database, but if you think you have a sample, I can try."

"I might, but you have to promise it will be confidential. I have a mirror that only she uses. Nobody can know you got it from me, ever, not even her, especially not her!"

"I can try, but I can't promise. Things like that are guided by departmental rules that may not offer that kind of flexibility."

"Weren't you telling me earlier that you were stuck unless you could find her real name?"

I'm not sure which is worse, having a client argue with me and win, or having a client with safety pins and rings stuck through almost

60

every visible part of his face show more common sense than me. "Okay, get me the mirror and I'll see what I can do."

"Do you promise not to tell anybody where you got it?" he asked, "Cross your heart?"

The question sounded childish even before he added the cross your heart part, but I needed that mirror to find the girl and earn my fee, so I promised. He stopped short of insisting that I cross my heart and hope to die.

He left the office, promising to bring the mirror to me Friday morning. I then proceeded to waste a day and a half trying to figure out why a girl who would leave her makeup mirror at Freak's place wouldn't ever find time to share her real birth name with him. I also wasted some time wondering how I was going to get Blake to run it for prints without telling him how I got it.

11   Revealing Mirror

I was sitting at my desk contemplating these issues Friday morning at 9:17. That's when Freak came into my waiting area and rang the buzzer. I hit the remote to slide the picture over the window, then opened the door to let him into the office.

As I sat back down, he gently set a four inch square mirror wrapped in a plastic sandwich bag on my desk. As I looked at it, he sat down in a client chair daring me to comment. It obviously wasn't a makeup mirror.

A faint white residue was visible on the mirror's surface, but even without that, the most naive person on earth would recognize its purpose. I mentally kicked myself for not considering that makeup isn't the only reason a Deep Ellum girl might need a mirror.

I took turns staring at the mirror and then at my client thinking the comment he was daring me to make might occur to me. It didn't, and eventually, he got tired of waiting, "What, no judgmental comments about my lifestyle? No condemnation of my friend? Or are you too naive to recognize what you are looking at?"

"I've seen coke mirrors before, Freak. I sort of figured you hired me to find the girl, not judge her, or you. You do realize though, that when they run this for prints, everybody's prints will turn up, including yours. I won't have to tell them where I got it if your prints are on file."

"My prints are on file, I did two years of ROTC in high school, but they're not on that mirror. I've never touched it. She brought it by one night, and as far as I know she's the only one who has ever touched it."

"So you two have his and hers coke mirrors, huh? How sweet!"

"I knew if I stayed here long enough, you'd get judgmental on us. I think she does coke because she knows she shouldn't and it makes her feel like she's a rebel. But most of the other people I know who snort, do it to ease the daily pain of living. Since I've never suffered pain, I've never needed anything to ease it."

"If you say so, Freak," I said supportively, "But not all pain is physical, and your condition doesn't make you immune to the entire human experience."

"Damn, I never thought Dudley Do-Right would be encouraging me to try drugs. And don't say it: I already know your friends don't call you Dudley Do-Right."

"Neither do my clients. I'm not encouraging you to do drugs; I'm just saying that most people who indulge in them don't need a legitimate reason."

Freak sat there looking at me for several minutes. He had something to say and was trying to decide whether or not to say it. I'd seen the look many times over the years, and I knew that the best way to get to hear it was to remain silent. Most people hate silence and will say things that sometimes shouldn't be said just to keep from being forced to endure it.

He obviously didn't hate silence as much as most people, since it was almost 20 minutes before he came out with it, "She's not going to get hassled about the coke when your friend identifies her, is she? I mean he's not vice or whatever department arrests drug users, is he?"

"Well, if he does, at least you'll know where she is," I joked.

"You're not funny, Man. I don't want to find her that bad."

"Don't worry about it. She won't be hassled." I said with more confidence than I actually felt. "My friend is most definitely not in vice. Besides, the officers in vice are usually more worried about hassling the sellers, not the users. That's what it takes to get promoted high enough to start bringing in the really lucrative bribes."

My low opinion of the vice department was mostly a reflection of Blake's low opinion of them. I hadn't spent enough time with anybody there to form a real opinion of my own. Of course, in the time I had spent, I hadn't seen anything to make me think Blake was wrong, either.

At any rate, Freak was satisfied and was out the door a few minutes later, but not before making it clear he would be checking in daily for updates. Nervous, interested clients are the norm in this business, but most have telephones and will occasionally wait for me to call them and report any progress.

Freak is definitely not the norm in any way, shape or form. I just accepted that I would be seeing him in my office or hearing from him regularly until I had the answer that we hoped that coke mirror would provide. We both hoped that would be soon.

Over the years, I would estimate that Blake had done over 100 favors for me that could have gotten him fired. However, I had only requested a handful of them. His tendency to be generous to a fault was something Ana Marie was trying to cure with no success, but I tried not to take advantage of it unless it was important.

Anything related to solving a case for a paying client could be classified as important, and this was no exception. Plus, since this was a paying client who had already left a retainer and understood that certain expenses would be necessary to solve the case, it was a rare opportunity for me to return some of Blake's generosity.

I called Blake's office, and he answered on the first ring. "This is Blake."

I was surprised to hear his voice instead of Ana Marie's, but I recovered, "Did Ana Marie quit, or did they demote you to admin and give her your job?"

"You aren't funny, Buddy, but it's good to hear anybody joking today. Ana Marie is out sick, and this place is in shambles."

"Well, I was calling to see if I could treat you to lunch, but if you are too busy…"

He interrupted, "You treat? I'm never too busy for you to treat. What time does Lenny's open?"

"I was thinking Morton's, but if you prefer Lenny's, I guess I could change my mind."

"I assume this has something to do with your case. I'll make the time, but it will have to be a late one. Does 1:30 work for you?"

"Sure, that's fine. And yes, it does have to do with the case."

I'll admit that Blake and I are friends, but I'm convinced that the main reason he is usually willing to help me out is because I'm usually searching for a missing person. He truly believes that all missing persons can be found, and more will be found alive, if everybody cooperates.

Even so, I knew I was pushing it by asking him to run a fingerprint check on a coke mirror. The fact that I wanted him to run the prints without telling him where I got the mirror made it far more than simply asking for a favor.

I've seen Blake bend over backwards to help people he didn't even like just because it might help find somebody who was missing. I needed him to do more than bend over backwards here; I needed him to do somersaults around the rules of the Sheriff's department to get me information on a case about which I was not sharing any information.

That is why I was sitting at the back of Morton's bar with a view of the door at 1:25 that afternoon. Morton's is a national chain and certainly isn't the best steakhouse in Dallas. Nick and Sam's on Maple or Al Beirnet's on Cedar Springs would be the frontrunners in that race.

However, Morton's is conveniently located downtown, is open for lunch and is pretty darn good for a chain restaurant. More salespeople had closed more lucrative deals over a steak at Morton's than at any of the 300 plus golf courses in the Metroplex.

I'm not a salesperson, but I needed to make a sale if I was going to have any chance of earning a fee from my client. Blake arrived at 1:35. On a Friday at noon, there's a long wait for a table. Since it was Thursday after the lunch rush, we were shown to a table almost immediately. In addition to perfectly prepared steaks and large portions, Morton's offers service that is hard to beat.

Blake had the prime rib and baked potato, while I had a chopped steak and fries. The salads arrived quickly, and the entrées were ready by the time we finished them.

Morton's fare is so far above my usual lunch fare that I feared that my taste buds might never accept the return to what I'm used to having for lunch. Still, I'm not going to complain. After all, it is an expense account lunch even if Blake refuses to help out, and even though I decided not to bring up the subject while we were eating.

Our conversation while we ate was entirely sports related. Will the Rangers stay in first place? Can the Cowboys win the Super Bowl this year? Are either the Mavericks or the Stars going to go further in the playoffs next year than they did this year? Our consensus was no on all four questions, but we gave the Mavericks the best chance and the Rangers the least.

Okay, so we're not exactly original thinkers when it comes to the fortunes of local sports teams. At least we got through a delicious lunch with no depressing talk about missing people. In our line of work, that is an important key to maintaining any degree of sanity.

As I was paying the check, Blake saved me the trouble of deciding just how to broach the subject of the favor I needed him to do for me. "So, who do you want me to kill?" he asked.

"Nothing that drastic, but thanks for offering."

"Actually, I didn't offer; I just asked. I was hoping it might be somebody who deserved to die, anyway, like maybe one of our County Commissioners."

"Well I'm sorry to disappoint you," I said kindly. "All I want you to do is run a mirror for fingerprints."

66

"Oh, you want me to kill my career and leave the Commissioner's Court intact. Seems like a waste of time. What's in it for me? And who are you trying to identify?"

I hate to lie and the truth is often inconvenient, so not for the first time I told a half-truth, "I have a reason to suspect that my client's missing girl held a mirror that I acquired while I was investigating her possible whereabouts. If she's on file, this might be a break in my investigation."

"Where did you get it?"

"I came across it in the course of a perfectly legal investigation for a client."

Blake leaned back in the comfortable chair that Morton's has at its tables and stared at me suspiciously. As the person doing the selling in this negotiation, I knew it was best not to be the one to break the silence.

After a short time that seemed like an eternity, he spoke, "You are so full of crap, you could almost ruin this fine meal, but bring the mirror over to the house tonight, and I'll have the prints run."

When I got back to my office, the light on the answering machine was lit, so I guessed that I had a message from my client. It was a logical guess, given that he had said he would be checking in regularly and he wasn't sitting in a client chair.

Instead, it was Blake, "Hey, Man, thanks for the best lunch I've had in weeks. Since you are dropping by tonight anyway, why don't you see if Emily can come with you? We'll play some cards or dominoes or something. Jade is always complaining that we hardly ever have y'all over, and this is a perfect opportunity."

I called Emily at her office and told her about the invitation. "Let's do it," she replied quickly enough to let me know she agreed with Jade. "But I have one condition."

"Just one? Sounds too easy, what is the condition?"

"You boys have to limit the shop talk. Last time the four of us got together, Jade and I learned enough about detective work to get us both through the Police Academy with honors, but we never even finished the first bridge rubber."

"Fine, I promise to keep the shop talk to a minimum. But if I recall, we didn't finish the rubber because we lost the first set and were losing the second, and you simply hate to lose."

"Possibly, but if you'd paid more attention to the game and less attention to the discussion of police procedures maybe we wouldn't have lost the first set."

She probably had a valid point there. Bridge is a game I play pretty well, and Emily is very good. But when I'm not concentrating, I tend to overbid, and we usually lose when that happens.

Even if she was wrong, it wasn't worth debating, so I didn't. "I promise to pay attention to the game tonight."

———

Since Blake and Jade live in Irving, much closer to my place than Emily's, we agreed that she would pick me up around 7:00. Of course, I realized that meant I should expect her sometime between 7:30 and 8:00.

That gave me three hours to think of something I could do to help my client. Unfortunately, three hours wasn't enough time for me to think of anything helpful. Mostly, it was time for me to think that I really needed Blake to find something helpful on that mirror.

I didn't come up with any ideas that would help my client, but I did get a visit from him. I tried to assure him that the investigation was progressing. He seemed satisfied with my report, even though I wasn't as convinced as he was.

I left the mirror in the sandwich bag, dropped it in a Ziploc bag, and tucked that bundle securely into a backpack to transport it to Blake's when Emily picked me up. If there was a useful print on that mirror, it wasn't going to be lost because I wasn't careful with it.

Emily picked me up at 7:15, early by her standards. I had told Blake to expect us about 8:30, so I called him to let him know we would be there a little earlier.

"Hey that's great, see you then. Oh, I'm glad you called." He paused briefly before continuing, "Jade insists that we keep the conversation light. She doesn't want to hear about missing kids all night."

"No problem, Emily pretty much gave me the same instructions. Plus, I really need a night of light conversation, anyway."

"Cool, Jade was worried that you were wanting me to solve your case for you tonight. Oh, one other thing, she says bridge is not an option. We're either playing Trivial Pursuit or dominoes."

Blake hates Trivial Pursuit almost as much as he loves Jade. So I put him out of his misery as quickly as possible, "Let's make it dominoes then. It will give Emily and me another chance to disprove one more racial stereotype."

"I know how you hate racial stereotypes, but even if y'all do win, it won't mean that one's not true. It could just mean you're not really white."

"I'll take that as a compliment, but you've seen me play basketball, so you know better."

"Good point, Casper," he said laughing. Then, he hung up before I could point out that my friends don't call me Casper.

I told Emily that we would be playing dominoes because Jade insisted. On the drive to Irving, we took turns reminding each other of the keys to playing and winning at dominoes.

I had been playing dominoes since my days on the high school basketball team. Emily had only started playing since she started dating me and hanging out with Blake and Jade. That's probably why she's only a little bit better at it than me.

Blake is still better than either of us. Even if he weren't, I would never jeopardize his standing in the black community by suggesting otherwise. But Emily and I are pretty good, and Emily is far more competitive than either Jade or Blake.

As Emily pulled off Highway 183 onto O'Connor, I was looking forward to a friendly, but competitive night of dominoes. I was also looking forward to a night devoid of discussion about missing people. It turned out I would have to settle for one out of two.

I knocked on the door of their house on Northgate. Jade answered almost immediately. No matter how many times I see Jade, I can't get used to how small she is. Slightly less than five foot tall, and thinner than she is short, she is the smallest adult I've ever known.

As Blake came into the living room from the kitchen, the stark difference in their size struck me again. Emily and I sometimes joke that we only hang around with them because they're one of the few couples with a greater height difference than ours.

——

70

I handed Blake the bag with the mirror. He put it in his briefcase; then turned to me, "So, now that I have the evidence, why don't you tell me where you got it."

I again replied, "I came across it in the course of a perfectly legal investigation for a client."

Blake smiled. "That sounds vaguely familiar; let's get started on the bones."

I was careful not to start any conversation about our cases. Several times, though, Blake would either bemoan his lack of progress or chide me for taking the case I had taken. He also mentioned that the mayor had upped the reward from $250,000 to $500,000.

To be polite, I kept commiserating with him on both counts. Jade and Emily both took the earliest opportunity to change the subject each time Blake went there.

We split the first two hands with Jade and Blake winning the first, and Emily and I winning the second. Midway through the third hand, I noticed that Emily was smiling her Cheshire cat smile. It only took me a few seconds to figure out what she was smiling about.

When I'm distracted, I tend to overbid. When Blake is similarly distracted while playing dominoes, he tends to tip his hand by playing too fast when he has a good hand and too slow when he doesn't.

Emily had noticed before I did that Blake was tipping his hand. Once I also realized it, the rest of the games weren't close. As I laid down a three-six to empty my hand for the fourth straight time, Blake just shook his head as he counted up the points left on his and Jade's tiles.

"Hey, Ringer, why don't you freshen our drinks while I do the dishes. I've had to do it so many times; somebody else should do the real kitchen work."

When it's just Blake and I playing, 'do the dishes' isn't the term we use for losing a hand and having to shuffle the tiles. However, around the ladies we try to keep it polite.

Emily came into the kitchen to help me with the drinks. I grabbed two beers for Blake and me, while she poured two more margaritas. She kissed me before we walked back out. "Don't get overconfident, dear. They might still come back and win."

I doubted it, but I nodded. When we got back to the table, Blake was still complaining about losing so many straight hands. Jade decided to change the subject.

"Well, Emily, it looks like you guys might actually win tonight, and from what I'm hearing, neither of our men is going to find any missing girls any time soon. So let's talk about something important. Like when are you two getting married, and do I get to be in the wedding party?"

I didn't even have time to propose or panic before Emily laughed faintly and smiled at me with just the slightest hint of a wink. The way she had of smiling and winking simultaneously always brightened my day.

I returned her smile and started thinking again about how Emily and I had agreed years ago that a wedding vow was seldom a contributing factor to a strong relationship. While I was thinking about that, I simply looked into her blue eyes and was amazed again by just how beautiful she is.

Emily interrupted my reverie, "Oh please, no wedding talk! See how he's looking at me, now? Married men almost never look at their wives that way, present company excluded, of course. But, he looks at me that way every time he sees me, and I bask in it every time. What kind of fool would I have to be to risk giving that up, just to have another ring to wear?"

She held up her hands to show off the beautiful rings she already wore before continuing. "Besides which, I love having my own place. I can create a virtual pink jungle paradise with all the lace and flowers and fur-trimmed accessories I want, with never a thought towards balancing it with masculine touches."

That visual image made me smile. Emily was right about the difference in our taste. While I loved to take an occasional safari into her feminine jungle, I couldn't quite imagine how it would be to sleep with a fake mink throw on my bed every night.

When we finally finished playing dominoes and discussing the pros and cons of marriage, Blake asked again about the origin of the mirror, and I answered as before, "I came across it in the course of a perfectly legal investigation for a client."

"Of course you did." He sounded a little sad as he continued, "All your investigations for all your clients are perfectly legal. I'm the only one who breaks the law for your clients."

Emily decided to come over to my place for a night cap. We were both tired when we got there, so we skipped the night cap and turned in.

Saturday morning, she had no trouble convincing me to take the weekend off with her. Her busy season had just ended, and there wasn't much I could do on the case until Blake got results from the mirror.

We spent most of Saturday at Trader's Village flea market, then went to her place where she cooked dinner for us. I don't love flea markets like she does, but I do enjoy the atmosphere and the people-watching.

Sunday afternoon, we went to Arlington for the Rangers' game. She doesn't love baseball as much as I do, but she loves the ballpark experience and the food. We both enjoyed that the Rangers beat the Twins and their ace Johan Santana five to two. It was a great weekend, but it didn't help my client any.

It was extremely late when I got home Sunday night. If I had known how Monday was going to turn out, I probably would have tried to get more sleep. Either that, or I might have chosen to get out of the detective business entirely.

13   Arresting Convergence

My phone rang at 7:17 on Monday morning. If this kept up, I was going to have to give serious consideration to throwing it away, and living without a phone the way Freak does. Of course, that would make it hard to make a living, but 7:17 in the morning is too early to wake up, and a ringing phone is a terrible way to wake up at any time of day.

I finally found the receiver and managed to mumble something which I hoped sounded like a greeting. It must have been close enough, because I then heard the voice of Jesse Reynolds, who owns Right-on-Time Delivery where I sometimes work. "Hey, Ace Ventura, made a fortune in the detective business, yet? Or can you use a little money bad enough to help out a friend?"

Of course, my friends don't call me Ace Ventura, but Jesse is a pretty good guy and even with Freak's retainer in the bank, money is hard to turn down. Besides, until or unless Blake was able to identify the girl I'd been hired to find, there still wasn't much I could do to solve my case.

I replied, "If you promise to quit calling me names, I'll try to help you out. What do you need?"

"Two of my best guys called in sick, and we've got a million stops to make this morning. If I can't find someone to step in, I'll have to try to do some myself, and you know how many years it's been since I've been useful on a bike."

"If only to save some poor bicycle from suffering a fate several hundred pounds worse than death, I'll help you out. I hope my kindness doesn't keep me from solving this big case I'm working on, though."

"I'm so desperate, I'll even let you insult me about my weight and pretend I'm keeping you from a case. Can you be ready by eight? I've got a dozen pickups that need to be delivered to the courts before nine thirty."

I would have traded more insults with him, but I was going to have to hurry to retrieve my bike and start by eight, so I told him I would be there and switched into hurry mode.

I like my office, but it doesn't exactly have a place to store a bicycle, so I keep my bike in the back of my van. Of course, my office also doesn't come with a parking spot, so I keep my van in the parking garage at Republic Center on St. Paul.

One good thing about the Republic Tower garage is that it's only a few blocks away. Another is that it is relatively safe since it is underground, has valet during the day and is locked at night. The best thing about it though, is that my friend Gus manages the place and lets me keep my van there at no charge.

At 7:47, I was on my bike and earning money. During rush hour in downtown, a fifteen minute walk can be a twenty or thirty minute drive depending on how many one-way streets and uncooperative traffic lights are involved. On a bike, however, an aggressive and fortunate rider can almost always cover the same ground in ten minutes or less.

All of which may explain why an aggressive bike courier can make more money than an honest detective. By the way, couriers don't actually get paid extra for scaring the hell out of pedestrians as we pass by at forty miles per hour. It's simply a fringe benefit of the job.

Jesse wasn't exaggerating as much as usual about the number of courthouse deliveries. By eight thirty, I had picked up twenty envelopes from about a dozen lawyers to deliver to various county courts in the Records Building on Main and the Federal Building on Commerce.

I started on the eastern part of downtown, picking up one envelope from an independent attorney in a storefront office on Olive Street. Then I worked my way back through the prestigious firms in Thanksgiving Tower and the 1700 Pacific building where I picked up most of the work.

From there, I went south to pick up three more envelopes from the Poverty Law Center on Main Street. Two more stops on Main and I was ready to deliver the pickups.

I first delivered all the envelopes to the various judges' clerks at the Federal Building. Finally, I dropped off the last envelopes to the appropriate county clerks on several of the floors of the Records Building at 9:17.

Since the Records Building is about the distance of a routine fly ball from the George Allen building where Blake worked, I was not surprised to see Ana Marie as I left the building to get back on the bike and back to making money. I was a little surprised that she saw me first and walked over to talk.

She got straight to the point, "Are you undercover or just trying to make sure you still have a way to make a living after you get Blake fired?"

"I'm just doing somebody a favor. Blake isn't the only person who can do that, you know."

"Oh, I know that, Amigo, I just enjoy thinking of you as the receiver of favors. It makes Blake look better. If I have to work a thankless government job with no chance of promotion, I can at least find ways to make it less mundane."

"And canonizing your boss makes it less mundane?"

"Well, I haven't made him a saint, at least not yet, but 'Santo Harrison' does roll off the tongue." She exaggerated the rolling of the 'r' in Harrison just to remind me that even though she normally spoke English like an Ivy League professor, she hadn't totally discarded her heritage.

"Besides," I reminded her, "until Saint Blake gets back to me with the results from the mirror, I can't do much detective work. Helping out with these deliveries gives me something to do other than sit in your lobby while I wait."

She smiled a little as she replied, "Gracias a Dios para su bicicleta."

—

76

No parting comment seemed appropriate, so I moved along without one. I was glad to have learned that her occasional complaints about Blake's favors to me were mostly in jest. At least, that's what I took from our chat. I had no idea what, if anything, Ana Marie took from it.

I spent the rest of the morning as a bike courier. A little after noon, Jesse told me we were caught up and asked me if I needed him to pay me now. I told him, no, that I wasn't kidding about being on a case and headed for home.

I got back to my office just before two o'clock. Blake was sitting in my client chair, and it was obvious that he wasn't happy even before he yelled at me, "What the hell are you trying to pull!?"

I had no idea what he was talking about, so I sat down at my desk and smiled what I hoped was a pleasant smile. "Are you still mad about losing Friday night, or is something actually bothering you?"

"Don't try to change the subject on me, Tenspeed. Where did you get that mirror, and why are you horning in on an official case of mine without telling me?"

"I told you, I came across that mirror in the course of a perfectly legal investigation for a client. I had and still have no reason to suspect that it is related to any official investigation. As I told you earlier, my client did not file a police report, preferring to rely on my skills."

"You've obviously delivered so many envelopes from law firms that it's rubbing off on you. You're starting to talk like an attorney."

I could tell he meant it as an insult, but I could think of many things worse than sounding like a lawyer. One that immediately came to mind was sounding like an angry cop. At the moment, I didn't see any advantage in discussing the things I was thinking. Waiting patiently may well be my best talent, and this seemed like an excellent opportunity to put it to use.

I didn't have to wait patiently very long. He broke the silence with a whisper that was somehow more emphatic than his earlier scream, "One more time, where did you get that mirror?"

His dark brown face was flushed with an anger I'd never seen directed my way, but I only had one answer. I started to repeat myself, "I came across it in the course of a perfectly..."

His interruption was no longer a whisper, "You tried that. I'm not buying it. I want the truth, now!"

"That is the truth, Blake. If you want me to tell you any details that might be related to that truth, you need to give me a reason."

We sat and looked at each other for awhile. His gray eyes were barely open. I could tell he was trying to decide what to say next, but I couldn't decide why. He reached for his cell phone twice, but stopped each time.

Eventually, he shook his head slowly, and then said, "I was ordered not to tell you something. If I tell you and anybody finds out I did, I'll be fired. This isn't Ana Marie trying to make you feel guilty, I'll definitely be fired. If I tell you, will anybody find out?"

"Not from me, they won't. You know that, or you wouldn't even think of taking the risk."

He sighed, "Yes, I know it. I guess I just needed to hear it from you. The prints on the mirror belong to Katherine Elizabeth Hightower."

This time I wasn't silent as a strategy; I was completely struck dumb. Could Freak's missing girl really be the daughter of the mayor of Mesquite? It seems impossible, but how else would he have a coke mirror with her prints on it?

I tried to get my mind to accept the idea, but it didn't work. Instead, I kept thinking of absurd possibilities, none of which, upon later reflection, did anything to contribute to my self-esteem.

—

The least ridiculous was that Freak had stolen the mirror from her at some time. Obviously, even Freak wouldn't bring me a stolen mirror to give to the police. As I said, I wasn't proud of any of the theories.

Blake tired of my waiting, "So, I'll ask again: Where did you get that mirror?"

Even to me, my answer sounded lame, "I can't tell you."

Blake jumped out of his chair, slammed his fist on my desk and screamed again, "You can and you will!"

"I can't, Blake. I made a promise. You know I keep my word. If you didn't know that, you wouldn't have even considered trusting me enough to tell me about the prints."

"I know. You think you have to be honest Abraham 'freakin' Lincoln."

"This is Texas, Blake. Sam Houston is our standard for honesty. Mr. Lincoln's just a Yankee with a funny hat."

"Sure, whatever. Look, I like you, you know that, but there's only so much I can put up with, even for you. You are going to get us both in more trouble than we can handle. Promise or no promise, you have to tell me where you got that mirror."

"Why is it so important? Unless her prints are the only ones on the mirror, you and your bosses should have a lead or two to follow before harassing me becomes the only option."

"So now you want to tell me how to do my job?"

"No, it's just that the mirror was obviously used as a coke mirror, so you have probable cause to bring in anybody whose prints are on it for questioning."

"Possibly true, but we also have probable cause to bring you in as a material witness. They let me come and talk to you instead of sending someone with an arrest warrant as a favor to me."

"What a favor. Did they give you an arrest warrant?"

"No, I'm either supposed to know the source of the mirror or have you behind bars by day's end. Do I need a warrant, my friend?"

"No, I'll let you take me in without one. However, in jail, I'll have no chance to find the girl or get an okay to tell you where I got the mirror. It's your choice, but I don't see how that will help us find the girl." I deliberately emphasized the word 'us' just like he'd emphasized the word 'friend'.

"You'll get two phone calls a day in jail, and we'll find the girl. You're good at what you do, maybe even better than you think you are. However, the department does manage to find people without your help sometimes."

"Are you going to cuff me?" I asked as I stood to let him take me in.

"No, you want to make any calls from here before we go?"

Now that I knew the situation, I was worried that Freak might show up for a progress report, so I declined. On the way out, I locked the outer office door for a change and headed across town with my friend taking me to jail.

14   Distasteful Quarters

By 6:30, I was processed, booked and sitting alone in a cell with time by myself to think. I probably should have been thinking about how to get released, how to find Katherine Elizabeth Hightower or how to get out of my promise to Freak.

Instead, I was thinking about how ironic irony could be. This morning I had been welcomed into some of the most prestigious law offices in Dallas. I had delivered important documents to the courtrooms of the very judges who were entrusted with the duty of determining the futures of the residents at Lew Sterrett.

Only a few hours later, I was one of the people in a cell in Lew Sterrett needing the services of a lawyer to convince one of the judges that my future should not include an extended stay here. I had used one phone call to let Emily know where I was, and that I might be here for an extended stay. My second call needed to be to a lawyer.

It might have been nice if I could have retained the services of any one of the high-profile attorneys whose administrative assistants and paralegals had been so happy to see me this morning. Unfortunately, even with most of Freak's retainer still resting leisurely in the bank, there was little chance of that.

Instead I called Daniel Leeds, the attorney I always call. His machine answered, "Greetings, your attempt to converse with the solicitor has been intercepted by an electronic recording device. Please communicate your needs at the conclusion of this outgoing message. I will commence on your behalf, immediately upon learning the details of your supplication."

Daniel had a knack for using two fifty cent words when one ordinary word would have worked just fine. When I first met him, I presumed all lawyers did that, but I've learned much about lawyers since then.

After I left him a message explaining as much of the situation as I felt appropriate, I initially regretted not calling him from the office. On further reflection, I doubted that it would matter. The district attorney was determined to make me sweat, and it didn't seem likely that my attorney could prevent it.

The county of Dallas has over 200 attorneys on its payroll. I've probably met about half of those, and I like most of them. Only a handful get under my skin, and only one do I truly despise.

So, of course, I was not surprised when Blake told me that Douglas Kenth was the attorney on my case. I don't know if Napoleon syndrome is real or not, but if it is, he is the textbook example.

He's about five foot six and tries to compensate for his height with the worst attitude of anybody I've ever met. His attitude around me is even worse, since I learned that he hates being called Dougie even worse than he hates being more than a foot shorter than I.

I wasn't looking forward to being around D.A. Kenth again, but other than that, being in jail is not nearly as bad as most people assume it is. Of course, most people have never been in a jail or a prison, so they don't distinguish between a county jail and a federal penitentiary.

County lockup isn't like a trip to Six Flags or Disneyland, but it is nothing like a stint in prison. In prison, you are locked up with people who have been sentenced to years or forever behind bars, some of whom have given up any hope of ever being free again. Not surprisingly, these people represent real and recognizable danger.

Fortunately, for me, I was locked up at Lew Sterrett, a county facility, with a collection of 'miscreants' who mostly hadn't paid speeding tickets on time or had gotten drunk at the wrong time and place.

This meant I had to spend the night in a cell that was almost exactly the same size as my bedroom on Young Street. I also had to share it for a short while with a scared kid who sniffled for the entire hour and forty-five minutes it took before his parents got him released.

———

I laughed occasionally while he was there thinking about how he would describe his cellmate and his reaction to being in the 'graybar hotel' when he tried to impress his friends with the story of his incarceration. My guess was that the only true part of the recounting would be my height. I finally realized that every time I laughed, he whimpered more, so I decided to desist.

Since I had not yet located my attorney, the county lawyers left me pretty much alone. Nothing mucks up the system more than people being questioned without their attorneys present. Being locked up is probably harder for someone who gets locked up after years of living in luxury. For me, it was mostly a temporary change of address. It certainly wasn't the Anatole Hotel, but it wouldn't kill me.

Of course, it would lessen the chances that I would find Katherine Elizabeth Hightower, or learn why my client also wanted to find her. Now that I knew who I was looking for, I should have been back in my element. Instead, I was in jail.

I knew it wasn't Blake's decision for me to be here. I started wondering about the man whose decision it probably was. They had been looking for Katherine Elizabeth Hightower for a long time with no luck. As soon as I get involved in the search, I'm put in jail.

I couldn't help but wonder if my not being able to find her from here was the reason I was here. Douglas Kenth might have me put in jail just for fun, but he could also have a reason. I wondered if he had any connection with the Mesquite City Council.

I was still manufacturing conspiracy theories and trying to connect Dougie to as many as possible when I finally fell asleep sometime after midnight. I slept better than I should have all things considered. Even so, I had been awake for several hours when I was taken to talk to my lawyer at 9:15 the next morning.

Daniel has been my attorney ever since I entered the detective business. At the time, he was making a nice living specializing in representing detectives. He and the old man who hired me at Pegasus had been fraternity brothers at SMU in the sixties. I'm not sure if that's how he ended up specializing in detectives, but it seems likely.

Daniel had mostly retired after he had a stroke two years ago. However, he promised me that as long as I kept Pegasus Investigations afloat, he would represent me. He did not look happy about that decision as he stood to shake my hand. For a small man over sixty years old, he has a firm handshake.

He had already met with the district attorney and got right down to business, "I presume that you have no intention of divulging the circumstances which resulted in the mirror in question coming into your possession."

"Right, I made a promise, and I intend to keep it."

"I am indisputably cognizant of your tenacious proclivity to honor your promises regardless of the potential repercussions. Therefore, I shall not endeavor to convince you to renege on this one. However, as your barrister, it is my professional duty to inform you of any expected consequences. Failure to disclose, at a minimum, the name of the person from whom the mirror was attained in all probability will eliminate any present potential of a release from your current state of incarceration."

He looked even more disappointed about that than I felt, but he continued in his own inimitable and wordy way, "The district attorney has reclassified your status from material witness to person of interest. Person of interest, as you are indubitably aware, is merely a less actionable term for suspect. Having accomplished this status change, he will precipitously endeavor to have you conveyed into court to be interrogated regarding the mirror and its heritage."

"How soon, and what happens when I refuse to answer?"

"In all likelihood, that event will transpire this very afternoon, perhaps as immediate as four o'clock. Failure on your part to provide a satisfactory response will afford him the opportunity to charge you with contempt of court and obstruction of justice."

"So he charges me with something and puts me in jail. I'm already in jail, doesn't seem like that big a deal to me."

As Daniel shook his head, his piercing blue eyes seemed to bore through me. "Currently, you may effortlessly secure your discharge from this august facility by providing the answers they desire. Should the impasse reach the unfortunate zenith of a contempt of court or obstruction of justice conviction, your release could not be attained with such ease."

"And as my attorney, how do you plan to keep that unfortunate conclusion from happening?"

"Unfortunately, my options are dreadfully paltry. Client privilege does not extend to private investigators, it is limited to attorneys. I will contend that no evidence of a crime has been established, thus preventing you from being a person of interest..."

I interjected, "Won't they use the coke residue on the mirror as the crime?"

"That avenue is not available, for the curious reason that the only residue found on the mirror was baking soda. I wish I could state that that development was likely to assist you; unfortunately, it is my practiced opinion that you are in jeopardy nonetheless."

"Not that I mind, but did you consider coming to see me and letting me know you were working on this, maybe getting my side of the story before getting the details from the county's attorneys?"

"As your attorney, your interests are mine. I chose to first meet with them so they would not presume that I had cognizance of your agenda and would, therefore, not consume hours attempting to devise a technique which would coerce me into divulging it."

He paused to wait for a response from me. He didn't get one, so he continued.

"By convening with them first, my taciturn compatriot, I created the opportunity to ascertain what they know; full disclosure is such a magnificent law, without revealing anything at all about our position. Besides, you knew I was engaged, as you did leave a message for me."

"Well, that explains why I always hire you when I need legal advice."

"You regularly employ me because I allow you to prevail yourself of my services at a fraction of the customary pecuniary amount. My advice right now is that you not become optimistic about your likelihood of returning soon to hearth and home."

I had a home, but I doubted that it had a hearth. I made a mental note to look up hearth in a dictionary when I got a chance.

My attorney didn't like my chances of getting out of here any time soon. That couldn't bode well, but I knew Daniel would do all that he could. The question was if he could do anything or not.

At the moment, I was more interested in the fact that the mirror wasn't used for cocaine. It didn't escape me that I wouldn't even know this important fact if my attorney hadn't discovered it for me. Daniel may not have an office in a high-rise on Elm Street, but he definitely knew how to do his job.

15   Unexpected Guests

I was taken back to my cell fully expecting to have several hours alone to consider the implications of this new and surprising fact before being taken to court. Instead, Blake and Dougie Kenth paid me a visit.

Today, with me in a cell, Dougie definitely felt like a little emperor, and it was obvious as soon as he spoke, "So, the lanky gumshoe doesn't want to cooperate with the real investigators." He turned and looked up at Blake, "I told you that if you kept hanging around with useless wannabes something bad would happen."

As usual, I didn't like his attitude, and I especially didn't like him turning it on Blake. So I decided to take the offensive. I jumped up quickly and stood as close to them as the cell bars permitted.

"He has to hang around with useless people, Dougie, he works for the same County Government that you do. I, on the other hand, do not. Tell me what you want to tell me, then get out of my face."

I briefly looked down at what has to be the least effective comb-over in the long, sad history of ineffective comb-overs; then added, "Or I should say get out of my chest." I'm certain his friends didn't call him Dougie, but I don't know if he has friends. And since I started doing it, many of his associates have started doing it.

In spite of himself, and the fact that the cell bars separated us, he jumped back a few feet when I started toward him. There wasn't anything he could do about it to save face now. Blake was trying not to laugh and mostly succeeding.

He bowed up as best as a man giving up over a foot in height can be expected to bow up. "Don't mess with me on this; you have information on an important case. No matter what it takes, I am going to get you to cooperate. Where did you get that mirror?"

"As I told the arresting officer, I came across that mirror in the…" Blake had heard it so often that he joined me for the conclusion, "…course of a perfectly legal investigation for a client."

Dougie was not amused, but Dougie was never amused by anything that didn't make him feel powerful. Even though he is a District Attorney, nobody respects him at all, so he should have been used to not feeling powerful. Everybody else was used to him not being amused.

He shot me his most intimidating look, "You can clown around all you want, Shoofly. If that girl isn't found because you didn't tell me where you got that mirror, I will make sure you hang for it." Realizing that I was not intimidated, he turned on Blake, "Whose side are you on, Blake? This does not reflect well on you."

"Side? I'm not on a side. I get paid to look for missing persons. I'm trying to find a girl who is missing. When I heard you say you were coming down to talk to this witness, I wanted to make sure I was here to learn what could be learned."

"He's a person of interest now, not a witness; and what did you learn?"

Blake smiled at Dougie, then looked at me. "Should I tell him what I've learned so far?"

Dougie exploded, "What the hell are you asking him for? You will tell me what you've learned, now!"

"Well, if you insist, I've learned that you are an emotional little twit who isn't qualified to be an attorney, let alone work for the county as one. You have questioned an incarcerated person of interest without his attorney being present and without even advising him of his right to have his attorney present."

As Blake spoke Dougie backed away as if he were being threatened. Blake didn't move, he just calmly went on, "To make matters worse, you have also threatened the same person, in the process demonstrating an embarrassing lack of familiarity with the laws of this state. I don't know how y'all did your executions up in Michigan, but here in Texas we use the electric chair."

As Dougie continued to back away, I suppressed the desire to laugh, but it wasn't easy.

"When, and if, this person of interest decides to sue the county over your inexcusable incompetence, you will have the opportunity to see whose side I am on. I'm certain you won't like what you learn, and I am certain I won't care. Until then, I strongly suggest that you should get as far away from me as you can get and stay there."

Dougie left with as much dignity as he could muster, which was virtually none. I was just glad he left. I told Blake, "I don't have this much fun at home. I should have you arrest me more often."

"Look, you know I'm sorry about having to do that, but don't forget you are still in deep trouble. The longer that girl stays missing, the more likely it becomes that this case will end in a funeral instead of a joyful reunion. If that happens, the esteemed counselor Kenth will be hell-bent on charging you with accessory to murder."

"Hell, Blake, he'd kill her himself if he thought it would keep me here. His hatred of me is less of a secret than my opinion of him. That's one reason I need to get out of here and start looking for her."

"Well, I'm going to go try to find this missing girl. I've spread my other cases out among my staff; I'm full-time on this one now. Try to get yourself out of here, so you can be full-time on it, also. Breaking a promise isn't a cardinal sin, I don't think."

"Thanks for the advice, Blake, and thanks for everything." I held my hand through the cell door and we shook before he left. Whatever happens, I will always cherish the memory of Dougie trying and failing to intimidate an inmate and a subordinate at the same time.

As expected, at four o'clock I was escorted to a squad car wearing the orange jumpsuit which the county had issued me. I was taken over to the Frank Crowley Building to answer questions in front of a county judge about a missing girl and a mirror. My attorney was already at the defendant's table when the bailiff took me in.

Daniel smiled and nodded subtly at the Judge's bench. I followed his gaze and noticed that for the first time since Freak had been waiting for me in my office, I had caught a break. District Judge Lamont Walker was presiding.

Judge Walker has a well earned reputation for making decisions based on the facts and the situations rather than relying entirely on the letter of the law. I had often heard him describe his judicial style as concentrating on the intent of the law to reach a fair ruling.

He is also a world class domino player who has never lost to Blake or me, even though we've had many chances. I've heard it said that Lamont Walker put the dots on the dominoes, but I don't think it's true.

Of course, the only one I've heard say that is Lamont Walker, but even if he didn't invent them, he's studied them extensively. Daniel probably didn't know that, but it didn't matter much. Judge Walker is too honest and professional to cut me much slack, but I could at least hope for a little.

Daniel and I sat silently at the defendant's table while Judge Walker examined the documents which Daniel and Dougie had previously submitted. He read them all thoroughly, and went back and reread several of them. After what seemed to be an eternity, he put all the documents down.

"So Mister Kenth, you contend that this person of interest should be charged with contempt of court and obstruction of justice."

"Yes, your honor." Only Dougie could look smarmy while answering a simple question, but somehow he managed it. He continued, "The County would prefer, of course, that he simply cooperate with the investigation, but he has thus far refused."

Judge Walker looked toward us, "Mr. Leeds, is your client willing to cooperate at this time? It does seem to be the simplest way to resolve this issue without the need for criminal charges. Charges, by the way, which can not reflect well on a person in his profession."

"Your honor has demonstrated cognizance of my client's profession. His is by definition a profession in which a certain amount of jeopardy is unavoidable. One of the multitudes of risks is that his voluntary cooperation with law enforcement will lead to an unjustified expectation of complete subservience. In this particular case..."

Judge Walker cleared his throat, which Daniel knew was meant to interrupt him. "Mr. Leeds, your command of the language, whichever language it is you are currently commanding, is clearly impressive as always. I'll ask the question more specifically, 'Is your client going to tell the court where he got that mirror?"

"I will reluctantly accept the potential consequence of oversimplifying a complicated situation with a monosyllabic response: No."

Nobody bothered to mention that Daniel's response had not, in fact, been one syllable. I certainly didn't mention it. I simply sat at the bench trying to look as cooperative as a person who is not cooperating can look. I don't think the orange jumpsuit helped.

Judge Walker shuffled the documents on his desk again, then addressed Dougie, "Mr. Kenth, please tell the court why you believe the defendant's stance justifies criminal charges at this time."

Dougie probably didn't use as many fifty cent words as Daniel, but he proved that day that he could string many big words together when he wanted to do so. His diatribe was probably not as long as it appeared to me, but it was definitely long.

In effect, he brought into question my right to have an investigator's license, my right to withhold any information whatsoever, and my right to specifically withhold the information relevant to this case. By the time he finished, I was even questioning some of those rights myself.

The judge had stopped him twice to advise him to focus on the specifics of the case and not attack the defendant's personal character. I was grateful for that. Still, the situation didn't look good for me.

Dougie spent about fifteen minutes on the subject of my silence putting the girl in danger. He brought up some sad and sensational cases of kidnapping that had been in the news recently and suggested that I could be subjecting her to extended torture with my silence. Then he continued with a flourish.

"Your honor, this man is deliberately impeding an important investigation by refusing to cooperate. In addition to risking a girl's life by this action, he is mocking the fine men and women in law enforcement; he is mocking the very existence of a civilized system of government, and by extension, he is mocking this court and everybody in it, including you!"

He paused for effect, but nobody reacted, so he concluded. "His refusal to cooperate as any law abiding citizen would cooperate has stalled an official investigation, wasted the tax-payers' money, and unnecessarily added to the courts' docket. If the court does not indict him on these charges, it will be a slap in the face to every person working to serve the public interest."

The sound of his hand slapping down on the table was still echoing in my ear when the Judge turned to Daniel, "Mr Leeds, please tell me why you do not believe your client should be indicted on these charges. And Mr. Leeds, please keep in mind that some of us have other cases and would like to get home sometime this evening."

"Your honor, counsel for the defendant thoroughly appreciates that all concerned have a desire for expedience in these proceedings. However, it would not behoove the court to keep the wheels of justice speeding along, if in so doing, the court allows the wheels of justice to speed over a citizen's constitutionally protected civil rights. Therefore, counsel courteously requests authorization to approach the bench."

"Very well, both attorneys may approach the bench."

I was almost certain that Daniel borrowed the 'wheels of justice' line from an old television show, but I couldn't remember which one. I wouldn't have thought he and I had ever watched the same shows, but I still felt sure I had heard a version of that line before.

Daniel and Dougie were at the bench for about 15 minutes before turning around. I wasn't sure what had transpired, but the frown on Dougie's face had to be a good sign for me. Daniel's face, as usual, couldn't be read.

After conferring with the bailiff, the Judge spoke, "At this time, the court will defer a decision on charges. The defendant will remain in custody as a material witness. A new hearing will be scheduled for Friday morning. At that time, both counselors will be permitted to call witnesses."

Before the bailiff came to escort me back to my cell, Daniel tried to convince me that this was a major victory for us. Since no charges had been filed, I could still get out of jail simply by telling them a few details about the mirror.

Of course, he used twice as many words and four times as many syllables than needed to explain it, but he did manage to somewhat convince me. The problem was that I still had no intention of breaking my promise.

Suddenly, I remembered the story of King Pyrrhus. He's the ancient king whose troops defeated the Romans in battle, but suffered many casualties in the process. I wondered how many more Pyrrhic victories it would take before my commitment to honor my promise was undone.

By 6:15, I was back in my cell contemplating the sad fact that I was going to miss date night with Emily. I had been coping with incarceration fairly well, until that realization hit home; now I was depressed and angry.

16   Welcome Visitor

I stewed in my cell for less than two hours before a guard came to get me. "Your attorney is waiting for you in one of the consultation rooms."

I couldn't imagine what Daniel would want to consult about so soon after what he considered our major victory. However, since it gave me something to do other than miss Emily, I was glad to follow the guard through the corridors.

When we got to the consultation room, Daniel was waiting outside the door. "My new intern is assisting on this case and awaits us within. Please comport yourself in a professional manner during our conference."

"Sure, Daniel, I'll try not to embarrass you in front of your employee."

I couldn't imagine why Daniel would be worried about my professionalism. We'd known each other almost two decades, and I couldn't remember a single time when I had failed to conduct myself in a professional manner.

I also couldn't imagine why he'd hired an assistant. After all, he had nearly retired. Maybe seeing that I was somehow keeping Pegasus Investigations afloat had inspired him to seek a successor to keep his law practice going. If that was it, I hoped his intern did a better job of it than I have.

The guard escorted us inside, and I immediately knew why Daniel had warned me to be professional. Even with the warning, it was all I could do not to rush over and kiss Emily and hold her tight.

She sat at the table impassively pulling papers out of an oversized attorney's briefcase, looking exactly like a competent and devastatingly gorgeous lawyer in training. I presumed she also had to fight the urge to kiss me and hold me tight, but it certainly couldn't be seen on her face.

94

I sat across the table from her and simply gazed into her beautiful blue eyes. We smiled at each other while I wondered if my client was even worth protecting at the cost of being separated from someone who loved me enough to be a part of this charade.

My self-reflection was interrupted by the guard, "You have the room for one hour to consult. You know the drill, Counselor. You know how to summon me if you wish to end the conference sooner."

As the guard turned to leave, Daniel tapped his shoulder, "Actually, Miss Street will debrief our client unaccompanied. This is an essential aspect of my instructional curriculum. I'll wait with you."

When they were gone, Emily rushed over, and we hugged and kissed. I could have gladly spent the entire hour or all eternity in that embrace, but all too soon we were sitting at the table again. At least this time we were sitting side by side holding hands.

"You didn't think you could get out of date night just by getting thrown in jail, did you?"

"Of course not, darling, I just figured this was a good way to make sure we didn't spend date night drinking wine with obnoxious suburban yuppies."

"City Manager Cannelly did seem to be a bit full of himself, but I'm not sure the company here is any better. Besides, I thought last week's date night ended quite well. I don't think tonight's will be as nice."

I had to agree with her, "Good point, Ms. Street, or may I call you Della?"

"You should call me Emily, darling." she said as she reached into her briefcase. "Oh, by the way, I brought you something."

She pulled out a paper sack from Stefan's deli and proceeded to lay out two meals for us. Compared to Morton's, this may not have seemed like a feast, but after a full day in Lew Sterrett, it seemed like the finest meal ever.

While we ate, we just chatted like any couple on a date. Meaning, of course, we discussed ordinary things like how the day went. For obvious reasons, we skipped over my day and discussed hers, instead.

I have spent all my life trying to avoid having to work in a normal office. Still, I love hearing Emily talk about her office. Part of that is because I love Emily, but some of it is because she obviously loves what she does. Also, since I've met most of her co-workers at various company functions, I also know who is who when she discusses them.

Unlike last week's date and its discussion of Spanish wines, I was intently interested in tonight's chat. I hung on her every word as she discussed the promotion she had applied to get. We had just finished eating when she starting discussing her competition, which allowed me to give her my full attention.

"Alyssa and LaDonna both applied, but I don't think they have much chance. The company really values education and certification, and neither has gotten her C.P.A., yet."

"I thought I remembered Alyssa saying at the Christmas party that her New Year's Resolution was to complete that by the end of March."

"That is what she said." Emily smiled, "But, then she met Lewis at a New Year's Eve party, and she suddenly had a new resolution. Anyway, I'm pretty sure the competition is going to be Bob Jacobs. He has the same level of education that I do. Also, he's been with the company longer than I have."

Bob and Emily had dated briefly long before I entered the scene, and they remain friends. I tried not to hold that against him, and he made it fairly simple.

Every time I've talked to him, he seemed like a truly nice guy. Granted, I hate that he's far more handsome than me, but I can usually forgive a guy for having one or two faults.

"Well, that scoundrel better darn well not steal your promotion. But, if he does, it will give me the excuse to kill him I've been seeking."

96

"You kill an innocent man? Hah! You can't even keep your cute tush out of jail when you haven't done anything. Speaking of jail, are you going to get out of here soon? If not, we need a J.P. in here to marry us. I understand only spouses are allowed conjugal visits."

"Well," I joked, "if I have to stay here awhile to get you to commit, I guess I can."

"No, be serious, Babe. We only have this room a little while longer. I need to know what to do to help you."

I brought her up to date on the complete situation. She listened intently as she always does when I discuss a case.

"I don't think that there's anything you can do. Daniel is going to try to find my client and convince him to come forward. "If that doesn't work, I don't know. I made a promise; I don't intend to break it. Eventually, even Dougie will realize there is no point in keeping me here. I don't care how long I have to stay here; I will not break a promise."

"Even to get out of jail and take me on a real date?" she asked.

"If promises are only kept when they're convenient, then they aren't really promises."

"Ooh, Nickie, I just love it when you act all noble, especially when you do it in an orange jumpsuit. I'll find your client for you and convince him to do the right thing."

I didn't have any friends who called me Nickie Charles either, but Emily was much more than a friend. Besides, this was definitely one time when I didn't mind if she wanted to pretend she was Nora Charles.

As much as I hated to admit it, I needed all the help I could get at this point. A martini (or five) might have been nice too, but that was too much to hope for.

17   Surprise Ally

When you are in jail, time passes slowly, unless you're asleep. So I didn't feel guilty about still being asleep at 10:25 Thursday morning. I might have slept all day if I hadn't been roused by the sound of a guard's voice.

"Up and at 'em, Sleeping Beauty! You have a visitor."

As we walked through the corridors to the consultation room, I speculated about who was visiting me. Dougie or Blake would have come to the cell. Emily would be at work, so I decided it was probably Daniel, my attorney. I wondered what he would want. He probably was going to try again to convince me to cooperate.

The guard led me into one of the visiting rooms and I couldn't have been more shocked by who I saw. It was an attorney all right, but it most definitely wasn't my attorney.

Larry Joe McCoy isn't just an attorney. He may well be the most famous and/or infamous defense attorney in Texas. Since Texas has more famous and infamous defense attorneys than any place east of California, that's saying something.

As usual, Larry Joe was wearing neatly pressed Wrangler blue jeans and a pearl snap shirt with his cowboy hat and boots. His typical attire makes J.R. Ewing look like a Yankee. There is no doubt that as a lawyer, he is hard to beat. I'm still always amused a little when I see him in his hat and boots.

Larry Joe is about 6'5, so with his hat he could seem to be as tall as I am. I think it bothers him a little that I'm taller than he is, but I know it bothers him that I know his dark little secret. Not many people know it, but the famous Texas Defender, Larry Joe McCoy, was born in Upstate New York with the given name of Lawrence Joseph McCutcheon.

He went to law school at St. Mary's in San Antonio and fell in love with the stereotype and decided to live it. He changed his name and became his own personal version of the quintessential Texan. He also became an incredibly successful attorney.

He started out doing estate planning, but had transitioned to high profile criminal defense a few years ago. Since this year was the first year in the last five that he wasn't on D Magazine's list of top lawyers under the age of forty, I presumed he had recently turned forty.

As soon as the guard left, Larry Joe spoke, "Are you enjoying your stay here in the hoosegow, Mr. Poirot?"

"My friends don't call me names from Agatha Christie books, and even in here I don't have to talk to my enemies."

"I'm not your enemy right now, Pardner. Be glad I didn't call you, Miss Marple. We might be on the same side this time. A client who keeps me on retainer asked me to check in and see what I could do for you."

"I thought you got rich by convincing juries that your guilty clients were innocent. It's hard to believe you are on retainer for clients looking for chances to get innocent people like me out."

"You're about as innocent as a coyote in a chicken coop. What's hard to believe is that my client, whose name will not be mentioned during this conversation, actually convinced me that a part-time, low-rent investigator like you could help him find that missing gal."

If I thought I was shocked when I saw Larry Joe waiting for me, I didn't truly know what shock is. Could Freak Show really be a regular client of Larry Joe McCoy? I knew Freak made good money from his performances, but Larry Joe McCoy's clients were normally those with so much money that they didn't need to work.

Larry Joe had built his reputation for success on impressive theatrics, not candor, but he usually reserved any actual dishonesty for the jury. However, even though I couldn't immediately think of any reason why he would lie to me, I was still cautious. While considering the implications, I decided to just do what I do best.

After a few minutes of silence, he continued, "My client and I understand that you're still here because you have refused to reveal any information about the mirror and any unsubstantiated relationship the district attorney might believe it has to a missing person they are seeking."

"Either that or I'm here because Dougie Kenth is a jerk."

"That's always a possibility. I enjoy the fact that when he prosecutes a case I'm dang near guaranteed an acquittal. Still, he is as irritating as a saddle-sore on a rainy roundup. Either way, do you want to get out of here or not?"

"Sure, but I could have been out of here before I got here, if that was all that I wanted."

"Of course, you also want to get out without betraying any trusts or hurting your reputation for discretion and integrity." He almost sounded like he could relate to these concepts as he spoke, "Tell me what you told the District Attorney when he asked you about the mirror in your cell."

I had no idea how he knew Dougie had come to my cell, but I saw no harm in repeating, "I came across that mirror in the…" Larry Joe turned it into a duet at the exact point that Blake had joined in earlier, "…course of a perfectly legal investigation for a client."

There was no way that Dougie had told Larry Joe about a conversation which had left him humiliated, so Blake and Larry Joe must have talked about this. I wasn't sure what that meant, but I knew Blake would have a good reason for cooperating with Larry Joe.

"Okay, I'll bite. Your client, or should I say our client, wants you to get me released. Can you do it?"

"Since you didn't kill anybody in front of 40 witnesses using camcorders, of course, I can get you out. The question is, will I?" He looked at me briefly before continuing, "I don't always do what my clients ask, you know."

100

"I've heard that. It may be the only thing we have in common."

"No, we also have a client in common, and I need to get you out of here in order to serve his interests. Can we put aside any past differences to work together on this?"

I didn't doubt for a second that Larry Joe would have a plan to get me released. He always had a plan. Normally, he had a plan and a backup plan and a backup plan for his backup plan. Unlike me, his plans usually worked.

The past differences he had mentioned mostly involved times when his plan freed somebody that I or Blake thought should have stayed in jail. The shoe was definitely on the other foot today. My plan was to find a girl, and his plan was to get me released. It was an easy decision.

"I can if you can. What's your plan?"

He reached into his briefcase and pulled out a tall stack of papers. As he handed them to me he said, "The first plan is to take the offensive. It looks to me, Pardner, like they've been keeping you in here because they don't think you have any rights. If you were in here because you'd done something wrong, you'd be protected by the Bill of Rights. But since you haven't done anything they think they can run roughshod over you, like ..."

It sounded like he was getting warmed up and I really didn't want to hear another of his colloquialisms, so I interrupted, "Easy now, save the speechmaking for the juries and judges, I just need to know what we are going to do to get me out of here."

"In general, what I'm going to do is make the county more afraid of what will happen if you stay here than they are afraid of what will happen if you are released. In particular, we are going to put that fear into Mr. Kenth."

The smile on his face when he said 'Mr. Kenth' was barely short of demonic, and I realized we had one more thing in common. He continued, "That's what I'm going to do, Partner. What you are going to do is sign these documents."

"And what exactly are you suggesting I sign?"

"These documents will authorize me to represent you and file lawsuits on your behalf against the County and Mr. Kenth for wrongful arrest, wrongful imprisonment, improper interrogation and assorted other violations of your civil rights."

"You expect me to just sign these papers without reading them?" If I sounded incredulous, it's because I was. It wasn't like I had any reason to trust Larry Joe.

"No, I expect you to be as stubborn as a mule with a bellyache. Please feel free to read every word. My time is valuable, but I can always bill it to our client."

He leaned back to allow me to read the documents. I wondered how long the guards would let us have in this room, but I suspected Larry Joe would have anticipated this and started reading.

I started reading the documents and realized quickly that I wasn't going to be able to make a good decision about whether to sign them. It was like reading a foreign language newspaper account of the Super Bowl. I recognized all the proper names and some of the common words, but I couldn't make much sense at all out of the rest of the text.

With my eyes still reading, I told Larry Joe, "I'm not signing anything until my attorney looks at these."

"Now, you didn't just fall off a turnip truck, right? You do realize that your lawyer may tell you not to sign these so he can keep billing you without helping you any?"

I didn't like him or what he was suggesting, and I responded accordingly, "Not all attorneys are like you, Lawrence. Some actually care more about their clients than they care about their fees. I'm not signing anything that Daniel Leeds hasn't reviewed. "

"Daniel still has his shingle out? I thought he'd put himself out to pasture ages ago."

He paused briefly before continuing, sounding more like a distinguished attorney than one of the Dukes of Hazard for a change. "The profession is well-served to have Counselor Leeds still practicing. Out of respect for a true gentleman, and for the sake of my client, I'll ignore your insults."

I couldn't resist, "All of them? Even the ones I haven't said out loud, yet?"

I was amazed when Larry Joe actually took the high road, "For now, anyway, but you really should learn to be nicer to people who are trying to help you."

"As soon as I learn how to tell who is trying to help and who isn't, I'll try to be nicer. Until then, you can leave these documents with me and I'll have Daniel review them on his next visit."

I wasn't surprised when Larry Joe objected; objecting is pretty much his stock in trade. What surprised me was his counter-proposal, "I can't leave these here; Mr. Kenth would love nothing more than to again violate your rights by confiscating them. I'll deliver them to Daniel personally for his review."

18   Bad News

After my meeting with Larry Joe ended, I was escorted back to my cell. I had plenty of new things to think about, but none of them seemed to make any sense. The more I thought, the less sense I was able to make of most of them.

Freak having an attorney didn't seem too unlikely. He makes his living doing stage shows that involve human pincushions, pierced suspensions and a number of other things that offend much of the world.

I accept that it makes sense that he might keep an attorney on retainer. All it takes these days is two offended people to have the makings of a class-action lawsuit. Since Freak could offend five to seven hundred people in the blink of an eye, it might not make sense for him not to have an attorney on retainer.

But, Freak doesn't just have an attorney on retainer. Apparently, he has the best defense attorney in Texas on retainer. I couldn't think of a reason why Freak would need a defense attorney on retainer, let alone the most expensive one in the state.

I'd seen his performances before, and while they are definitely not for the faint of heart, there is nothing illegal involved. Granted, Jim Morrison was arrested years ago for pretending to show his privates on stage. However, in Freak's performance, his privates were the only thing not shown.

At 2:45, I was again escorted to the consultation room. Daniel was waiting for me alone with a large sheaf of papers. "Larry Joe visited me. His creativity astounds me with regularity. These stratagems might have eluded my cognitive ability indefinitely."

"Will they work?"

"With certainty, but you must append your signatories where we have designated."

"So, is it we now? I would never have thought you'd want a partner in your practice. But I guess I was wrong. I hope you and McCoy enjoy a long and prosperous partnership."

"I've cooperated with him previously. He possesses a brilliant legal mind. This might be a prudent occasion for you to distance your mind from any perceived past injustices, my young associate."

It had been quite a while since I'd been accurately called young, but he was right, so I moved on. "Should I read any of these documents before I sign them?"

"You may peruse any of the motions which it pleases you to peruse, but I've analyzed every asseveration. Every delay in signing could exponentially delay your release and subsequent reunion with your paramour."

He might be nearly impossible to understand, but Daniel definitely knows how to make a convincing argument. I started signing. By the end of the day, Blake came by my cell to tell me I would be released the next morning.

"Can you call Emily and let her know?"

"I already called her; she said she'd be here waiting to pick you up as soon as you're processed out."

I hoped Emily wasn't hurting her chance for promotion by taking a day off on such short notice. But even with that concern, I slept well for the first time since Sunday night.

I also woke up early. I had been awake for several hours, when a matronly guard came to my cell to escort me out. After I was dressed like a free man and had signed the waiver stating that all my possessions had been returned intact, she escorted me to the lobby. It was just after noon.

As Emily rushed over to kiss me, the guard muttered under her breath. "I don't understand what pretty ladies like you see in these deadbeats."

Emily didn't say a word in response. She just looked up at me with those delightful blue eyes and smiled at me with a look that said, "Don't worry, we know what it is."

The truth is that I don't really know what attracts her to me, but I guess it doesn't matter. What matters is that she loves me as much as I love her. I know how lucky I am to be with her, and I don't want that to ever change.

So, I just looked at her and returned the smile. "It's great to see you so soon after my release, but you didn't need to take time off. I can walk from here to my office."

She didn't say anything until we were in her car. Then she smiled her cat that ate the canary smile and looked up at me, "Of course, you could, but we aren't going to your office, dear. We're having lunch together, and I know there's no chance of getting a decent lunch at your place. Besides, I'll more than make up the time at work this weekend."

"So where are we going, then? I'm sure I'm not too presentable after my time in jail."

"That's for me to know and you to find out. And you're always presentable in my eyes."

She pulled onto Stemmons Freeway and then took the first exit onto Harry Hines. I knew immediately where she was headed. Keller's on Harry Hines is an old fashioned drive-in restaurant which sells beer in long-neck bottles and specializes in deliciously greasy burgers.

Sitting on the tailgate of her Chevy Blazer, enjoying Keller's specialties, I wondered how many guys had eaten here shortly after getting released from jail. Whatever guess I came up with would probably be low, but I knew none had better companionship.

"Did you have anything to do with getting McCoy on the case?"

"Maybe a little; I saw in the Dallas Observer that Freak's troupe was performing at Reno's Chophouse Wednesday night."

She seemed a little hesitant to continue, so I prodded, "And?"

"Well, I knew you wouldn't want me to go down there alone, even if I am a big girl, so I asked Bob to go with me. Of course, I explained that we were going to help you out."

"I presume he agreed. Getting you killed in Deep Ellum would guarantee him the promotion you deserve."

"Actually, you know what he said? He said he'd do anything to help you out, and if I didn't feel comfortable in Deep Ellum, he'd go down there without me. I'm beginning to think he's just using our friendship to get you to hire him at Pegasus."

"Sure he is. Everybody at Penney's wants to work for a struggling detective agency. If I do need to hire, I should put up recruiting posters in the break room."

"You might be surprised, dear. You might be very surprised."

She had that look she always gets when she knows that nobody knows what she's really thinking. Usually, when she does that it means nobody but me knows what she's thinking. This time I had no idea either.

"So, you went to Reno's," I said as soon as I gave up trying to figure out what she was thinking.

"Yes, and it turned out to be simple. I showed the bouncer your picture and asked if he had seen you with Freak recently. He said he had. Why does he call you Larry Bird, by the way?"

Tall, white guys like me get called Larry Bird because he's the most famous white basketball player in the last twenty years. Since Emily has a better chance of preparing me for the C.P.A. exam than I have of explaining this to her, I just said, "Sam the Man has a strange sense of humor."

"Anyway, he took us to a private office and brought Freak in to talk to us almost immediately. I asked Freak to go tell you that you could break your promise. He said he couldn't do that, but that he could do something better. I tried to get details from him, but he just said the legal system will always work best for those who know how to work the legal system."

"I never thought about it that way, but I bet he's right."

"I should say so! If he'd been wrong, I'd still be baking files into cakes instead of feasting on this messy delicacy."

Even when she's only brushing poppy seeds off my chin, Emily's touch always makes me feel like the world exists only so the two of us can be together, and that every day that we don't touch is a sad day for the world. As I gazed in her eyes, I could tell she'd missed touching me as much as I'd missed being touched. Her hand lingered just a moment less than I wished it had, before she let the rest of the world return.

"I thought Freak was acting crazy, but obviously I know what he meant now. I kept after him, and he eventually promised that if you were still in jail on Monday, he would come forward to get you out."

"Well, it seems to have worked out fine. Thank you. And thank Bob for me when you see him. That guy just keeps making it harder and harder for me to dislike him."

At 2:50, she dropped me off at my place. We both had busy weekends ahead of us. She also had a staff meeting scheduled for Tuesday afternoon, so we agreed to have date night near her office in Plano.

The shock of being in jail had worn off. Now, I was trying to come to grips with the concept that Freak had given up going to strip clubs because of Mayor Hightower's daughter.

I spent Friday night and all day Saturday back in Deep Ellum retracing steps I had already been over. However, now that I knew the girl's name, I was able to get a little bit more information.

What I learned served mostly to confirm what Freak had told me about her habits and activities. After spending another weekend in Deep Ellum, I spent Sunday in my office compiling my notes. I had a meeting scheduled with both the attorneys for Monday afternoon.

———

I knew I was going to be the least affluent person in the room for that meeting. I also accepted that I would be the least intelligent one there. I was darn sure not going to be the least prepared. By the time I turned in Sunday night, my stack of notes was at least as thick as the papers I had signed while in jail.

The phone rang Monday morning at 7:07. The theory that nothing good ever happens after two in the morning is well known, but the corollary to this rule, that nobody calls before 7:30 in the morning with good news is less well documented.

I knew when I heard Blake's voice on the other end of the line that this call was not going to be the exception. He wasted no time proving me right. "Katherine Elizabeth Hightower's body was found this morning beside a trash dumpster Uptown."

It only took me a few seconds to grasp the importance of the specifics of what he had said. People who die of natural causes, especially wealthy young people, are almost never found by trash dumpsters.

"I presume that the Dallas Police Department suspects foul play." I finally said.

"Nobody will go on record until an autopsy is complete, but I think it can be assumed that foul play is suspected."

I called Emily to let her know what had happened. We'd been together long enough that she understood that an investigation, especially one involving a murder could affect our time together, just like her job and long hours often did.

Since the girl was no longer missing and had been found inside Dallas city limits, Blake no longer had an official interest in the case. It was now official Dallas Police business, and Blake and I were both outsiders.

However, he had been involved and had enough connections that he offered to take me to look at the scene as soon as the crime scene team had finished their work. My meeting with the two attorneys was postponed for obvious reasons.

At two o'clock, Blake and I were standing on the corner of Boll and Howland looking at a small fenced-in trash dumpster at the end of a strip mall across the street from the auxiliary parking lot of a seafood restaurant and bar called the S&D Oyster Company.

On a Friday or Saturday night, the parking lot would usually be packed. The parking lot is less than 100 yards from McKinney Avenue, but when the place isn't that crowded, it is more convenient to park at the main lot right on McKinney.

It took very little investigation to establish that the employee who found the body, took out the trash at six every morning and four every afternoon Monday through Saturday. Since he had found the body this morning, it was pretty obvious that the body had been dropped there between four o'clock Saturday afternoon and six this morning.

The S&D Oyster Company and surrounding area is a bustle of activity from Friday happy hour until the bars close at two a.m. Sunday morning. That makes it a safe bet that the window of opportunity to dump a body can be narrowed to early Sunday morning through early Monday morning. The key question, of course, is who put the body there.

I didn't have a theory, but I knew the police would soon have a ready made suspect. It wouldn't matter very much if he did it or not. What would matter is that he would be an easy suspect for the cops and the media to accept.

Once the police confirmed it was a murder, I wasn't going to be able to keep Freak out of this for long. The question was, did I even want to try? I've already spent over four days in jail on this case. There has to be some limit on the amount of time a man is expected to spend in jail for somebody he doesn't like.

If Freak did kill her, I wouldn't be the first investigator hired by a guilty client. For some reason, though, I didn't believe that he killed her.

Perhaps not coincidentally, I also wasn't as sure as I once was that I didn't like him. Freak is definitely an acquired taste, but he had helped me solve a case once, and he had hired me, and paid cash money to do so.

Blake and I looked around the dumpster and the surrounding area for a little while pretending that we might notice something that the crime scene team had missed. The only thing I noticed was that it was the only dumpster in the area with a fence around it.

I mentioned that to Blake, but we both realized that we were wasting our time. He offered to take me back to my office, but I decided the walk might give me time to think.

19   Attorney Privilege

Murder isn't my specialty. Finding people is my specialty. Unfortunately, I didn't find Katherine Elizabeth Hightower, and now I was investigating a murder, not looking for a missing person. I knew enough about investigating murder to know the police were going to want to know about that mirror.

I knew they were going to ask me about it again. I just wasn't sure how soon they were going to ask me about it. I also suspected that since the mirror was now evidence in a murder case, a return trip to jail was a real possibility for me.

I was still trying to decide what I was going to do about it when I got back to my office. For the second time in a week, I was surprised to see Larry Joe McCoy and his ten gallon hat. This time he was sitting in my waiting area with a firm grip on his briefcase.

I nodded at him as I walked past and unlocked the door to the inner office. As soon as we entered, he got to the point. "What are you going to do, Pardner?"

I waited until I was at my desk, and he was also seated to answer. "Don't call me Pardner, and I haven't decided. Did he kill her?"

"I call everybody Pardner, don't take it personally. I'm not sure if he killed her. I doubt it, and I certainly hope not."

"Guilty clients are harder to defend, huh?"

"Not always, but I don't like defending friends if they're guilty. It makes it hard to keep from getting emotionally involved. Besides, they were in love, and that's a terrible way for love to end."

"How in love could they have been if he didn't even know her name?"

"Look, I know you're a skeptical bastard. Usually that's not a bad thing. Right now, I'm just asking you not to do anything rash."

I wasn't used to Larry Joe asking anybody for anything. He had built his successful reputation by telling people to do things. Of course, I had built a less successful reputation by not liking to be told what to do, and he knew that.

"Is there any particular rash thing you want me to avoid doing? Or do you want me to steer clear of all rash behavior until further notice?"

"I want the same thing I always want, Pardner. I want to make sure my client gets a fair shake if it comes to a trial. The D.A. could make a jury think that Freak Show is Jack the Ripper if he gets to try him by that name. I've already started the process of changing his name. But if you give him up now, they'll try to prosecute him as Freak Show. If they do, that will make my job much harder."

"How long is it going to take you to change his name to Snow White?"

"We're changing his name back to his given name. I hope to have it official by Friday, but it could stretch into next week. However, if he gets connected with this case before it's done, it could drag on for weeks or worse. That's why I came here to ask for your help."

Early in the conversation, I realized breaking my promise to Freak hadn't even been one of the choices I was considering. If I went back to jail, I went back to jail. There are still worse things. I had wanted out earlier, mostly so I could find Freak's missing girl.

Now that I knew the girl was dead and that every law enforcement agency in the county would be trying to solve the case, that didn't seem as important. I also realized that without McCoy's help earlier, I might have still been in jail.

Still, I couldn't help but enjoy the rare treat of having Dallas' most aggressive attorney politely asking for my help. It was almost enough to make me wish I kept a journal. Of course, the facts that a girl had been murdered and my client would soon be a prime suspect made it impossible for me to truly savor the moment.

I was still trying to arrange my thoughts and decide how long I could keep McCoy in suspense when he broke the silence. "Damn, Helen

Keller, I always forget how long you'll go without speaking. How well do you know your client?"

"Well enough to know what he does for a living and that he can afford to pay my fees. In my line of work, that's all I usually need to know."

"Then you do realize that he doesn't make enough with that stage act of his to afford my fees, right?"

"The thought had crossed my mind. I'll admit I never envisioned you as being that big on the pro bono aspect of legal practice."

"You might be surprised, Pardner. But we can discuss me, and your opinion of me, some other time. I'm working for my client right now, and we need your help."

"Yeah, you went over that, you want me to keep Freak's name out of the case until you get it changed to something less offensive to people who actually serve on juries, instead of making up excuses to skip jury duty. Truth is, you wasted your trip over here. I promised Freak not to reveal where I got the mirror unless he cleared it. He hasn't, so I haven't, and I won't."

"I guess your client knows you better than you know him. He told me I didn't need to make this trip, but I didn't believe him. I told him we should expect you to demand more money to buy us time."

"Like you said, we can discuss me, and your opinion of me, some other time. Anything you should tell me about my client?"

"There are several things you need to know. Can you meet us at my office Wednesday morning at ten?"

"Unless, I'm back in jail by then, I can be there."

"You won't be. It will take at least 48 hours for the crime scene and forensics teams to do their work and compare notes. After that, if they decide a crime was committed, they'll start issuing warrants and arresting people."

"You know more about these things than I do, but I didn't expect to go to jail last week, either. Anyway, I'll want Daniel Leeds at the meeting tomorrow."

"Good idea, once our client meets Daniel, I'm sure he'll want to add him to the defense team. Of course, we hope it doesn't get to trial. But if it does, Daniel will be a great help."

He pulled a pendaflex folder out of his briefcase and set it on my desk. "Everything you should know about your client is in here. Bring this back to the meeting on Wednesday, but you're free to make copies of anything you think you need."

As I picked up the folder, he glanced around my office skeptically. "You do have a copier, right?"

I nodded and pointed toward the door to my living room. It wasn't really a lie. I had a copier right across the street at the library, and it only charged fifteen cents a copy.

We shook hands before he left, and I watched him start walking past Neiman Marcus toward his office. It was less than a ten minute walk from my office to his, but it wouldn't have shocked me to see him call a cab or have a limo waiting to take him.

He passed Neiman's and was nearly to Elm Street when I noticed a heavy-set man in a non-descript blue polo shirt and khaki slacks walking twenty yards behind him, matching his pace step for step and stopping each time Larry Joe did.

While I contemplated the significance of Larry Joe McCoy, the Larry Joe McCoy, being tailed as he left my office, something else occurred to me. Not once, in the entire time he had sat in my office, had he used one of his trademark colloquialisms.

I wasn't sure what, if anything, either of those facts signified, but I knew I was going to be checking to see if I was being tailed when I went to McCoy's office. I also knew if he called me Helen Keller again, I would have to hit him. A man in my line of work can only take so much.

After McCoy and his shadow were out of sight, I turned my attention to the folder. It looked like I had homework to do again.

I spent several hours reading through the documents in the folder that night. It did, in fact, contain information about my client that I should know. Actually, it contained more information about my client than I've ever known about a client, or anybody else for that matter, in my entire career.

Freak had not been lying when he told me that he was in ROTC for 2 years in high school. Since I've never heard anybody lie about being in ROTC, that didn't surprise me. That may be the only thing in the entire folder that didn't surprise me.

Pretty much everything else in the folder Larry Joe left stunned me. Even so, three things stood out as I read through it. First, Freak's parents had both died in their thirties while he was just a teenager. Second, they were incredibly wealthy when they died.

The third, and certainly most important thing I learned from perusing the dossier, was that Freak is almost certainly going to die at about the same age that his parents had, and he has known it for a long time. I had known that Freak was incapable of feeling physical pain, but I had not known the cause or the severity of the consequences.

I turned in that night wondering how I would have spent my younger years if I had known I was going to die young. I doubt if my first choice would have been to change my name and create a stage show involving piercing and hooks.

On the other hand, you never know how you'll react to something like that, if you've never faced it. I've never faced it, so I may never know. I do know I slept fitfully weighing those options and knowing that I would probably never totally understand my client.

20   Three Forks

I woke the next morning feeling relieved to be alive and grateful that I will never know what it's like to know you are going to die young. Freak, on the other hand, knew that he was going to die young before most of us really understand what dying is.

I am already older than Freak is ever likely to be. He also knew that he would never have to worry about money, since his parents had left him a trust fund that pays him fifty thousand dollars annually, provided he is either gainfully employed or enrolled in an institution of higher learning throughout the year.

Like both his parents, Freak was born with congenital analgesia. To summarize the stacks of medical reports on my desk, congenital analgesia is a rare condition which leaves a person completely unable to feel pain. As a result, victims often hurt themselves without knowing it.

Children with the condition require constant monitoring and supervision. Those fortunate enough to survive to adulthood almost never live past their early thirties. Freak's parents were able to afford constant care for him as a child, but even their fortune didn't prevent the condition from catching up with them. His mother died his freshman year of high school when her appendix burst.

For most people, a problem with an appendix causes a stomach ache which leads to a hospital visit and corrective surgery. Since she never felt the stomach ache, she never went to the hospital and died at thirty-seven years old. Living to thirty-seven is considered almost a miracle for someone with congenital analgesia.

The cause of his father's death four months later was never fully determined. This is not unusual given his condition. Many victims die from injuries which are never identified. After years of being scarred and bruised internally by injuries which are never noticed, and thus never treated, the cumulative affect eventually results in death.

By the time Freak joined the ROTC as a seventeen year old junior at Mesquite High School, he was an orphan with a large trust fund and a complete inability to feel pain. Not surprisingly, he got into a few fights. More accurately, he apparently got into many fights.

I presume that he won the ones which resulted in Larry Joe having to defend him against assault charges. When he attempted to hit me that time in Deep Ellum, I would have guessed that he had never won a fight. Of course, I didn't know then that he couldn't feel pain. With Larry Joe McCoy as his attorney, he had never been convicted which wasn't surprising.

As I read through the reports of the assault charges against Freak, I noticed a repeating pattern. In almost every case, the person who Freak allegedly assaulted was either picking on or actually accosting a freshman or sophomore.

I read through the affidavits relating to over two dozen incidents, which almost always included comments from freshman or sophomore students lauding his efforts to protect the underclass from bullies. All seemed to follow the same theme: a bully was hitting me or picking on me, and this guy showed up and stopped him.

One comment, in particular, struck me as overwhelmingly important. A sophomore girl's statement included the following sentence, "He came in and saved me like Superman rescuing Lois Lane. If he hadn't shown up when he did and hit that bastard, I might have been raped or killed or worse."

A rational adult might wonder what exactly would be worse than being raped or killed. Of course, since a sophomore girl made the comment, several things, such as not being popular, could qualify. However, that wasn't what was important to me. What was significant to me was that the sophomore girl who made the comment was named Katherine Elizabeth Hightower.

118

I knew that was significant. I didn't know what it meant, but I knew it meant something. I doubted if it meant anything that would help convince a jury that Freak didn't kill her. If Freak knew her in high school well enough to get into a fight on her behalf, how did he not know her name when he hired me to find her?

If the folder contained anything else significant, I missed it. I read everything in it at least twice. I took the folder to Daniel's office to make copies, being too frugal, even with a client's money, to pay fifteen cents a copy at the library for that many pages. Then I returned to my office and read everything again.

Mostly though, I just listened to a small phantom voice in my head saying over and over, "He came in and saved me like Superman rescuing Lois Lane." It was the voice of a young girl who would never know what it felt like to be an old lady, and I wanted to know why. I also wanted to know if I could have saved her if I'd acted more like Clark Kent and less like Sam Houston.

Tuesday night was date night. If Emily wouldn't let my being in jail keep it from happening last week, I wouldn't let a dead girl's voice in my head interfere with this week's date. Besides, I had already made reservations for dinner at Emily's favorite steakhouse, III Forks, and we had agreed to meet at her office at 5:30.

At 4:04, I took one more look at the two pictures of Katherine Elizabeth on my Post-it board, locked up the folder in my desk and went to my room to change clothes. At 4:22, I was appropriately dressed in a navy blue pinstripe suit. I decided it was close enough to after-hours, so I locked my outside door and walked down to get my van.

I briefly exchanged pleasantries with Gus at the parking garage and had my van on Woodall Rodgers at 4:31. As I made the loop over to North Dallas Parkway, I popped in Robert Earl Keen's 'Number 2. Live Dinner' cassette and cranked the volume.

Neither 'I'm Going to Town' nor 'Five Pound Bass' were loud enough or strong enough to drown out the voice in my head. However, 'Sonora's Death Row' seemed to fit my mood a little better. By the time "Amarillo Highway' and 'The Road Goes on Forever' finished, the phantom girl's voice started to fade.

As I turned onto Legacy to pick up Emily, Robert Earl was singing, about selfish crime and precious time. When I parked by Emily's Blazer in the J.C. Penney corporate office parking lot at 5:17, the final song on the album; 'I'm Coming Home' was just ending.

I knew I wasn't going to be really coming home until I knew who had killed Katherine Elizabeth Hightower and why. I also knew I was going to find out if her Superman had killed that young Lois Lane. If he did, I was going to make sure I found a way to hurt him, even if I had to provide the kryptonite myself.

I always enjoyed meeting Emily at her office. Of course, I always enjoyed meeting Emily anywhere. Her office, though, gave me a chance to watch the people with real jobs going home for the day. It usually reassured me about my career to see that they didn't seem any happier after a day in their real world than I did after a day in mine. Today, I just kept thinking about a girl who was never going to experience the real world.

At 5:53, the girl's voice finally left my head. It was replaced by the lovely vision of Emily walking across the parking lot wearing a white blouse with a peter pan collar under a black jacket with a knee length skirt and pumps.

I got out of my van before she reached it, and we hugged and kissed. It was the first time since I'd answered Blake's phone call yesterday morning that I felt happy to be a person. After last week, I was determined not to ruin Emily's date tonight, so I didn't say a word about Katherine Elizabeth or the voice in my head as we drove to III Forks in her Blazer.

Every dining room at III Forks is named for one of the heroes in the fight for Texas' Independence. We had reserved a table for two in the Fannin room, named for Colonel James Walker Fannin, who was shot by a firing squad in 1836. Given the mood I was in, that somehow seemed fitting.

We were seated in a lovely booth beneath a picture of a couple embracing on a deserted street. The red leather seats were comfortable as always. The table was pristinely set, the lighting was romantic, and Emily was gorgeous and perfect as she always is. Still I could not seem to get out from under my own little dark cloud.

I tried my best. After we ordered, pepper steak for her and prime sirloin strip for me, we talked about her promotion hopes. Then we lightly reprised our frequent discussion about whether 'Dogma' or 'Chasing Amy' is Kevin Smith's finest movie. As usual we ended up agreeing to disagree.

We also talked about traffic, music, weather and American Idol. When I told her I missed the days when game show winners just took their money and went away, she just shook her head, and turned her attention to the rest of her meal. I had already finished eating, so I sipped my iced tea and watched her.

She eats like she does everything, with a graceful precision that makes it seem that she is the only one who knows exactly how it should be done. Normally, I enjoy watching her do whatever it is she is doing. Somehow, even as I watched her, the phantom voice invaded my head again, "He came in and saved me like Superman rescuing Lois Lane."

When Emily finished eating, she smiled sadly at me, "Obviously, you aren't really here in this lovely restaurant with me. Where are you? How bad is it? And how can I help?"

Emily has always been able to read me like that. I thought I could fake it for one evening, but I should have known better. I'm not that good at faking, and Emily isn't that easily fooled. Of course, I wasn't entirely sure I could still think properly at that time. Nothing I had done since I accepted Freak's retainer reflected particularly well on my ability to think.

I was still thinking of the best way to answer when she continued, "Okay, Silent Bob, spill. You told me the girl's body had been found, but you haven't told me why you are such a mess."

"She might be dead because my client killed her."

"Freak killed her? I don't believe that. Are you sure?"

"Right now I'm not too sure of anything. How do girls view the relationship between Lois Lane and Superman?"

"I'm going to assume you aren't trying to change the subject. Most girls see Lois Lane as the girl they want to be: competent, confident and in control. They view Superman as her perfect match, even if the two of them never connect. Why do you ask?"

I told her everything I had learned and suspected about Freak and Katherine's connection. I included everything, especially the girl's comment. The only thing I skipped was the phantom voice rattling around in my head.

When I finished, Emily asked, "How does all of that lead you to think Freak would kill her. His history seems to suggest he'd be more likely to save her than hurt her."

"Well, he hired me to find her, but lied about not knowing her name. That is suspicious. It indicates that he didn't want her found, just wanted to make it look like he did."

"My love, I think you've been out of high school too long. For every sophomore girl who thinks a senior boy is Superman, there is usually a senior boy who doesn't even know she exists. The girl usually forgets him after awhile and decides somebody else is Superman."

The light started to come on for me. "If Katherine Elizabeth never decided he wasn't Superman, what would she do?"

"She'd obsess about him, draw little hearts with his name on all of her notebooks and book covers."

"You sound like you are speaking from experience."

"Every woman in America can speak from that experience. We were all sophomores once. Eventually, as juniors or seniors we meet a guy who does know we exist, and we move on."

Just like that, it made sense, "Unless, of course, you spend your junior and senior years at an all girls' school. I think Superman is the wrong movie."

"What do you mean? What's the right movie?"

"Grease; she couldn't get him to notice her as she was, so she became a girl he couldn't help but notice. That's how she spent two years at Ursuline Academy without connecting with anybody. She was too busy. She was busy preparing for her final scene as Olivia Newton John, when she showed up at the carnival in a black leather outfit and knocked John Travolta's socks off. Or in this case, she showed up in Deep Ellum with blue hair and completely wowed Freak."

Emily nodded, "That would explain why she never gave him her real name. She didn't want him to know she was the same girl he'd ignored in high school for fear that he would ignore her again."

"So Freak didn't know her name, and I sat in jail, instead of finding her while she was alive. What the hell was I thinking?"

"You were thinking that keeping promises is one thing that makes you who are. And who you are is somebody I love very much. I recommend that you quit blaming yourself and find the person who really is to blame."

As usual, Emily's advice was sound. Also, as usual, I felt much better for having spent time with her. But, it was still going to be quite some time before that phantom voice was going to quit coming back in my head. When it finally left for good, it would be replaced by the sound of a gun being fired at me from very close range.

21   Thanksgiving Tower

That night I dreamt over and over about Clark Kent and Lois Lane. Only, in my dreams Clark wore safety pins and other body jewelry instead of goofy glasses and an ill-fitting suit, and Lois had blue or pink hair and high cheekbones. Every time Lois died, I woke up in a cold sweat with her voice in my head. Every time I went back to sleep, I dreamt about them again.

Not once in any of the dreams did Clark Kent leave the familiarity of Deep Ellum where he was virtually invisible to dump her body in Uptown where he would attract more attention than Marilyn Manson at a Girl Scout meeting. For that matter, not once did he dump her body anywhere.

When I finally woke up for the last time Wednesday morning, I had a theory about why the body was found where it was. I was also fairly certain that Freak hadn't put it there. What I still needed was a way to learn who had.

I left my office at 9:10 for my meeting with Larry Joe and Daniel. I deliberately allowed myself almost an hour for a ten minute walk because I suspected I would need to take the scenic route. As I left my office, I tried not to look at the heavy-set man in a non-descript beige polo shirt and black slacks standing across the street, simultaneously ignoring me and the homeless people beside him on the library's steps.

As I walked down Ervay, I stopped to look in the Neiman Marcus window just long enough to confirm that he was following me. Judging from my brief glimpse at the mannequins on display, short skirts and high heels were going to be in style again this season. At least, they would be in style for the ultra-rich.

The man in the polo shirt stopped when I did and stared at the blackened out window of what used to be a nice little patio bistro. So, instead of turning left on Elm to Larry Joe's office, I continued on to Bryan Street and turned right to the Plaza of the Americas building.

Three decades ago, when the science fiction movie 'Logan's Run' had been filmed there, the Plaza of the Americas had been a futuristic looking building. Now it is just another tall building with an ice skating rink.

More importantly to me, the rink is in the center of the plaza and can be viewed from all levels and offers a view of all levels. This makes it easy to confirm if somebody is tailing me. Plaza of the Americas also has enough staircases, elevators, escalators and exits to make it fairly easy for me to lose the tail.

I had confirmed the tail before I entered the building. So instead of circling the rink and looking behind me, I walked directly to the northeast corner and went down the steps toward the exit. I knew my tail would hurry to follow and rush out to the street to catch up with me in time to see which street I took.

Instead, I ducked into the men's room and waited long enough for him to get out onto the street. Then, I doubled back to the stairwell and up to the second floor. I took the skyway over to 2100 Ross. From there, I weaved my way back to the underground walkways which connect many of Dallas more prestigious buildings and a few of the less prestigious ones.

By the time I got on the escalator leading from the walkway up to Thanksgiving Tower, I was confident that nobody had followed me. At 9:53, I entered Larry Joe's lobby. I walked up to his receptionist, an attractive and extremely voluptuous young woman with shoulder length black hair and sparkling black eyes. I handed her my card, "Mr. McCoy is expecting me."

She pointed me to a chair. "Yes, he is. Counselor McCoy has a guest; I'll let him know you're here."

An engraved wooden nameplate on her desk revealed that her name is Adriana Karamanlis. Her translucent fuchsia blouse and black side

125

slit skirt revealed much more. I concentrated on reading the nameplate and not watching her as she took my card into Larry Joe's office.

Having had more than a little experience waiting in lobbies for high-profile attorneys, I was shocked when she ushered me in at 9:59. When I entered, Larry Joe and Daniel were seated at a conference table only slightly larger than my office.

Daniel tilted his head about a quarter inch as a greeting, and Larry Joe spoke, "Come in, Rockford."

"My friends don't call me Rockford."

Larry Joe sighed, and replied in a clipped voice that indicated an extremely high stress level. "I may not be your friend, but my client and I appreciate what you have done for us."

I corrected him. "You mean what I did for him. Where is he?"

"As you like it; I thought it would be wiser to have this conversation without his presence. I've known him since he was a child, and I do not want him burdened by bad news at this time. Did you read the file?"

"Yes." I handed him the folder, "and I made myself a copy for future reference."

"Yes, Daniel mentioned that. If you had just told me you don't have a copier, I would have gladly had Adriana do that for you."

Lying to associates is easier than lying to friends, and I still wasn't willing to admit to him that I didn't own a copier, "I'll remember that if I don't get my copier fixed before this case is over. You know our client better than I do, but why is this conversation bad news?"

"I thought you said you read the file. The incident with the girl when she was a sophomore invalidates a key aspect of my planned defense. The prosecution will instead have proof that he knew that she was the mayor's daughter. Once the police have his name, they will certainly arrest him."

"You knew that before you gave me the file. Isn't your job to get him acquitted, even if they do?"

"It is, but I'm not happy with the way things are developing. I'm not unaccustomed to having clients try to conceal things, of course. However, to have one lie to me, especially one I've known this long, is extremely troublesome."

"What is Freak lying to you about?"

"Even though I showed him the girl's statement, he insists that he didn't know her until recently and that he didn't know her real name. I told him if he wasn't honest with me, I couldn't properly represent him. I even suggested that he might need to seek another attorney."

"A display of ethics from an attorney with your reputation, I'm impressed. You're missing the point entirely, though."

Larry Joe cleared his throat and stared at me suspiciously, while Daniel looked impassive and remained completely silent. I sat there wondering if Emily knew she was smarter than two of the best attorneys in Dallas. I decided that she probably knew it, but that she would never mention it.

Finally, Larry Joe spoke, "Okay, what point is it that I'm missing entirely?"

"Your client isn't lying to you. He didn't have any idea that the girl he loved and hired me to find was Katherine Elizabeth Hightower."

Larry Joe leaned forward in his chair. "Okay, I'm listening, what makes you so sure?"

"In high school, Freak saw himself as the patron saint of the underclass, not the patron saint of one particular sophomore girl. He didn't fight for her because he knew her. He did it because that's what he did. You have dozens of examples of him doing that."

I waited for Larry Joe to argue, but he was simply listening, so I continued. "Do you think he knew the name and family history of every one of them? Sure, the girl saw him as Superman, because he stood up for her like nobody had stood up for her before. He didn't see her as Lois Lane; he just saw her as somebody who needed help. Do you really think Superman knows the name of every person in Metropolis that he's saved?"

Larry Joe leaned back, and the lowering of his stress level was palpable. He slapped his palm on his desk, "Dadgummit, that's righter than rain! I should have figured that out from the git-go. Why didn't I think of it?"

"Larry Joe, if I'd known you were going to revert to your Ace Reid cowpoke accent as soon as I restored your trust in your client, I would have definitely kept that to myself for a little longer. But, since you ask, the reason you didn't think of it is that you were never a sophomore girl."

Daniel smiled broadly, "Obviously, the pulchritudinous Ms. Lockaby has been entreated to exercise her impressive mental faculties on behalf of Freak's defense consortium. I trust her fees and any related expenditures will be included on your expense reports."

"By all means, include them, I'll be as happy as a hog in slop to pay'em myself. Hell, I may need to hire the pulchi... pulchit... Hell, whatever Daniel called her. I may need to hire the little gal myself. And you, my tall friend, may have plum missed your calling. That Superman analogy would have sold most juries even if it weren't as dead-on as an 1873 Winchester. If this gets to trial, I'm stealing that speech lock, stock and barrel, just exactly the way you said it."

I don't know if an 1873 Winchester is an accurate rifle or not, but somehow I doubt it. Larry Joe's Texas idioms excel at making him sound like a native Texan, but can't be counted on for historical accuracy. His ability to influence a jury, on the other hand, can definitely be trusted.

"You're welcome to it if it will help Freak, but I'd rather prove Freak didn't kill her and avoid a trial altogether. I'd also like to find out who did kill her, and I presume our client wants to know that, as well."

"I'm sure he does, and by the way, his name isn't Freak Show anymore, so we're ready to proceed if it comes to that."

"When will we know if it's going to come to that? Do I just hang out waiting to be arrested again, or should I go in and tell them where the mirror came from?"

"Well, that's pretty much up to you, but I've got my eyes and ears open over on Hall Street. If they issue a warrant for your arrest, I should know it before a judge even gets asked to sign it."

"I'll need to talk to Freak before that happens. Do you know where he's hiding?"

"He's not so much hiding; he's just being his usual reclusive self. I saw him at his home this morning. Go see him now, if you want. Adriana will give you the address."

Talking to my client seemed like a good idea. I couldn't think of anything to be gained by sitting in a swanky office in Thanksgiving Tower. So, I stood, shook hands with both attorneys and walked to the reception area.

After Adriana had given me Freak's address, McCoy called out, "Oh, somebody followed me here from your place the other day. Make sure you lose any tails before you get to Freak's place."

When I was out of McCoy's office and in the elevator, I looked at the paper Adriana had handed me. Freak's address was on Adolph Street which is in an older part of Dallas just east of Central Expressway less than half a mile from Deep Ellum.

Homes in that area range from houses that are nearly mansions to apartments which are barely more than slums. Now that I knew my client's financial status a little better, I could guess on which end of that spectrum his place would fall.

I wasn't at all surprised that he lived that close to Deep Ellum. Since he doesn't drive and spends most of his time at the bars in Deep Ellum, it made sense to live close. What did surprise me was that below Freak's address, Adriana had written her name and phone number and put little hearts around both.

22   New Look

I left Thanksgiving Tower pretty much the way I arrived. I circled around the underground walkways that I call tunnels to make sure I wasn't being followed. I reached the staircase leading up to what had once been the Titche's Building without any appearance of a shadow.

As I ascended to surface level, I looked out the window on Elm Street and saw the man in the polo shirt standing at the corner of Elm and Ervay. He was furtively trying not to make it obvious that he was alternately looking at Thanksgiving Tower and glancing up Ervay toward my place at Ervay and Young.

Facing that direction made it impossible for him to see me as I climbed the rest of the stairs. It also made it obvious that he had given up the tail long ago and came outside hoping to catch sight of me. Since I had snuck past him, he was in for a long day in the hot sun. I felt a little sorry for him as I turned right to the first floor concourse.

Seven decades ago, this building had been Titche-Goettinger Department Store's signature broad-front store, but that time was a distant memory. The store closed in the 70's and sat empty for years. Only recently had developers turned the building into luxury lofts that I'm not even close to being able to afford. Luckily, I can still afford to stroll though the lobby which costs nothing.

Normally when I am in this building, I take some time to admire the photos of Dallas taken years before I was born. Today, I was more interested in slipping out the Main Street entrance and continuing east to Freak's place without being followed.

As expected, Freak's house on Adolph is closer to being a mansion than a slum. Although it is only about fourteen to sixteen hundred square feet, it probably is appraised somewhere between three hundred thousand and a half a million dollars.

My surprise at seeing Freak in my office last month couldn't possibly compare to my shock when a very nervous looking Freak opened the door in answer to my knock. Dressed in cargo pants and a long-sleeved denim dress shirt with no visible piercing or tattoos, he looked less like the star attraction in a freak show than I did.

Even his hair was back to one color and styled like any typical twenty-something yuppie would wear it. He invited me in, and I followed him into a spacious living room with high ceilings, hardwood flooring and an ornamental fireplace.

I wasn't positive, but I was pretty sure I still hadn't said a word when we each sat down in one of the four matching upholstered reclining rockers. The décor of the room was typical nouveau rich, except for the two dozen or more pictures of Katherine Elizabeth framed and hung throughout.

While I was counting the different looks she had in each, Freak broke the silence. "I finally shocked you, didn't I?"

"Finally? Since I've known you, 'shocked' has been too timid a word for my reaction to almost everything I've seen you do. Hell, I didn't think I could be more shocked than I was when I found you waiting in my office for me last month."

"Bullshit! That just surprised you a little, like when I asked you to let me hide out at your place that time. This time you're really shocked. I can see it in your eyes."

Actually, when he had asked to stay at my place, I really hadn't even been surprised. People who could do it had threatened to kill him then, and I figured he didn't have many options. If anything had surprised me about that, it was that I had let him stay with me.

I finally asked the obvious question, "So what's with the new look? Are you going undercover?"

"Larry Joe tells me I'm probably going to be arrested soon and tried for murder. He suggested I adopt a more innocent look. Since he thinks I killed her, he wants me to look presentable while he lies to the jury."

"Even if that happens, isn't the trial a long way off?"

"Larry Joe says the D.A. might try to show the jury my booking photo. It's a cheap trick, but the D.A. is not above cheap tricks. Larry Joe says if it's done right, he's not sure he can prevent it. Rather, he's not sure my lawyer will be able to prevent it. Damn it! He's been my attorney forever, and now he's not even going to represent me. I think he's afraid I'm going to ruin his damn winning percentage or..."

His face was getting redder and his voice was getting louder and shriller as he went on. I almost had to shout to interrupt, "Calm down, Freak."

His voice returned to normal, but the anger and sadness were still visible on his face. "He's known me since before I was born, and he's going to desert me. Why should I calm down? Why doesn't he realize I didn't, couldn't have done it?"

I wanted to answer the question, if for no other reason than that I hate to see a grown man cry. Apparently Freak hated to be seen crying because he ran up the stairs before I thought of anything to say.

I walked around the room looking at the pictures of Katherine. Several were actually pictures of the two of them together. If I overlooked her blue or green hair, and his body jewelry, the pictures looked very much like pictures of any young couple in love.

One picture in particular looked familiar. In it, Freak and Katherine were sitting on a sandcastle framed by the setting sun behind them. They were kissing and their arms were interlocked with their hands touching so that the thumbs and forefingers formed a heart. Suddenly, I realized why it looked familiar. In my living room, I had an almost identical picture of Emily and me.

I was still looking at that picture when Freak came down the stairs fully composed. He saw that I was looking at it and answered the question I didn't ask.

"Yes, we posed for that because I saw the same thing at your place. I thought it was the most romantic pose I'd ever seen. I still do, in fact. Maybe, when I'm in prison whoever makes me his bitch will take one like it. Or better yet, maybe I'll get the death penalty. At this point I don't care. My girl's dead. She was carrying my child, so my baby's dead; and my own godfather thinks I killed them."

"What does your godfather have to do with any of this?"

"Larry Joe is my godfather. Didn't he tell you?"

"No, he didn't. But, he also doesn't think you're guilty," I stated confidently.

"What makes you say Larry Joe doesn't think I killed them? He told me this morning to look for a new attorney. Do you know one I should call?"

"That was this morning; things change."

"What changed? Why did he change his ..." Freak hesitated; then looked directly at me, "You talked him out of it, didn't you? You talked him out of quitting on me. You hate me, and you convinced him that I was innocent, didn't you?"

He was staring at me like he was daring me to disagree as if it was an accusation. I carefully evaluated his points. Did I talk Larry Joe out of quitting on Freak? I probably did. Did I convince him that Freak was innocent? I might have. Did I despise Freak? I once did.

Now, I just felt bad for him. Losing loved ones is always difficult. Losing the only loved ones you have left has to be harder. Losing a loved one carrying your unborn child is worse than I can imagine. I hope it always will be.

"I didn't do much. I just reminded him that high school is different than adulthood. People sometimes forget that after they graduate. You don't need to look for a new attorney, you still have one. In fact, you have two at your disposal if you want or need them."

"Two lawyers? Why would I need two? And who's the second?"

"Daniel Leeds, my lawyer, has worked with Larry Joe in the past, and he'll help any way he can. But we're getting ahead of ourselves. We don't even know yet if it was murder. She…"

Freak interrupted, "They!"

"Okay," I acquiesced. "They might have died accidentally somehow."

"But you don't believe that, do you?"

I decided to change the subject, "Tell me, Freak, did you lose all the body jewelry or just the visible ones."

"The only one I still have is the handcuff key on my left tit. It's permanently attached. It fits a bracelet we made her out of a pair of handcuffs she told me she'd had for years. She promised to wear the bracelet as long as I wore the key, so I had the key attached permanently."

"Permanently, how is that possible?" I asked, in spite of realizing that I probably didn't want to know.

"It's called a break-off screw, once the bar is screwed through the piercing, the head of the screw breaks off and it can't be removed without a jeweler's saw. It's normally used for couples looking for a permanent chastity device, and you don't even want to know where or how they attach them, trust me."

"I trust you on that. I definitely trust you."

"If you trust me, tell me the truth. They were murdered, weren't they?"

"If they weren't, I really will be shocked. Generally, when a body is found by a trash dumpster, murder is the cause of death. When a body suddenly shows up by a trash dumpster in an entertainment district in the wee hours of the morning, it's almost a certainty."

"Which means they'll be all over you about that mirror again soon, right?"

"Almost certainly."

"You've done more than enough to protect me. When they do, just tell them what they need to know. I'm ready for whatever happens."

"It could be soon, you know."

"I said I'm ready. You think I like this look? Who killed them? Why? It doesn't make any sense." He had difficulty talking, and I expected him to lose control again, but he recovered.

"I don't know, Freak. The police will look into it. They usually solve their murders, especially high-profile murders. Let's not give up on them too soon."

"You're not quitting on me, are you?"

"No, I'm not quitting. I'm on this with you as long as you want me to be. I'm just saying the police solve more murders every day than I've ever solved. We should wait and see what they come up with before we get too worried."

As I left his place, he looked less worried than he had when I arrived. I don't know if I looked more or less worried. I do know neither of us looked nearly as worried as we should have been.

23   House Party

As I approached my office, I saw the shadow in the polo shirt standing again on the library steps. Two uniformed officers flanked him. If I had ever wondered if he was a cop, I didn't wonder about it anymore. Unfortunately, if Mr. Perlini added a secret entrance from the tunnel to my office, I haven't found it.

Lacking tunnels, I simply hustled in and locked the inner door behind me, noticing as I did so that my answering machine was flashing. I opened my living room door, so I could see the library from my desk.

The three cops stood passively, trying to pretend my return didn't interest them. Only polo shirt's animated conversation on his cell phone suggested that they'd noticed me at all. I pressed the button on my machine and listened to four messages all left in the last thirty minutes.

The first was Blake, "Hey man, it's Blake. I'm hearing rumors that they're trying to get a warrant to search your place. If you have anything to hide, and I'm sure you don't, get it hidden and quick. Call me, or better yet, don't."

McCoy's message followed almost immediately, "This is McCoy; Hall Street is hopping like a one-legged jackrabbit. They're aiming to get warrants for you and everybody else they got a name to hang one on. I'm fixin' to look in on my client; then I'll call on you. If you ain't there, I'll know what to do. Daniel's heading straight to your place. Try not to let anybody in till he gets there."

Another from Blake followed, "Hey, it's me again. It's not just a search warrant; they're planning to arrest you as a material witness and for accessory to murder. I think Kenth wants you more than he wants the killer. I'm coming over. Try to stay out of sight 'til I get there."

Daniel's message was longer than the other three combined, but told me nothing the others hadn't already covered. I erased all four; then glanced out my window again. Polo shirt was still on the phone, apparently waiting for word from headquarters that the warrants were ready to serve.

I grabbed the remote control and raised the picture which covers the window to the waiting area. I didn't know who would be coming, but I saw no reason for its existence to become public knowledge. I also locked the exterior door and closed all the interior doors.

If the search warrant only stated 'office', my living areas would be temporarily off limits. With Daniel on his way, I was certain of that. Next, I set about getting rid of everything I could think of to hide.

I popped the tape out of the machine, grabbed my notes and the copy of the file on Freak I had made at Daniel's and went to the kitchenette. I may not be much of a cook, but as Emily often points out, I can burn with the best of them. In a matter of moments, everything that connected me to my client went up in smoke.

I threw the ashes in the shower and turned the water on high to wash it down the drain. I heard the doorbell ring, but I wasn't quite ready to answer it. First, I changed into shorts and a tee and stuck my head under the faucet to create the illusion that the shower had been running for personal hygiene reasons.

I then lit two of the candles Emily brought over when I moved in and listened to the bell ring again, accompanied by persistent knocking. I turned off the shower and glanced in the mirror. When I was sure I looked freshly showered, I called out, "Just a minute!"

I waited exactly two minutes before opening the door. I realized immediately that my ruse had been wasted. Blake and Daniel came inside from the landing, and the man in the polo shirt still stood on the library steps talking on his cell phone.

Blake wrinkled his nose, "Damn, Emeril, what did you burn? Hasn't Emily taught you not to do any cooking?"

Daniel glanced around; then added, "Of greater consequence, did you not consider that displaying more than a scintilla of culinary accoutrements would more preponderantly cultivate the illusion that you had incinerated edibles, as opposed to evidence?"

As usual, he made a good point, even if I almost needed a dictionary to understand it. I quickly pulled a couple of unwashed dishes and forks out of the dishwasher and put them in the sink with the pot. As I did so, I saw Larry Joe walking past Neiman's toward my office. My legal cavalry had arrived faster than City Hall could process the warrants.

As I invited him in, Larry Joe looked stressed again. He barely acknowledged Daniel or Blake before talking, "I presume you got my message. Did you go over there? Did you talk to him?"

"Yes, and yes," I answered. "Assuming you are asking about my client. I thought you were going there also."

"I did, but he wasn't there. How did he look?"

"He looked like the president of the local chapter of the young Republicans club should look. He certainly didn't look as stressed out as you do."

"Well, ain't that finer than frog's hair? Guess I got myself all worked up for nothing."

For the second time in one day, I had calmed Larry Joe down enough to cause him to revert to his fake Texas accent. I definitely need to quit doing that. Any comment I might have made became moot, when I again heard the doorbell ring.

I expected it to be the officer in the polo shirt with warrants in hand accompanied by his uniformed sidekicks. Instead, it was Dougie Kenth. I don't know which surprised me more, that the D.A. was apparently serving his own warrants or that he didn't barge in when I opened the door.

"Blake's here, isn't he? I'd like to speak to him, if I may." He sounded like a door-to-door salesman who had become accustomed to rejection.

As much as I normally enjoy it, for some reason I just couldn't be rude to him. I guess it's because he asked so politely to speak to Blake. "Yes, Blake's here. Come on in."

As Blake heard his name, he appeared at the door from the waiting area to the office. Dougie stepped inside and addressed Blake, "Actually, I need to speak to you privately; come outside a minute."

"No thanks, Dougie. It's a little too hot for outside discussions today. Everybody in this office is more famous for their discretion than I am, so it won't hurt you to discuss it in front of them. Besides, it must be important, or you wouldn't have come yourself."

Dougie's normally pale face turned beet red, but he managed just barely to stay in control. "It's more than just important, but you're right. Even if we discussed this privately, you'd probably just relay the entire conversation first chance you got."

Blake's response was direct, "Yes, I probably would, but I won't have to if you'll just tell us what brings you here." He went back into the office, and Dougie and I followed.

When we were all in the office, Dougie addressed Blake again. "Well, I was going to ask you to talk your friend into cooperating with us. However, since I can't even talk you into cooperating with me, I'll try a different tactic."

Dougie looked at me as he continued, "I couldn't bully you into telling us where you got that mirror. I realize now that I shouldn't have tried. Things have changed now. There's a dead girl involved, and I need to know. Where did you get that mirror?"

Out of habit, I started to answer, "I came across it in the course of…"

Blake stopped me from finishing, "Everybody here knows that a girl is dead. That's why you got the warrants. If you aren't planning to bully anybody, what do you plan to do with them?"

Dougie looked almost human as he sighed, "If I had a warrant, maybe I would try to bully somebody. God knows I don't have much of a plan as it is. Unfortunately, without a Judge's signature, a warrant is just a useless piece of paper. All the warrants presume murder as the cause of death, but the Medical Examiner's office hasn't officially declared it murder. Without murder established, I couldn't get the warrants signed."

Larry Joe managed to fake a sympathetic tone, "Son, this here ain't your first rodeo, either. Why in tarnation would you suggest murder if you ain't seen a supporting coroner's report?"

Dougie's response was both exasperated and angry, "Oh, I saw the coroner's report. If that report doesn't support murder as the cause of death, I don't know if I've ever seen one that does."

Now, it was Blake's turn to be exasperated and angry, "You've seen the report? It hasn't even been filed yet. I checked before I headed over here. What in the hell are you pulling here, Dougie?"

"Sorry, I should say I saw the preliminary report. You're right, the final report isn't filed, and I don't know why not. They examine a body which has been found in a location where it couldn't possibly avoid discovery for more than thirty-six hours. The autopsy shows that this recently discovered body has been dead for at least four weeks, thus proving that the body was moved weeks after death. How long can it take to conclude that murder is the cause of death?"

Blake nodded, "That's pretty suggestive, I'll admit. I even agree with your conclusion; however, it's also relatively circumstantial. The medical examiner's office doesn't usually rely much on circumstantial deduction."

"It is more than circumstantial when the autopsy reveals blunt force trauma to the head, multiple contusions on both arms, and significant internal bruising." Dougie looked smug again, "Wouldn't you agree?"

Blake shrugged, "I couldn't agree or disagree. I haven't seen the coroner's report, so I don't know what the autopsy reveals."

"Dammit, Blake. I just told you what it says. Don't you see why we need to cooperate? We all know that girl was murdered." He turned to me, "Look, you can refuse to cooperate until I can get the warrants if you want. But I know you; you're a decent guy all things considered. You also know as well as I do that when a girl gets murdered, the murderer is usually somebody close to her. What will you think of yourself if your client gets away with murder because of you? I know you don't want that."

Daniel had been silent for a long time, especially for him. He ended his silence, "I'd advise prudence, Mr. Kenth. Any insinuation, which rationally can be construed as an accusation, would be ill-advised in the presence of a multitude of competent attorneys. Such an allegation would be actionable even if the accused individual were not represented by the aforementioned counsel. If you inculpate my client regarding a death which isn't indubitably a murder, jurors would doubtlessly concoct fiduciary rewards larger than Dallas County's treasurers care to contemplate."

"Look, I'm not accusing anybody of anything. I just came here asking for help. You see the problem I have. I can't accuse your client or anybody else. Until the medical examiner declares she was murdered, I don't have a crime to accuse anybody of committing."

Dougie turned his palms up. "I don't want to arrest him for murder. I just want to ask him some questions. It'll show my bosses that I'm working. All I'm asking for is a little cooperation. Trust me, I always remember favors."

"Dougie, I don't trust you as far as I can throw you, but I can't think of any reason not to cooperate." I addressed Larry Joe and Daniel, "Any reason you know of for me not to tell him what he wants."

Daniel just shook his head. Larry Joe paused a second before answering. "General principle would be good enough. But Hell, whatever's fixin' to happen is gonna happen whether we like it or not. Ain't no reason to buck if you're gonna get rode anyhow."

I don't always agree with that sentiment, but this time I did. I told Dougie Freak's real name and gave him the address on Adolph. He jotted it down in his notebook and left without saying a word.

"Damn," Blake said after Dougie was gone, "You'd have thought he might have said thanks."

"You might have, Blake. I wouldn't have. I'm just glad he didn't try to steal my guest towels."

Daniel and Blake laughed politely at my lame attempt at humor. Larry Joe didn't bother. He just shook his head. "I've got a plumb bad feelin' about this. I don't trust that polecat when I know what territory he's fixin' to piss all over. I sure as hell don't trust him when he acts like a schoolboy beggin' the schoolmarm to let him clean the blackboard."

"None of us trusts him, Larry Joe. I thought we had agreed that this was our best option. If you didn't want to give him our client yet, I could have taken the heat. I don't mind bucking, you know."

"Sure, Pardner, I know you can buck with the best of them. We all agreed not to buck for now, but that don't mean we're right. Santa Ana's boys all agreed to take no prisoners at Goliad, too. General Houston sure made them pay for that, and I'm afraid we may pay for this."

Several things were wrong with Larry Joe's analogy, two of which were that Santa Ana never asked for his troops' agreement and that Dougie Kenth is no Sam Houston. However, I didn't have the energy to debate him on it. Plus, I suspected he was at least partially right.

As the two lawyers and Blake left, Larry Joe told me to drop by his office in the morning for another copy of Freak's file. He also promised to keep me informed of anything that developed.

I thanked him and hoped for Freak's sake that nothing would develop quickly. Knowing how slowly city hall generally acts, I really didn't expect anything dramatic to happen soon.

I made notes of what Dougie had said, then spent the rest of my evening recreating all of my notes on the case. Dougie's rant hadn't

142

convinced me that Freak had killed her. As much as he bothered me sometimes, I just couldn't see Freak as a killer.

However, I was as sure as Dougie was that she was murdered. I also knew that he was right about how frequently victims know their murderers well. It wasn't going to be enough for me to believe Freak was innocent. I needed, for my sake to be sure, and for his sake to prove it.

It was well after midnight before I turned in. I set my alarm and tried to sleep, but I couldn't shake the feeling that I was missing something important. By the next day, I would know what it was. I would also know that I couldn't have been more wrong about how quickly city hall could act.

I woke up to the sound of the alarm, which isn't the most pleasant way to wake up, but at least it isn't the phone. The alarm is just as loud and abrupt, but it doesn't require me to speak to it. All I have to do is hit the snooze button, and repeat as needed every nine minutes.

After the third time, I realized I must have set the alarm for a reason and dragged myself out of bed. By the time I had showered and shaved, I remembered why I'd set the alarm. I thought about calling, but decided just to walk over to Larry Joe's office.

I spent two and a half minutes making sure I wasn't tailed and still made the trip in fourteen minutes. Adriana greeted me with an icy stare and a question that struck me as inappropriate, "You're not married. Are you gay?"

"I didn't realize those were the only choices."

"They're not, but you also aren't divorced or a convicted felon."

"You did a background check on me?" I'm sure my voice probably sounded less incredulous than I actually felt; at least I hope it did.

"Of course, do you think I give my phone number to every loser who comes into this office?"

"Oh yeah, you wrote your phone number under Freak's address." I had forgotten about that.

"Actually, that's why I'm here. See, I put that paper with my copy of Freak's file. But then I, sort of, accidentally, burned the file, and Larry Joe suggested you could make another copy for me."

"You want a copy of my phone number? Or ..."

"Freak's file, Adriana. You're a charming girl, but I'm not really looking to adopt..."

"You're not old enough to adopt me; I'm not even ten years younger than you. But, I get it; you aren't going to call me. You could have just told me that. I'll go copy the file." She didn't look happy as she went to make copies, and I wasn't sure why I felt guilty.

Adriana returned a few minutes later with the file. "You know, most men your age like younger women."

"I suspect that's true. Personally, I like women of all ages. But I like one woman more than all the others, and her name is Emily. I'm sorry if you thought I was single, just because I'm not married, but I'm not available."

"Does Freak know about this Emily?"

"I'm not sure why you're asking or if it's any of your business, but yes, he does. I've been with Emily since before the first time I met him. He calls her Chameleon Lady."

"Damn that boy! He sits here raving about what a great guy you are and never mentions that you aren't available. He really needs to learn to keep his mouth shut."

I'd never thought of talking too much as one of Freak's faults. I'd also never suspected that he ever raves about what a great guy I am.

"Even if I were available, should you really trust Freak's opinion? I'd think you would have better ways of choosing your dates."

"Well, you're the first man I've ever heard him say anything nice about. That piqued my interest. Then you strolled in here and you're taller than Troy Aikman and almost as handsome, so I took a chance. I guess I made a mistake."

"I wouldn't call it a mistake; it just didn't work out. I am flattered. Thanks for copying the file for me."

"You're welcome, try not to accidentally burn it this time. For what it's worth, I think Freak's probably right about you."

"I just hope we're right about him."

"You are. If he were going to kill somebody, it wouldn't be her."

I took my leave and was back in my office before it occurred to me to wonder who Adriana thought Freak might have been willing to kill. At one time, I thought I was high on the list, but apparently, that isn't the case now, if it ever was.

I studied Freak's file again, this time thinking about who he might kill if he ever would. Based on his history of defending the defenseless against perceived attackers, I decided he would only kill someone he thought was attacking somebody.

Since the only potential murder victim in this case hadn't attacked anybody that I knew of, Adriana was probably right. Murdering his girlfriend certainly didn't fit Freak's profile. Of course, his girlfriend may have attacked somebody Freak wanted to protect.

Also, she may not have actually been Freak's girlfriend. All I knew for sure at this point is that I didn't know anything for sure. Not knowing anything for sure is pretty common for me, so I was still studying the file when the phone rang at 11:14. During office hours, I try to sound professional when I answer the phone, "Pegasus Investigations."

"Hey Pardner, you gonna be free later this afternoon?"

"I'm not your partner, Larry Joe. And I'm never free. I can make myself available this afternoon if needed, but first I'd like to know what's going on."

"I'm hankering to find that out myself. Our client's in the hoosegow, and I'm moseying over there now."

"I thought Dougie couldn't get a warrant. Why is Freak in jail?"

"That's what I'm aiming to find out. I'll know the lay of the land by this afternoon. I reckon Mr. Kenth pulled a fast one on us, but I ain't sure how or what right now."

"Okay, what do you want me to do?"

"Nothing you can do, yet. I'll find out what's going on soon, then we'll figure out what to do. The girl's pa is meeting me here at two. Can you amble on over here about three?"

Only Larry Joe would schedule a meeting by asking someone to 'amble on over'. I agreed to meet him at his office as requested. That left me about three hours to think about what was happening. My client was in jail less than a day after Dougie said he wouldn't be arrested.

That either meant something had changed, or Dougie lied to us yesterday. Since I don't like him, my first instinct was to presume he lied. However, I couldn't actually remember any time that he'd lied in the past, at least not outside the courtroom.

At 2:32, I gave up on the file and headed over to Thanksgiving Tower. I didn't think I had any secrets to keep at the moment, but I was still going to shake anybody who tailed me.

I didn't see anybody, but just to be sure I slipped in the south entrance of Neiman-Marcus and spent a few minutes looking at jewelry that costs more than the gross national product of several countries.

I still hadn't noticed a tail as I exited north. If anybody can tail me unnoticed through all the glass and mirrors in Neiman-Marcus, they're too good for me to shake. I walked over to Stone Plaza, strolled past Campisi's and went to see Larry Joe.

The tempting aroma of Campisi's pizza was still on my brain, when I greeted Adriana at 2:51. "He's expecting me."

She responded with a two hundred watt smile, "I know, but if you keep meeting me here like this, maybe Emily will get jealous, and you'll be available after all."

"Don't count on it. She's not the jealous type."

"Well, that presents interesting possibilities as well." She finally turned the smile down a notch, "Have a seat, he should be free any minute."

Two minutes later, Mayor Hightower came out of Larry Joe's office followed by a woman that I presumed to be his wife. The mayor looked like he always did, like a combination of every stereotype of how a politician should look. I'd probably seen him five or six times over the last few years, and he always looked exactly like he looked now.

His dark brown hair was perfect, except for a few strands which strategically fell across his forehead to make it clear that he wasn't wearing a toupee. His blue eyes and white teeth couldn't have been more of either. His forehead showed just enough wrinkles to suggest the maturity needed to be a leader without even hinting at a lack of youth.

His wife, on the other hand, didn't look like the perfect example of anything. Having never seen her before, I had presumed it was jealousy talking when Bethany had insulted her looks at Vino100. It was not.

Mrs. Hightower didn't have any particularly bad features. It was just that none of her features matched any of her other features. If you handed a young boy a stack of pictures of various facial features and asked him to paste them together on a sheet of paper, the resulting mishmash might well look just like Bunny Hightower.

The mayor didn't even look my way as he held the door open for his wife. As his wife went through, he leered at Adriana in what I guess he thought was a surreptitious glance. Some men can do that without being noticed. Mayor Hightower isn't one of them.

As he turned and followed his wife out the door, Adriana smiled at me and held her left hand to her forehead with her thumb out and her forefinger in the air. Even at my age, I recognize the unofficial youth sign language symbol for loser.

I smiled at her, "Now I see why I piqued your interest. Compared to him, Quasimodo would be a nice catch."

Larry Joe stood in the doorway to his office and cleared his throat, "If you're done tryin' to court Miss Adriana, come on in. Our client's in a fix, and we need to discuss things."

Adriana blushed, and I followed him into his office. He closed the door, and we sat at his conference table. When an attorney with Larry Joe's track record says his client is in a fix, it doesn't take a genius to realize that things aren't going well.

———

148

25   Jail Visit

"For the record, I wasn't flirting with your administrative assistant. We were just discussing Mayor Hightower's charm or lack thereof."

"I know that, Lochinvar. Your commitment to Miss Emily is plumb legendary. But Adriana gets so depressed when my guests don't flirt a little, that I feel obliged to gussy up her ego every once in awhile."

"My friends don't call me Lochinvar, but Emily will appreciate the vote of confidence. What's going on? Why did you ask me here? Why is Freak in jail? What kind of fix is he in? Should Daniel be here? What did the mayor want? "

"Damn, Lochin... sorry. I won't call you that, but you're askin' more questions than a virgin on her wedding night."

"Maybe so, but I think I'm just as likely to get screwed soon. That gives me the right to ask as many questions as I can think up. It also gives me the right to get some answers."

"I reckon you're right, but I'm running just as low on answers as you are. About all I'm sure of is that our client is in jail, and Mr. Kenth is every bit the low-down varmint we thought he was."

"Not exactly startling information, but I thought Dougie couldn't get an arrest warrant until the coroner's report was official."

"It seems it ain't as hard to get arrested in this town as the district attorney led us to believe. Our client has been charged with obstruction of justice and withholding evidence related to the girl's disappearance."

"Basically the same thing they used to hold me. How long will it take to get him out?"

"Might take awhile, ain't gonna be near as easy as it was with you. Freak ain't got your reputation, nor does he play dominoes with any local judges. Besides that, they think he killed her."

Larry Joe shook his head as he continued. "That makes the county a bit harder to intimidate. Plus, as soon as they get a coroner's report declaring it murder, those charges ain't gonna matter much."

"Does all that mean you can't get him out at all?"

"No, I reckon I'll get him cut loose sooner or later. That ain't the problem."

"It's not? Then what's the problem?"

"Are you familiar with Kubler-Ross's five stages of grief?"

Suddenly, I really felt guilty. I'd just been thinking about who had killed her and deciding if it was Freak or not. I'd forgotten all about the loss he had suffered. My thoughts went back to our conversation about Freak not going to strip clubs recently.

"I think so. I never knew who defined them, though. Doesn't it go denial, anger, bargaining, depression and recovery?"

"That's close enough. Being arrested seems to have leapfrogged him right into depression. He's got it about as bad as I've ever seen."

"Is he suicidal?"

"I don't think so, but with his condition that might not matter. He hasn't eaten today, and he could starve himself to death without even feeling a belly ache."

"Anything we can do?"

"Not that I can think of. Some good news might help, but good news seems to be scarcer than hen's teeth at the moment."

"Why don't you give me the details on the bad news? Maybe we can turn up some good news in there somewhere."

"I certainly hope so." His Texas accent disappeared as he got down to business.

"We don't have very much in the way of details, but here's what we know. Mr. Kenth convinced a judge to sign a warrant based on the time differential. Since Katherine Elizabeth was reported missing on June 8th, and he hired you on June 21st, the Judge agreed that he could have been withholding evidence related to an ongoing investigation."

"But how? We didn't know she was the same girl at the time."

"You didn't know, but nobody at city hall really believes he didn't. How many people don't know their girlfriend's real name?"

It was a rhetorical question, so I didn't answer it. I thought back to the day he hired me and the time he and I spent in Deep Ellum looking for her. Even I hadn't really believed him then. It was only after he reluctantly gave me the mirror which he thought was a coke mirror that I really believed he didn't know her name.

If the coroner's time of death was correct, and I have no reason to doubt it, she had already been dead more than a week before he hired me. The D.A. probably would have found that suspicious, as well. No wonder my client was in jail.

I continued rehashing the case in my head until Larry Joe spoke, "Nothing to add? I know you're famous for silence, but we are supposed to be working together here."

"Sorry, I was just thinking." Suddenly, I realized what had been nagging at me all day. "How accurate are time of death estimates? Is it a certainty that she was dead for five weeks before she was found?"

"They're pretty certain. I've occasionally been able to create 'reasonable doubt' regarding one, but only if the coroner isn't thorough or has questionable credentials. I seriously doubt if we could do that here. Do we need to impugn this one?"

"I don't think so. How quickly can we get a meeting with our client?"

"We might get it done this evening, certainly no later than tomorrow morning. What are you thinking?"

"I'm thinking we may have that good news we've been seeking. I need to ask him a question to be sure, and I don't want to tell you the question until I ask him."

"I wouldn't exactly call that working together, but I'll go along. Let me make some calls, and I'll see how quickly we can see him. How important is it that we see him tonight?"

"For the case, it's probably not important. For Freak, it may be crucial. You realize he's never felt unexpected pain before. He always knew his parents were going to die about when they did. This is new to him. You said yourself that depression has set in. The first night of being truly depressed is always the hardest. Alone in a jail cell can't be the best place to spend that night."

"Okay, I'll try to make it tonight. I'll call you as soon as I get it arranged. I hope you're right about having found good news."

I stood up to leave, "I do too, Larry Joe. I do too."

I got back to my office about four o'clock. I immediately spread out my notes to make sure I wasn't missing something. Freak hired me on June 21st. According to the coroner, the girl had died at least a week before that.

Unless Freak had lied to me, or I hadn't asked the right question, my client couldn't have killed her. I really needed to ask the right question. If Larry Joe couldn't get us visitation this evening, Freak wasn't the only one who might do something drastic. I really wanted to confirm my theory soon.

Larry Joe's call came at 6:16. "We can visit him at seven. I pulled in several favors to make it happen, and we're only promised fifteen minutes."

"Fifteen minutes will be more than enough. Should I come by your office or meet you there?"

"I don't care. I just hope you know what we're doing."

We decided to meet at the jail. We were sitting together in a consultation room when a guard escorted in our client. The word 'depressed' didn't really describe how he looked.

Wearing the requisite orange jumpsuit with all of his body piercing and art either gone or hidden; he looked barely alive. If I hadn't seen him without the body art at his place earlier, I wouldn't have even suspected that this was our client.

"The guard said you have a question for me." His insolent voice, which bordered on petulance, reminded me that he was indeed the client. I'd heard that voice several times now. It wasn't exactly growing on me, but I could certainly forgive it this time.

"I do. How many times did you come back from Vegas, while your show was amazing the tourists last month?"

Larry Joe started to say something, but thought better of it. Freak just stared at me for a little bit before answering. "That's your question, the question that was so important I had to miss American Idol on the tube to come here and answer?"

The thought of Freak watching American Idol in jail was too disturbing to contemplate, but I did want an answer. "Yes, that's the question. Will you answer it?"

"Sure man. I didn't come back at all. It's an eighteen hour ride. We did two shows a day. Even if somebody would have driven me back, there was never a chance to come home."

"It's less than a three hour flight."

"I don't fly; it's not safe."

Inside I was happy, but I knew I should press. God knows, Dougie would. "Haven't you heard? Flying is the safest way to travel."

"Not for me, it's not; too many risks that could kill me without me even recognizing them."

"I know you don't like to drive, but I don't know why, maybe this was the one exception. Why don't you like to drive?"

"Not that it matters, but I almost killed somebody during driver's ed. I don't not like to drive, I won't."

I kept pressing, "Some risks are worth taking to be with the one you love, or to kill somebody you don't. Maybe you drove back to Dallas and got back before anybody noticed you were gone."

Larry Joe had had enough, "Stop it! If you want him to prove he doesn't fly or didn't leave Vegas, do it another way. What does any of this prove anyway? Where's the good news?"

"It proves our client is innocent of murder. It also proves he didn't withhold evidence or obstruct justice. Everything that happened to that girl happened while he was twelve hundred miles away."

Larry Joe addressed the client, "When were you in Vegas?"

"End of May through Flag Day, June 14th. What does that prove?"

I answered him, "Everything, if we can prove you were there. Any witnesses who can vouch for your being there the whole time?"

Freak thought for some time before answering, "I don't know. The show's cast varies nightly based on who is in town and available, I doubt if anybody was there the whole time."

"What about the manager, wouldn't he know you were there the whole time?"

"I doubt it. He only showed up to a couple of shows while we were there. Truthfully, I don't think he likes the act."

"That shouldn't be a problem, we should be able to find enough witnesses to prove you were there the whole time. We'll just hire somebody out there to check into it."

Larry Joe didn't like that plan. "It would be better if we had one reliable witness to prove it. The prosecution can make it hard for several people to establish an alibi. People's memories aren't always fool-proof. The more witnesses we have to use, the greater the chance he can prove one of them wrong about something. If that happens, everybody's credibility gets called into question."

The guard entered the room, "Time's up. I need to escort him back to his cell now."

On the way out, Freak looked back at me. His face showed some signs of vitality again. "Go out there; find somebody who can prove I was there. There must be somebody, and you always get people to talk. I know you can do it."

"I don't need to go out there; every city has qualified investigators; we'll hire one who knows the city."

"Please do it yourself. I know I can trust you."

The guard had him out the door, before I could answer. The last thing I wanted to do was take a trip to Las Vegas in July. I turned to Larry Joe, "You know anybody in Vegas who can handle this?"

"Not off-hand, but I'll make some calls. Why don't you come by my office tomorrow morning around ten?"

I agreed and we parted ways. I really hoped Larry Joe would turn up an operative in Vegas who could handle the investigation. I don't have anything against Vegas, but I didn't want to go.

I don't like to leave the Lone Star State very much. I don't like to travel on business very much. I very much don't like to leave Texas on business. There are no words to describe how much I didn't want to make that trip.

26   Travelling Companion

I no longer had any reason to worry about being tailed, so I left my office at 9:52 for my ten o'clock meeting with Larry Joe. At 10:01, I sat down in front of his desk. "Did you find anybody?"

"Well, I got two recommendations. But I talked to both and I'm not impressed. The first one seems to think his job is to invent an alibi, not find one. The second one didn't seem clear about the concept of alibi."

"Nobody else we can try?"

"I'll keep checking, but time ain't on our side. You should go."

I'd been expecting that. I'd had all night to think it over, and I didn't know what I was going to do until I heard my own reply. "I'll go."

"Great! I'll have Adriana make the arrangements. I knew we could count on you."

"If I even begin to suspect you didn't make a real effort to find somebody out there, you'll regret it for a long, long time."

"Honest, Pardner, I tried. I know you think I'm just another Yankee, but I hate leaving this great state as much as you, maybe more."

Looking around at the overwhelmingly Texan décor, I almost believed him. Of course, I was the one flying to the Mojave Desert, not him. I wasn't happy as I left his office, but I accepted that I had to go.

I expected to find my office empty when I entered it. I wouldn't have been surprised to see one of the homeless people in my waiting area. I definitely did not expect to see a drop-dead gorgeous young lady with long honey-blonde hair and Cupid's bow lips sitting in my waiting room

As I opened the inner door, I looked back at her and recognized that the blonde in my office was Bobbie Jo Nottingham. Instantly, the normal reaction that a man has when seeing a pretty girl was replaced with an extreme and irrational fear that can't possibly be described to anybody who has never felt it.

I nearly ran to sit behind the relative safety of my desk. After I was seated, I asked her as calmly as I could manage, "Are your co-stars here?"

"No, I know only too well how poorly you react around Skipper and Skippette, so I left them at home."

My heartbeat started to slow down to almost normal. The angelic, innocent looking girl with the high cheekbones and arched eyebrows sitting across from me looked as likely to be a part of Freak's revue as I looked likely to be the winning jockey at the Kentucky Derby.

As she usually does, she looked like she should have been the model in a car dealership commercial or perhaps the face in a magazine advertisement for toothpaste or a skin care product. The only time she doesn't look like that girl is when she is onstage in Freak's Absolutely Incredible Completely Unbelievable Freak Show and Burlesque Revue.

To be totally honest, she probably still looks like a model when she does her performance. But, since her performance consists of two tarantulas crawling over every inch of her barely clothed body, it doesn't seem that way to me.

As much as I'm not entertained by watching Freak stick needles through various parts of his body or suspending himself on meat hooks, I find Bobbie's performance to be much less entertaining and much more disgusting. Even if I didn't suffer from acute arachnophobia, I would be put off a little by her act.

I would especially be put off by her faux coup de grace in which she lets both spiders crawl inside her mouth. She then walks through the audience opening her mouth to show them to anybody who will look. She finishes the act by making it appear that she has swallowed both.

Even some of the people who attend Freak's show generally have a problem with that part of the act. I suspect that's the whole point. At any rate, she had assured me that her beloved pet tarantulas weren't in my office, so I turned my attention to the question of why Bobbie Jo was.

"What brings you here, Bobbie Jo? More importantly, what is so important that you left Skipper and Skippette at home to visit me?"

"Freak says you're going to Vegas."

I had only agreed to go fifteen minutes ago, so I wasn't sure how she knew it. "When did he tell you that?"

"He called me last night. He says you're going to prove he didn't kill her."

"If he said that, he has way too much confidence in me, and I only decided this morning to go."

"That's what I tried to tell him. But he insisted. He said he knew you would go, and he knew you'd find a way to prove he was there."

She paused briefly before continuing in a confident, almost defiant tone, "He is innocent, you know."

Such a certain statement coming from a sultry beauty like Bobbie might have carried more weight with me if I'd never seen her walk through a Deep Ellum nightclub with two tarantulas in her mouth.

Still, as I looked at her, trying very hard not to think of spiders, I realized that I was just as sure as she was. "Yes, I know he's innocent. And I know he has the best defense attorney in Texas. I hope that's enough."

"He doesn't think it's enough. That's why he so desperately wants you to go to Vegas. He thinks that since your specialty is finding people, you'll find someone to prove he was in Vegas the whole time."

"Well, he was right that I would agree to go, but he shouldn't get his hopes up. Even if I find somebody who can prove he was there, the chance of getting them to testify isn't good."

"I know, you'll have to overcome the whole whoosh thing. But Freak says you're great at that."

"He may think that, but I don't even know what the hell a whoosh thing is." I told her honestly.

"It's what they're calling Vegas' 'what happens here stays here' mindset these days." She obviously tried to say it without letting on that

158

she thought that anybody who didn't know that was too old to be on this case. She tried, but being a performer of sorts didn't make her an Academy Award caliber actress.

She managed to compose herself before she continued, "Nobody out there will want to talk to anybody about anything. That's why I'm going to go out there with you."

"That's why you're going to do what?" I asked. I was starting to get used to hearing things that made me incredulous. This time, I didn't even try to hide it.

"Going with you to Vegas, you'll need my help. You don't know anybody out there. I know everybody. I'll introduce you to everybody in the scene out there. Then you'll do what you do. You'll ask a bunch of questions, and you'll just sit around silently waiting for answers. And since I introduced you, they won't just walk away; they'll actually talk to you. Eventually, somebody will tell you something that will prove that Freak is innocent."

"Okay, so you remember how I work, but I'm hoping that nobody I question in Vegas this time will have two spiders in a velvet pet seat on their lap, like you did when I questioned you." I tried not to shudder visibly as I recalled that experience.

"But there is absolutely no chance that I'm going to Vegas accompanied by you and your eight legged companions. If I can't find something that will help on my own, then Freak can hire somebody else to take the three of you out to Vegas."

"I know how prejudiced you are about Skipper and Skippette. You really need to get over it, but I assume you haven't. Sam The Man has already agreed to baby-sit them while I'm gone."

Now, I really was impressed. I had been a little surprised that she left them at home to come and talk to me. The idea of her actually leaving the city without them was almost unfathomable.

Bobbie Jo was correct in assuming that I wasn't over my prejudice, as she called it, against her pets. Even so, I recognize complete commitment when I encounter it. No cat or dog lover anywhere is more committed to a pet than Bobbie Jo is committed to her two spiders.

"I appreciate the sacrifice you are willing to make to help Freak," I told her truthfully. "But I don't need you to come to Vegas. I know where the show was and who to talk to."

"But you don't know those people. If they even think you're pumping them for information, they'll get so quiet it makes you seem like a chatterbox. Plus, most of them are guys, and at least they'll agree to talk to you if I ask them nicely enough."

"How do you know so much about them? Did Freak give you the same list McCoy gave me?"

"No, Silly. I was out there with the show. The Vegas crowds always love my act."

For a brief moment, I entertained the hope that getting the charge against Freak dropped might not even require a trip to Vegas. If Bobbie Jo told the court that she was with Freak in Vegas, the verdict would be assured. No prosecutor would even try to overcome that, not even Dougie.

"Bobbie Jo, if you were there with the show, you just need to tell the D.A. that you were there with Freak the whole time, and everything will be fine."

"That won't work. God, how I wish it would. But I came back to Dallas for my Dad's birthday. I told Freak I would lie and say I was there the whole time, but he said it wouldn't work. Would it?"

"No, it wouldn't work. Don't even think about it. You start lying to the D.A., and you'll get yourself into more trouble than you can handle. And I know they won't let you take your pets to jail."

"Fine, let's go to Vegas and find a witness."

"I'm going to Vegas to find a witness. You just stay here and take care of your costars."

"Why won't you let me help? I already promised not to bring them. I even wore nothing with pictures of spiders today, and I packed my suitcase the same way. I know you don't like me, but Freak needs us to help him. He needs both of us to help! I'm willing to sacrifice and spend time in Vegas with you that will keep me away from my little lovelies. Why aren't you willing to sacrifice a little, too? After all, you're the one getting paid for this."

I really didn't have a good answer for that. In fact, I didn't even have a bad answer. More than likely, it was my prejudice against her little lovelies that made me not want her help. While I was trying to decide whether to give in, she continued.

"You know what? I don't even care. It's a free country, so I'm going to Vegas. If I have to hang out in the hotel's lobby until you realize that you can use my help, I will. But, you're acting like an iddy biddy widdle baby."

Only a girl as young and innocent looking as Bobbie Jo could even think of getting away with using such an expression. That didn't change the fact that she was right; I probably could use her help.

"If you promise not to bring any spiders or use the phrase 'iddy biddy widdle baby', I'll call McCoy and let him know you will be helping on the case. He'll get you a room and a plane ticket."

To Bobbie Jo's credit, she didn't gloat as she left my office. To my credit, I didn't have nightmares about spiders that night. Of course, it helped that Emily wanted to spend my last night in Dallas at my place. It also helped that we didn't spend much of it trying to sleep.

Southwest Airlines doesn't fly from Love Field nonstop to Las Vegas since the Wright Amendment restricts its flights. That's why Saturday morning Bobbie Jo and I were sitting side by side on the Trinity Railway Express riding from downtown Dallas to DFW Airport.

Actually we had both been sitting alone on opposite sides of the aisle until the third time a guy sat beside her and started hitting on her. The first two had been at least ten years older than me. Neither struck me as being as handsome as Troy Aikman or as wealthy.

The third looked like he hadn't been to a dentist since elementary school. After that one, she decided she'd rather sit beside me. I was pretty sure Emily wouldn't mind. "You think they'll leave you alone if they think you're sitting with your dad?"

Bobbie Jo giggled, "You're totally too young to be my dad. You're also tall and tough looking; they'll leave me alone. You know, that doesn't happen when I have my little lovelies with me."

I didn't believe I was too young to be her dad, but I was certain that having her pets around reduced her number of unwanted advances. I also knew this was going to be a tough trip. I'd been on the train to the airport for less than half an hour, and I already missed Emily. That was going to get worse before it got better.

Pretty soon I was going be 1200 miles from Emily, off my home state turf and trying to bring back information from a city that prides itself on holding on tightly to its secrets. I hoped Freak appreciated the sacrifice I was making on his behalf. Watching the guys on the train still eyeing Bobbie Jo, I doubted anybody on the train did.

Bobbie Jo was leaving loved ones behind for Freak, also. At least I was getting paid, and I could call Emily from Vegas. I've heard about people who call their answering machines when traveling so their cats and dogs can hear their voice. I wondered if Bobbie Jo would do that for Skipper and Skippette.

That line of thought led me to wondering about how much she must care for Freak to have insisted on making this trip. Maybe her Dad's birthday hadn't been the real reason she'd come back from Vegas. That also might explain why she was so sure he was innocent, and why she was willing to lie about leaving Vegas.

27   Sin City

Bobbie Jo and I managed the three hour flight from DFW airport to McCarron International in Las Vegas without incident and virtually without conversation. Right after take-off, the pilot told us that we would arrive in Las Vegas at 1:30 where the temperature would be ninety-four degrees.

Many of the passengers gasped, having apparently forgotten that they had boarded the plane in Dallas where the temperature was ninety-nine degrees. I managed not to laugh, but I did find it amusing.

We had adjacent rooms booked at The Orleans, and it only took eleven minutes to get to the hotel on the shuttle from the airport. By 2:27, I was unpacked and trying to decide exactly how I was going to start looking for a witness or witnesses that could prove Freak had been here for the duration of his show's run.

I thought about knocking on the adjoining door to see if Bobbie Jo had a suggestion, but decided against it. Instead, I spread out all my notes on the table in the sitting area and reviewed them hoping for inspiration. As I went over the notes for the umpteenth time, I barely even heard the knock from the hallway.

When I opened the door, Bobbie Jo stood there wearing a grey pinstripe suit with a knee length skirt and white blouse. She looked like she was planning to apply for an office job while she was here. I opened the door inviting her in.

"Sorry that I wasn't much for conversation on the plane. I should have warned you about that. I live for danger, swallow spiders for fun, and fear no man or beast. But flying scares me speechless."

The live for danger speech was borrowed from her stage act, so I'd heard it before. It was the first time I'd heard her admit to fearing anything. I suspected she didn't admit it very often.

"Don't worry about it; I'm not much for conversation anyway. Besides, you know how scared I am of your little lovelies, so we're even."

"You're not really scared of them; you just have a phobia about them because you don't understand them like I do. But I know you don't want to talk about them, and I don't either. We've been gone less than a day, and I already miss them."

"I know how you feel," I told her honestly.

"You already miss Emily?"

"I miss her. I miss Dallas. I miss being in Dallas because it's closer to her. Every mile the plane took us this direction took me another mile away from her, and I missed her more each mile."

"Damn, you love her every bit as much as Freak said you do. He told me once that if he could find a love like the one you two have he could die happy."

The longer I stayed on this case the more amazed I was with Freak's opinion of me. How was it possible that I'd made such an impression on him without even liking him?

I was still thinking about that when Bobbie Jo brightened. "Hey, I know something that will cheer both of us up. You game for a long walk, or should I call for a cab?"

"How long is a long walk?" I asked.

"Just past the college, let's walk it."

"Okay by me, do you want to change out of those heels first?"

"Hell no! I live for danger, swallow spiders for fun, and fear no man or beast. Besides, if I decide to call a cab, they'll give me an excuse."

As we walked east on Tropicana Avenue, Bobbie Jo told me anecdotes about Freak and the show. She never mentioned spiders, so I mostly enjoyed the stories. Some of the pitfalls and pranks of the entertainment community are funny no matter how disgusting the show may be.

I didn't really get the humor in the one where Freak's meat hooks weren't properly inserted, and he ended up falling fifteen feet down to the stage. However, she finished that story just as we passed the UNLV campus, and I saw a Sizzler Steakhouse sign beckoning on the right.

"Please tell me that's where we're going," I said as I pointed at the restaurant.

"Of course, it is. You think you're the only one who misses sizzling steak served with a baked potato and a salad bar with more calories than the steak and potato combined?"

"We've only been out of Dallas for six hours. How badly can we be missing it?"

"Bad enough. Let's have a steak and get Freak cleared quickly. We both need to get home sooner rather than later." I couldn't have agreed more, as we both ordered sirloin steak and a sweet iced tea.

I'd been wondering about something ever since Freak and I had taken the tour of Deep Ellum and this seemed like my best chance to ask about it. "Why did your brother loan y'all his tour bus for the trip out here?"

"Why shouldn't he? And how do you know he did?"

"It came up in conversation earlier in the investigation. Doesn't he need it? I thought up and coming bands had to be on the road all the time to make it big."

"Charlie Ray hasn't been touring since…" She looked out the window, and I saw a slight hint of a tear in her eye, but it was gone just as quickly as it appeared and she continued. "He's been working on some other stuff, trying to write new material."

I wondered what she was hiding, but I didn't want to know badly enough to press for it. Generally, when a tear appears, there are more where it came from, and I didn't want to see them. Instead, I just pressed forward.

"That explains why the bus was available, but why did y'all need it? Doesn't the revue have its own means of transportation? Surely, you aren't dependent on loans and charity, are you?"

"We didn't used to be. Don't tell anybody I told you this, but the show hasn't been profitable lately. Freak's just been keeping it going because he knows so many of us depend on the income.

"He loaned us his bus, because without it, Freak probably would have just blown this off. Charlie Ray doesn't like Freak much, but he'll do almost anything for me, so he offered us the bus, so I could make a damn living."

She stared at me, and I was almost certain I was going to see more of her tears. I almost did, but she somehow kept them from flowing and went back to her meal.

I managed to change the subject to our approach to learning what we came to Vegas to learn, and the rest of the meal was far less awkward and far more pleasant. After we ate, we agreed to take a cab back to the hotel.

Time is pretty much meaningless in Las Vegas. However, night people are always night people no matter where they are. The first person we needed to interview was the club manager, Barry Wade. Bobbie Jo said nine o'clock was the earliest we could expect to find him at the club, which was the only place she knew to find him.

She suggested we meet at the rooms at 8:30. It sounded like a plan, so I agreed. I called Emily. She answered on the first ring. Long distance may be the next best thing to being there, but it's a very distant second.

I was happy to hear her voice, but I felt even worse about being away. After we hung up, I went to look around the hotel. I'm not sure hotel is the right word to describe The Orleans. Where I come from, hotels don't usually have a seventy lane bowling alley, an eighteen screen movie theater, and half a dozen restaurants.

Since casino gambling isn't legal in Texas, we don't have casinos or sportsbooks in our hotels either. I'm not a big fan of gambling myself, but I quickly found that the hotel sportsbook had something of interest for me. People will gamble on almost any sporting event in the world, so the sportsbook at The Orleans has more than one hundred televisions showing different games.

On one of the televisions, the Rangers were visiting the White Sox. Even Pete Rose wouldn't place a bet on a Rangers-White Sox game, but I was happy to sit and watch the game. The Rangers got two runs in the ninth off Bobby Jenks and won three to one. I watched the Cardinals pound the Dodgers for a while, before heading back to the rooms.

When I got back upstairs, Bobbie Jo was ready to go, still dressed in the pinstripe suit. I wondered if I was underdressed in my khakis and polo shirt. "Should I change into better clothes to meet this Barry Wade?"

"No, you're overdressed, but I'm half a foot shorter than Barry Wade, and I'm a girl. He's an intimidating person, and I don't want to be intimidated. The power suit and the heels help me keep things even when I talk to him."

"Skipper and Skippette probably help with that too, when you have them with you," I suggested.

"Normally, they do, but not with Barry Wade. He isn't impressed or scared or even much interested in them. Given the range of acts he books, that's not that surprising. But as long as he can glimpse my legs in high heels, I can usually manage him."

"He sounds like a real peach of a guy," I said sarcastically. "So other than the fact that he likes to look at your legs, and I'm a little taller than he is, why do we think he might help us?"

"Well, you're a lot taller than he is, and these are really great legs. But mostly, because I think he has a soft spot in his little black heart for our friend Freak."

The phrase, 'our friend Freak' rolled off her tongue much easier than my ears accepted it. Still, I hoped Barry Wade did have a soft spot for 'our friend', since we really needed his help.

The cabbie did a double-take when Bobbie Jo gave him the address on Nellis Blvd. I guess since he picked us up in front of The Orleans, and we were dressed like a yuppie couple from the Midwest, he assumed he'd be dropping us off somewhere on The Strip, not out by the Air Force Base.

Wade's Place isn't very far from The Strip geographically. In fact, we passed The Strip on the way to the club. As far as the ambience is concerned, however, the Strip and his bar couldn't be further apart. Once we got there, the driver's double take seemed inappropriately tame.

The club, such as it is, sits above a pawn shop between a strip joint and a tattoo parlor. Not surprisingly the entrance was in the back and the staircase was outside. All of the glitz and glamour associated with Las Vegas was conspicuously absent. Once inside, only the slot machines made it clear we weren't in Texas anymore.

The place was surprisingly crowded. A third of the patrons wore their Air Force uniforms. Another third were Air Force personnel out of uniform presumably and naively thinking nobody could tell without the uniform. The final third looked like they had auditioned for the bar scene in Star Wars, but hadn't appeared normal enough to be cast.

Bobbie Jo led me over to Barry Wade shortly after we entered and told him that Freak had been arrested. He motioned us toward his office and said he would join us when he could. The office, like the rest of the club was cramped, dirty and just barely short of nauseating.

I noticed a shelf behind his desk with a stack of porno magazines and another stack of whiskey labels. Neither surprised me. I was still trying to get comfortable in a chair not built for comfort when the office door opened.

"So, Freak's in trouble, is he?" Barry Wade's soft voice seemed out of place from a man of his size. "And this affects me, how?" The

168

arrival of Barry Wade added little to the ambiance other than the odor of cigarettes mixed with something I couldn't identify. He sat behind his desk, which I noticed was on a platform and looked at us.

More accurately, he looked at Bobbie Jo. Mostly, he looked at her legs, but occasionally he looked at her breasts. He seldom looked at her face or at me. I looked at him almost constantly. He was about 6' and very fat, not in the way that athletes get heavy when their careers end, but in the way that overweight children grow up to be more overweight adults.

I assumed the question was rhetorical, so I made no attempt to answer it. Bobbie Jo followed my lead. Eventually he grew tired of the silence. "Neither of you can think of anything better to do than sit here and not say anything? Maybe you should just leave since I don't have anything to tell you."

Even with him perched on the platform behind his desk, I had to look down to address him, "I have several better things to do. Kicking your fat ass is the one I'm trying to talk myself out of doing. My girlfriend keeps telling me I should do less of that, and I sometimes take her advice."

Bobbie Jo started to giggle, but thought better of it. The sound of a giggle stopping in midstream is hard to describe, but it almost caused me to start laughing. I didn't think that would help the situation though, so I refrained.

"Does this girlfriend of yours know you're hanging out in the underbelly of Sin City with the spider training whore?"

I considered saying something to him about his description of Bobbie Jo, but thought better of it. She shouldn't need my help to deal with him, and even if she did, she probably wouldn't appreciate it. Instead, I just answered his question.

"No, she thinks I'm at an NRA meeting with Charlton Heston. What I want to know is this: Freak comes out to your place, does his show, and packs the place. Why don't you want to help him?"

Barry Wade laughed. Actually it sounded more like a snort than a laugh. "Packs the place? Did you not look around when you came in? This dump is packed when the stage is dark. Fly boys and locals who've been banned from every casino on the strip know they can always come here and lose money and drink. Sure, Freak's show draws a crowd, but it's not a crowd that even I try to draw. Mostly, it's weirdoes and losers who either don't buy drinks or don't tip. It's hard enough to get girls to wait tables here; a two week run with that audience takes me a month to re-staff."

Bobbie Jo asked, "If you lose so much money on the Freak Show Revue, why do you book us so often? I've only been with the show for two years, and we've played here five times."

"Hey, I've got to book something. It ain't like Penn and Teller are going to play this joint these days. And one of my best customers is a fan of your revue."

This could be the witness I was hoping to find. "That's a good reason; customer service is the key to a successful operation like this. Maybe, we should talk to your good customer."

"Hey pal, I don't need your sarcasm. This place may not be Caesar's Palace, but I make a living with it. My customers like it, and I do take care of them."

I held my palms to him apologetically. "I wasn't being sarcastic, Barry Wade. I'm just asking you to help me talk with this customer."

"What's in it for me?"

"The sooner I find out what I need to know, the sooner I leave Las Vegas. The sooner I leave Vegas, the less time I'll spend wondering if those Jack Daniels and Crown Royal labels stacked on the shelf behind your desk mean your customers aren't getting name brand drinks. I don't really care about the knockoff liquor, but if I hang around long enough, I might get bored."

I put a fifty on his desk. "Also, I can probably find another one of these, if I get to talk to that customer."

He surprised me by having enough class to not reach for the bill. "Okay, I'll tell you what I'll do. Give me a number where you're staying, and I'll pass it on to my customer. But, I don't promise that he'll call you. If he does, and I find out you harassed him, you'll wish you'd never left Dallas."

"I've been wishing that since I got on the plane. But thanks, I really do appreciate it." I wrote the hotel number on my business card and handed it to him.

Bobbie Jo smiled at him, "We both appreciate this, very much." Then, she stood up and kissed him on the cheek. "I can be very nice to people who are nice to me."

Barry Wade was still blushing and grinning as we got to the door. Bobbie Jo turned and looked at him with a fierceness I didn't know she had in her. "If you ever call me a 'whore' again, you'll learn just how trainable spiders can be. You do know they're not all harmless and lovable like Skipper and Skippette, don't you?"

28   Jesus Freak

If he had a reply, I didn't hear it as she timed her remark perfectly with our exit. We had to walk past the tattoo parlor, two hotels advertising hourly rates and several boarded up buildings before we found a cab parked in front of an adult book store.

The cabbie seemed a little embarrassed when I asked if he was on duty, but he said he was. He made me show I had cash, but once I did, he opened the door for Bobbie Jo. The ride back to our hotel was as devoid of conversation as the plane ride to Vegas.

As soon as we were dropped off at The Orleans, I asked Bobby Jo, "You know Barry Wade better than I do, will we hear from the guy?"

"I don't know the customer, so I can't be sure. I promise that Barry Wade will give him the number, though."

"Are you usually this confident?" I asked.

"About men? Always." She laughed a little. "The three best motivational tools for a man like Barry Wade are fear, lust and greed. We managed to give him all three. He'll do it, probably sooner rather than later."

She had a valid point; those were probably the three best motivators for most types of men. Much as I agreed with her, I didn't share her confidence. That's why I got up early the next morning to develop an alternate plan. I was still coming up empty when the phone rang.

I answered it, and a man with a very deep baritone voice replied, "This is Ezekiel James. Barry Wade tells me you wish to speak to me about The Freak Show Revue. May I ask why?"

"Of course, one of the performers is accused of a crime in Dallas which took place while the troupe was performing here."

"Not a minor offense, if you are going through all this trouble to investigate it. I presume the star is not the suspect?"

"Murder is certainly not a minor offense, and actually the star is a suspect. But, he certainly isn't the only member of the troupe under suspicion." I saw no reason to mention that I was the only one suspecting anybody other than Freak, since I wasn't sure which part of the show he liked enough to encourage Barry Wade to book it often.

"Oh! I see. That, of course, is preposterous. My calling requires my attention during the lunch hours; can you meet me at three o'clock?"

"Sure, name the place," I answered wondering why he thought it preposterous.

"Will the Denny's on The Strip be okay, Sir?"

I didn't bother to tell him that nobody calls me Sir. "That works fine for me. I'll see you this afternoon."

"One more thing, Sir." He hesitated before continuing, "Please do not bring the harlot with you."

Apparently, Bobbie Jo's part of the act wasn't the reason this customer had encouraged Barry Wade to book the troupe. I agreed not to bring her with me to Denny's and hung up the phone.

As soon as I hung up the phone, I heard Bobbie Jo knocking on the adjoining door. I opened it.

"Was that our call, or was it just Emily making sure you're behaving here in Sin City?"

"It was Skipper asking me to tell you that he and Skippette are moving back to South America."

"Ha! My little lovelies would never call you even if they could use a phone. They'd just instant message you pictures of each other until you either got over your phobia or went completely insane. Now, answer the question."

"It was our call, or rather my call. I'm going to meet with the guy this afternoon at three."

"You mean we're going to meet with him."

"No, he wants to meet with me alone."

"The detective meets the possible witness alone in an unnamed place. Wasn't that a corny premise even before you were born?"

"Probably, but I'm not meeting him alone. I'm just meeting him without you." I saw no reason to mention what he called her. "He apparently shares my prejudice against spiders. He asked me not to bring you."

"You should have tried to invite me, anyway. Perhaps you haven't noticed, being all in love with Emily like you are, but I do have a certain way with men. Did you even tell him my little lovelies are back in Dallas?"

"Spiders didn't come up in the conversation. Look, I appreciate the help you've given me so far, but this time I don't need your help."

"Fine, be that way!" She went back to her room and slammed the door closed.

At 2:48, I was sitting at a booth in Denny's. At 3:10, a thin man with graying hair came in and walked directly to my booth. I hoped he wasn't my date, but I expected that he was, so I asked, "Are you Mr. James?"

"Please, call me Ezekiel. Mr. James sounds so formal. He took off the sandwich board he was wearing and shook my hand. He was about six inches shorter than me and about a foot taller than the board. The front of the board read:

REPENTANCE

PSALM 90:8

Even What Happens in Las Vegas

Will Be Set Before the Eyes of God!

Based on the sign, I had no reason to expect this interview to go well. As he leaned the sign against a booth, I saw the back. It read:

FORGIVENESS

JOHN 8:11

Then neither do I condemn you

Go now and leave your life of sin!

As he sat down, he gently placed a satchel full of pamphlets on the table and took off his sunglasses and carefully put them in the satchel. With the signboard, he looked like a religious fanatic. Without it, he looked like a distinguished businessman or doctor.

I generally expect little good to come from talking with fanatics, religious or otherwise. However, it seldom hurts to start out nice regardless of expectations. "Thank you for agreeing to meet with me so quickly."

"Barry Wade made it sound urgent, and nothing you told me on the phone contradicted his tone. What can I do to help Mr. Show?"

"It is urgent, and I hope we can come up with something you can do to help him. But, I suspect Barry Wade made it sound urgent because I implied that I'd give him another fifty dollars if I got to speak to you."

"Yes, Barry Wade does have a weakness for such offers. Most men do, in fact. Barry Wade's weakness is greater than some. "

"And he speaks so highly of you; he even called you his best customer. Having been to his place, I didn't expect his biggest spending customer to be a Bible thumper."

"In this city, expectations are seldom accurate. I doubt if he thinks of me as his best customer because I am his biggest spender. I seldom even go to his place, except when Freak is performing."

"He said he only books Freak's act for you. If you aren't really a customer, why does he do that for you?"

"Because I introduced him to God's word and Jesus' forgiveness, which has in some small way helped him to fight his demons. He is grateful for that, although his battle is far from won. And for your information, I do not thump Bibles; I merely pass on the teachings of our Savior."

"That answers half the question, but it doesn't explain how you think having Freak perform there will help you spread the Savior's message?"

"Does it not? It does if you realize that Freak is probably a direct descendent of Jesus of Nazareth."

I had expected not to like what he had to say. But I hadn't expected to hear that. In fact, I could have spent a year trying to guess what he was going to say, without ever getting around to that.

I finally recovered from my shock enough to speak, "You do realize that 'The DaVinci Code' is not the third Testament, don't you?"

"Certainly, I realize that." His deep voice made it almost impossible to recognize his indignation, but not quite. "That does not mean everything in it is false."

"I'm scared to ask this, but I will anyway. Even if we accept that Jesus might have descendants, what would make you believe Freak is one of them?"

"Are you aware of his gift of not feeling pain?"

"Yes, but I'm not sure I'd call it a gift. It seems to almost guarantee a short life span."

His voice went from deep to almost commanding; a voice even Cotton Mather would have envied. "Short and pain free; our Creator most certainly had a reason to create such a condition. So I ask you, who was the first person on earth, upon whom He would see a need to bestow such a condition?"

I didn't answer, so he continued. "Surely, anybody even slightly versed in the Word can make the connection. It would be a person who only needed to live a short time, but would suffer greatly if not for this gift."

"I'm not sure that He was the first; I seem to recall some suffering and short lives in the Old Testament, also. But still, it's a stretch to assume that His descendants would share the trait and that Freak is one of them."

"I think not; not when you factor in that it is a hereditary trait most commonly found in the Ashkenazi-Jewish population. Add in the fact that this is the population which is also the most likely to be descended from His lineage."

He was on his soapbox now, and I let him go on, "Then, you look at the Dearborn Incident in which a similar human pincushion act, Edward H. Gibson staged his own crucifixion and it becomes more likely. My parents were in the audience for Mr. Gibson's performance and described them as almost identical to the shows Mr. Show puts on. When I learned that Freak's maternal grandmother's maiden name was Gibson, I became certain."

"I'll admit that you have more than one coincidence, but why would The Second Coming be working a pincushion act? Wouldn't you expect him to be in a ministry of some sort?"

"Firstly, there is no record of Jesus starting in the ministry until He was in his thirties. For all we know, He had His own pincushion act in Egypt or somewhere during His twenties. Secondly, given the money-changers who pass themselves off as ministers these days that might be the last career he would choose while biding his time."

Mr. James' voice became deeper and more commanding the longer he spoke. "However, I never said that Freak is the Second Coming. I have simply proven that he is descended from the First Coming. If he is the Messiah, that will be revealed in its own time."

I wasn't really convinced Mr. James had proven anything, but I learned a long time ago not to argue with religious fanatics. I especially knew better than to argue with religious fanatics when I wanted their help.

"Okay, I see your point." Like I said earlier, lying to strangers is getting easier as I get older. "How many of Freak's shows did you see while he was out here?"

"I saw them all. I never miss one while he is here."

"Even the matinees? What about your calling? Don't you have pamphlets to hand out and sinners to save?"

"I see no reason for you to mock my calling. Anybody can preach to church choirs. I try to introduce sinners to the power of the Savior. Las Vegas is an excellent place to find sinners. More accurately, it is a great place to find good people who are sinning and will eventually regret it."

I could tell that I didn't have the most perfect witness. A crafty prosecutor could probably bring his credibility into question with ease. Still, I continued the interview, "Did Freak miss any of the shows or were there any cancellations."

"Without Freak, there is no show, and there were no cancellations."

"So Freak did two shows daily for the entire two weeks? Will you testify to that in Dallas?"

"I will if Freak asks me to do so. If he is the second coming, and this is the crime for which he is here to be sacrificed, I would be doing God a disservice by testifying on his behalf. If he asks me to testify, then I will know this is not the case."

"I'm here at Freak's request; he will ask you."

"When he does so, I will testify."

Just like that, I had a witness. Granted, my witness was a little bit crazy, but I had a witness. My job was to find a witness. Larry Joe's job was to make the testimony stand up in court.

We exchanged business cards, and I went back to The Orleans feeling better than I had when I left it. I should have guessed Bobbie Jo would be waiting there with news that would derail my good mood.

—

178

29   Compelling Evidence

Bobbie Jo left the adjoining door open, so I shouted out, "Start packing, we have a witness. Dallas is only a plane ride away." Like I said, I was in a good mood.

Bobbie Jo walked into my room, and she didn't look happy. "I hope the Holy Roller isn't our witness."

"Hey, I know he's a little out there, but he'll testify that Freak was here the whole time. Larry Joe can turn his religious beliefs into a positive. After all, juries usually believe preachers, even if the rest of us don't."

"Even if they know he can't see for shit? Even if he doesn't have vision problems, when a jury learns that he never takes his sunglasses off, they'll doubt if his testimony proves Freak was here. In Barry Wade's place, a person wearing sunglasses can't positively tell Freak from you."

"What makes you say he never takes off his glasses? For that matter, how do you know who I talked to?"

"I followed you to Denny's. Then, I hung around until I saw someone I recognized. When I saw him walk in, I knew it was him, even though he never brought that silly sign into Barry Wade's joint."

It didn't help my self-esteem any to realize that although I could lose a shadow by the Dallas Police, I could be followed by Bobbie Jo without even knowing she was following me. Of course, I didn't expect her to be tailing me, but I probably should have.

I knew she wasn't happy about not being invited to the meeting. What did I expect her to do, hang around the hotel missing her spiders? I considered myself lucky she hadn't barged into Denny's and joined us. My mood wasn't helped by her assertion that Mr. James most likely can't see.

I wasn't happy, but still I called Larry Joe and told him about the witness. "I've found a witness who says he'll testify that Freak performed two shows daily, but there may be some issues."

"Ain't never been a perfect witness. That's why we have to coach 'em all up a speck. What issues?"

"Well for one thing, the guy's a real religious nutcase, walks around the Strip carrying a signboard and passing out pamphlets. Worse yet, he thinks Freak might be a descendant of Jesus Christ. In fact, he won't testify without Freak's blessing."

"Ain't that interesting? Don't recall the Messiah sticking needles in himself, but I've heard of stranger beliefs. I don't reckon that'll hurt us. We don't need a dependable character witness, just any ol' boy who saw that Freak was in Vegas for two weeks straight."

"Well, that brings up the other issue. Bobbie Jo is convinced that his vision is very poor."

"Hell, gals that look like her reckon every feller who doesn't cotton up to her is blind, gay or both. Maybe, he just likes his religion more than her looks."

"That might be true, but she says he never took his sunglasses off at any of the shows. She's afraid that even if he can see that makes it likely that his testimony might not mean much. Honestly, I agree with her."

"Well, that is a bit of a burr in the saddle, ain't it?" He paused, and when he continued his Texas speech had disappeared. "Even so, we have a witness. That's a start. We'll do some research on eyesight issues. There must be some that require sunglasses that don't involve blindness."

"Sure, find one, and then you can coach him up to pretend he can see well. I see why most people don't trust lawyers."

"I'm not going to coach him to lie. I just don't want the truth lost over a pair of sunglasses. You don't know he can't see. Have you even asked him about it?"

My mood was now completely soured. I was deciding between two or three possible retorts, when I remembered that Ezekiel James had put his sunglasses in his satchel when he joined me at Denny's.

I had a hunch that I needed to follow up on quickly. So I told Larry Joe, "I've got to go. Don't bother researching eyesight. I'm going to do some follow-up with the witness."

Bobbie Jo had gone back to her suite while I talked to Larry Joe, but the door was still open. While I looked for Ezekiel James' card, I called out, "Bobbie Jo, I need your help."

She still didn't look happy when she appeared in the doorway, "About time you figured that out. Why should I help you?"

"Because other than the fact that you're mad, and I have a plan, nothing has changed. We both came out here for one reason, and we both want to get back as soon as possible."

"Whatever. Tell me about the plan."

I told her; she agreed to help, and I called Mr. James to arrange a meeting. I don't follow my hunches very often, and if this one was wrong, I was going to feel like a moron. I was definitely pleased when Mr. James agreed to meet me in an hour at the same Denny's."

He was at a table when I got there. I shook his hand and sat down. His baritone again showed the slightest hint of indignation as he asked, "What's so important?"

"Well, I talked to the attorney representing Freak, and apparently eyesight is being questioned regarding all eyewitness testimony these days. When I mentioned to him that you wore glasses, he got nervous."

Lying to strangers was getting easier and easier, and he reached for his satchel, but didn't pull out the glasses or say anything, so I continued. "Anyway, he asked me to check that your prescription wouldn't cause us any problems. He really took me to task for not being more professional."

He interrupted, "Honestly, this is much ado about nothing. My vision is fine. I can put you in touch with my eye doctor if needed, but all of this could have been handled by phone."

He was getting offended and would probably have gotten onto a soapbox if Bobbie Jo hadn't chosen that moment to time her entrance.

Apparently pushed by a stranger, she fell into our table and managed to simultaneously push the satchel toward me and land side-saddle in his lap.

"Zeke baby, is that really you?" She cooed. Yes, she really cooed. I hadn't heard anybody coo since Emily and I went to a thirties film festival at the Majestic Theatre. I certainly had never heard Bobbie Jo coo, even to her spiders, but she definitely cooed.

He stammered something, but it didn't sound like English. While she continued to coo and he continued to stammer, I reached in the satchel and found exactly what I hoped to find: sunglasses, a wire and a digital recording device. It was an almost exact duplicate of the setup Sam the Man had confiscated in Deep Ellum.

"Uh, Miss! If you're through pretending to be Mae West, I really wish you would leave this man alone."

She slid off his lap, stood far enough from the table that he could see the withering glaze she gave me. It was only when she said her line, "Well, I never!" and stormed off that I realized that the girl storming away looked almost nothing like Bobbie Jo.

When he quit watching her exit, he turned toward me. He started to say something, then he started to reach for his glasses, on which I had a firm grip. He thought better of both ideas and simply looked at me.

For a change, I wasn't the silent one. "So, Ezekiel, when I look at the contents of this disk, am I going to find footage of harlots or circus freaks?"

"You have no right to ask me that. I'll thank you to return my property, now."

"Your thanks aren't needed, since I don't plan to return your property. I asked you a question, and I expect an answer."

His face was turning red, either from anger or embarrassment, or both, but his voice had softened by the time he answered. "Both. When I bought the glasses, my intent was to record shows like Freak's. Sadly, no man is without sin. I can only ask for strength and forgiveness."

"Well, don't look to me for either. All I do is investigative work. I don't even care how many harlots you've filmed. I just want to know how many of Freak's shows you recorded while he was here."

"All of them, if I'm there when he decides to proclaim himself the Son of God, I most certainly plan to have a recording of it. Had recording technology like this been available two thousand years ago, there would be no non-believers."

I doubted that, but it didn't matter much right now. I held my breath as I asked my key question. "Did you delete the recordings, or do you still have them?"

"I have them all, but I'm not giving them to you or anybody else for that matter!"

"Really? You won't share them, even if Freak asks? Seems like a small thing for a Messiah to ask of a believer."

"He may not even be the.... Never mind. You're right. My embarrassment is inconsequential compared to the magnitude of the situation. If the recordings will help, I will provide them."

Remarkably, it really was that easy. We flew to Dallas and presented the recordings as evidence, which turned out to be unassailable. Dougie's experts told him that if called to testify, they would have no choice, but to assert that the recordings were completely authentic.

Since each of Freak's performances differed slightly and had a slightly different cast, there was no chance Freak hadn't been there for the entire run. A few days after I got home, Freak was released.

The official search for Katherine Elizabeth's killer could now begin in earnest. A few days later, I learned that our efforts to free him had been a waste of time.

30   Surprise Gift

On the Monday after they released Freak, Dougie Kenth paid me a visit. I watched as he climbed the exterior staircase, crossed the waiting area and rang the bell at my door. His comb-over looked as pathetic as ever, but he didn't have his usual scowl.

I saw no reason for him to know about the secret window, so I grabbed the remote and slid the panel over the window before I answered the door. I opened it slowly and didn't say anything as Dougie slowly entered.

"Don't worry, I'm not staying long. I just wanted to thank you."

"You want to thank me? For what? Thwarting your case?"

"I wouldn't call it thwarting. I'm sure I'll be prosecuting somebody on the case soon. We aren't in the business of prosecuting innocent people. You saved my office a great deal of expense and embarrassment by proving his innocence."

"Well, you're welcome. As long as we're being such friends all of a sudden, who do you expect to be prosecuting for it?"

"It's hard to say, yet. The prevailing thought is that her family knows more than they're saying. One of them might even be a suspect, except that all three were in Mineral Wells the weekend that the body was dumped. Other than that, everybody she knew falls into two categories. The ones who knew her in Deep Ellum thought she hung the moon, and couldn't imagine anybody wanting to hurt her. At Ursuline, nobody knew her well enough to even speculate."

"Doesn't really sound like you're going to have a case to prosecute any time soon."

"Oh, I'm sure they'll turn something up soon. And when they do, we'll have to thank you again. We could have wasted months prosecuting the wrong guy." As he left, he stopped and shook my hand.

——

I couldn't ever remember a conversation with Dougie in which neither of us insulted the other. I also couldn't ever remember him thanking me or shaking my hand. I really had expected him to be mad, but I guess prosecuting the wrong guy is about the worst thing that can happen for a D.A., especially in a city famous for prosecuting the wrong guys.

After he left, I slid the panel away from the window. About thirty minutes later, Freak showed up. I let him in after sliding the panel back into place. As he sat down, he pulled off his backpack and set it gently on the floor, "Will they find him?"

I was used to not understanding Freak, so I asked, "Will who find whom?"

"Will the cops find the son of a bitch who killed them?"

"They should; they know you didn't do it; they are generally good at that sort of thing, and it is a high profile case. They'll find him or her."

"Well if it wasn't for you, they'd still be thinking I did it, but okay, give me an invoice, and I'll pay you what I owe."

He didn't say anything as I slid my chair over to the computer and printed out the invoice. I tallied my fees, listed my expenses and subtotaled it, then listed and deducted the retainer, which was only slightly less than the subtotal. I printed it out and gave it to him.

He pulled a pen and a checkbook from his backpack and wrote out a check and handed it to me. I noticed it was for the subtotaled amount of the bill, not the total after deducting the retainer. I figured he hadn't noticed, so I pointed out his mistake.

"No, the check I wrote is yours. You may not know what your work is worth, but I do."

"Freak, I billed you for my work. I'm not going to overcharge you just because you have more money than most of my clients. I have ethics, you know."

"Try to see it from my point of view, Colombo. If I live long enough, I'm probably going to need something investigated again

185

sometime. You sometimes don't realize it, but you're really good at this. How will I feel if I need a detective, and my one friend in the detecting business is out riding a bike instead of detecting because I was too tight with my parents' money to keep him in business? Keep the retainer for the next time I need you,"

I was about to tell him that my friends don't call me Colombo, when I realized that, in fact, I might have one who did.

He reached into his backpack and pulled out his pair of recording sunglasses and the digital video recorder that went with them and put them on my desk. "I want you to have these."

"I can't take these, Freak."

"You don't have to take them; I just gave them to you. If you leave them sitting there, someone will eventually steal them. But don't, they could help you stay in business if you learn how to use them."

"Don't you want to use these again?" I asked, "After all, the strip clubs are still open."

He just stared at me for several minutes while I wished I hadn't said it, but finally he said, "No, if she was right about that heaven and afterlife thing, I don't want to have to explain to her that I started going back to those places just because she died."

I didn't say a word. I just watched my friend and former client walk out of my office and wondered how long it would take for him to get over the only real pain he had ever felt. Somehow, I doubted if he ever would.

After he left, I realized that since I still had his retainer, he could still technically be considered a client. I didn't have any other clients at the moment, so I decided to stay on the case. Homicide isn't my specialty, but that didn't mean I couldn't try.

Since Dougie had mentioned that the girl's family seemed to be hiding something, I decided to go out to Mesquite to talk to them. Since I had no official standing, and very little unofficial standing, I decided just to pop in on them.

If the traffic is light, it would only take fifteen minutes to get from my office to the Mayor's house just south of Interstate 80. Of course, Dallas traffic is almost never light, and it was close enough to the rush hour when I left that it took almost an hour.

The house turned out to be a two-story plantation style home on a cul-de-sac. There were five pillars on the porch. The porch was about the size of my home office, and the rest of the house appeared to be larger than the entire building my office is in. The doorbell rang loudly, as I guess it must to be heard throughout a house that size.

Bunny Hightower answered the door reluctantly, as if she thought I might try to sell her something. With the door barely open and the chain obviously still on, she said one word in a very timid voice, "Yes?"

I introduced myself and explained that I was investigating her daughter's death. She didn't seem impressed, but she did gently release the chain and usher me into the house. I tried to hand her my card, but she turned away too quickly.

The inside of the house matched the outside with ornate chandeliers and hardwood flooring. A staircase straight out of 'Gone with the Wind' dominated two sides of the living area.

"My husband is upstairs. Have a seat and I'll go get him."

I tried to stop her, "Actually, you're the one I'd like to talk with."

"No, I should get my husband. He is..." I never heard the reason she thought she needed to get him because he appeared on the staircase before she finished the sentence.

"Who is this, Bunny, and what does he want?"

"He's from the police, dear. I think he wants to talk to you about Katherine Elizabeth."

He was downstairs with us before she finished the sentence. "Police, huh? Did he show you a badge?"

Bunny paled, "No, but…"

I interrupted, "I didn't show a badge. I'm not with the police. I'm a private investigator. I handed him the card I hadn't been able to hand his wife. I'm sorry about the confusion. I am investigating the case."

"Are you one of McCoy's minions, helping that shyster manufacture an alibi for that freak the cops just let loose?"

I never expected to feel an urge to defend Larry Joe McCoy's integrity, but I suddenly did. Fortunately, even though I felt the urge, it made more sense to let it slide. "No, I don't work for McCoy."

"It doesn't matter. We have answered the police's questions, and we have nothing to say to you."

I tried a couple of ways to change his mind, but nothing worked. Eventually, I gave up and left. The drive home was against traffic, so I was back in the office at 5:27. On the way, I considered the case. Obviously, I wasn't going to learn anything about Katherine Elizabeth or her family from her family. I only knew one other person who might know anything about them. It was a long shot, but I decided to try it.

I called Jack Cannelly's office and was pleasantly surprised that he was in his office that late. Even better, he agreed to meet with me at 9:30 the next morning. Either a city manager has more spare time than I would have expected, or he wanted to talk to me as much as I wanted to talk to him.

31   City Manager

Since the city manager had graciously agreed to meet me on short notice, I definitely wasn't going to be late. I set my alarm early in case traffic was heavy. In the morning, it normally isn't heading away from Downtown, but I wasn't taking any chances. I left my office 7:56, and as expected, traffic was almost non-existent.

That was fine with me; arriving early gave me time to grab a delicious and reasonably priced breakfast at Mama's Daughters' Diner just a few blocks north of the Mesquite Municipal building. Even after breakfast, I was still in the lobby of the city manager's office on Galloway Avenue at 9:17.

At 9:56, his receptionist ushered me into his office. He stood to shake my hand and spoke immediately, "So glad you could make it. I've been looking to buy some property in Dallas, and I need a real estate agent I can trust to handle the transaction."

On the drive out, I'd wondered if he would be upset about the deception at Vino 100. Apparently, he was.

"Look, I'm sorry about that. It wasn't really meant to trick you. It's just that Emily and I have noticed over the years that if we tell people I'm a detective, the rest of the evening tends to be spent answering inane questions about how exciting being a detective must be. Since being a detective isn't exciting, that gets old in a hurry. By the time the conversation turned to Katherine Elizabeth, it was far too late to tell you anything different. Even so, I do apologize for the deception."

"Oh, I accept your apology. In fact, I was just having a little fun at your expense. The funny thing is, on the way home that night, Bethany told me there was no way that you were in real estate."

I was very curious about that. "Really, how'd she know?"

"She said real estate agents never pass up an opportunity to distribute business cards or drum up business. But that's probably not how she knew. Bethany has an uncanny ability to read people. It's almost frightening sometimes."

"She must be a good actress, also. I never suspected that she didn't believe us."

"Yes, she's a good actress. To serve on as many committees as she does and pretend to like everybody on every one of them requires Academy Award caliber talent. I'm glad she does, though. She is invaluable in keeping me aware of potential trouble. I always tell people I learn things three ways. Somebody telephones, somebody telefaxes, or somebody tells Bethany."

It's an old joke, but to be polite I laughed as if I'd never heard it. It never hurts to be polite, especially when looking for help or information.

Jack continued, "Now that the cards are on the table, let's talk. I assume you called because you have some questions for me. But first, I'd like to ask you a couple. Is that okay?"

"That's only fair. I'll answer any question that I can. I do have a client to consider, so I may not be able to answer everything. But I owe you enough to answer what I can."

"I don't know that you owe me anything. But anyway, what happened on the case? The papers were reporting on the story as if the case was solved, and the police had the perpetrator in jail. Next thing you know, the police release the guy, and the investigation seems to have started over. I know that McCoy guy is supposed to be a hotshot trial lawyer, but I guess there's not even going to be a trial. Did he pull a fast one, or is the guy really innocent?"

"He's really innocent. I'm not just saying that because he's my client. He couldn't have done it. McCoy's team presented the police with an indisputable alibi for the timeframe when the girl was killed."

"Wow, why aren't the papers reporting that part?"

"The police aren't releasing any timeframes, so they can't release the alibi information. The papers could probably press them for it under the freedom of information act. They usually don't do that, though. Say what you want about the media, they generally don't want the scoop bad enough to jeopardize an investigation."

"And it's not one of McCoy's tricks? It really is an airtight alibi?"

"He was 1200 miles away. No alibi is ever airtight, but that is as close as one can get. They'll keep looking for any evidence that he came back, but unless they find something, they'll have to accept that he didn't do it. At the very least, they'll have to accept that they can't possibly convict him."

"But you don't think they'll find any evidence like that?"

"No, I don't think they will. He didn't kill her."

"You sound pretty sure of that."

"I am. I would stake my reputation on it."

In fact, I had staked my reputation on it. I wasn't sure how much my reputation was worth. But I did know how little it would be worth if I was wrong about Freak being innocent.

"Well that explains why the police are harassing everybody again. What can I answer for you? I'm sure I've already answered every possible question."

"You probably have, but the police aren't exactly publishing the answers for me to read. As it happens I'm interested in alibis myself. The mayor's family says they were all at their lake house when Katherine's body was left uptown."

"And you suspect they're lying? Why?"

"I wouldn't exactly say I suspect they're lying. But whenever someone is murdered, suspicion always starts with the immediate family. Have you ever been to their lake house?"

"We went out there once, right after they bought it. They had a big party there. I think it was a Fourth of July weekend, maybe six or seven years ago. Mineral Wells is a hell of a long drive to spend time with people we don't actually like."

"It is a long drive. Do you know why they bought it? I mean with all the lakes right around here, why would they buy a house at a lake almost two hours away?"

"Actually, I do. The mayor and his wife actually believe all that talk about the water being the fountain of youth. They go at least one weekend a month, even in the winter. Bunny swears that it keeps both of them young. If you need to know exactly when we went, I can check with Bethany."

"I don't think I need that, at least not right now. I'm more interested in the size of the place. How many rooms does it have? How many entrances? Anything you can tell me about it would be helpful."

"Well, I was there for a party, not doing a survey, but I remember it was smaller than I expected. I think it had four bedrooms, maybe five, certainly no more. The living area was large, but nothing like his house here. As far as entrances go, I remember that we went in a front door when we got there into a living area. There were bedrooms on either side and a back door led out to the boat house and dock."

"So somebody in a bedroom on one side could probably leave unnoticed, if they wanted to. Is there a garage?"

"I didn't see one, but I don't remember seeing the Mayor's Mercedes either, so there might have been. Is that important?"

"Probably not, but I think I'd like to pay the place a visit. Do you know the address or can you get it for me?"

"I'm sure Bethany still has the invitation, she never throws away anything that relates to city business." He picked up my business card and glanced at it before continuing, "I'll have her email it to you, if that's okay."

"That would be great. Again, I apologize for misleading y'all at Vino 100, and I thank you for your help."

"Don't worry about it. I may not like the mayor, but I feel horrible about what happened to his daughter. I'm especially ashamed of how I

192

dismissed the whole thing when we talked before. Thank goodness, I didn't say anything like that in front of anybody with loose lips. At least, I hope I didn't."

"Don't worry. If I'm good at anything, it's keeping quiet. Nobody will hear about what you said at Vino 100 from Emily or me."

"Thanks, but it still bothers me. I shouldn't speak ill of people even if I don't like them. I especially shouldn't have said anything bad about the girl and her family when I did."

He did seem truly disheartened over it. I tried to cheer him up the best I could, and we parted on better terms than I had any right to expect. I headed back to my office with at least a semblance of a plan.

I definitely wanted to know more about the layout of the lake house in Mineral Wells that served as an alibi for three of my suspects. I also wanted to know who besides the family had confirmed that alibi, if anybody had.

When I got to the office, the answering machine light was flashing. Before I could check the machine, the phone rang. I answered it with my standard professional greeting, "Pegasus Investigations."

"Thank heavens, you're there finally. This is Adriana. How quickly can you come to Larry Joe's office?"

I told Adriana I could be there in fifteen minutes; wasted five deleting three messages from her, one from Larry Joe, and another from Daniel. Then, I hustled over to Thanksgiving Tower. Obviously, something had happened, and it wasn't good.

Adriana ushered me into Larry Joe's office without even using the intercom to tell him I was there. Larry Joe, Freak and Daniel were all sitting down looking extremely somber. Adriana hadn't even closed the door behind me when Freak and Larry Joe both started talking.

Freak's voice was a little louder and much shriller, so I somewhat heard what he was saying, "…bullshit. … lying to protect some… said they'd handle it." He finally realized I didn't really understand him, and he stopped screeching. It helped that Larry Joe had stopped talking as well.

Freak looked at Larry Joe, "Tell him what happened. I'll be quiet."

Larry Joe waited until I had taken a seat and told me, "The coroner's report has been finalized. Katherine Elizabeth Hightower's death has been ruled accidental: the result of a botched attempt at an abortion. The police have concluded that she didn't want anybody to know she'd been pregnant, so she got somebody to attempt the abortion for her rather than go to a clinic."

I interrupted, "Surely they don't think that accounts for the five weeks it took before this 'abortionist' decided to drop the body behind a dry cleaner?"

"When she died, or so says the official report, whoever she got to do the abortion panicked and didn't dispose of the body for several weeks until he or she calmed down. They say they want that person for a possible manslaughter or obstruction of justice charge, but we all know it won't be a high priority."

"The mayor and her family are accepting this? After the way he was harassing everybody in the county while she was missing, I wouldn't think he'd buy that story."

"Apparently he's fine with it. He says it's partially his fault. His daughter knew how he frowns on sex outside of wedlock and probably didn't want him to know she'd 'had a moment of weakness'; his phrase, not mine."

My mind went back to the way he leered at Adriana the last time I'd seen him in this office, but I kept my thoughts to myself. There is a difference between appetite and action.

Freak had been quiet as long as he could stand, "So you understand why you have to get back on the case, right?"

"Actually Freak, I never got off the case. I decided since you left me a retainer, I could still consider myself retained."

Freak looked at Larry Joe again, "Can I have minute alone with Sam Spade?"

"Of course," Larry Joe got up to leave.

Daniel smiled at me and got up also. He turned to Freak and said, "As your solicitor acquiesces, so too will I abide." On his way out he addressed me, "Presently, an inquirer, not an advocate, is requisite. Notify me if that transposes."

After he left Freak asked, "Do you ever know what the Hell that guy is saying?"

"I usually know what he means, but other than that, not really. Why the private meeting? Isn't your attorney supposed to be your confidential representative?"

"Not on this. You know all of that is bullshit, right? She didn't have a 'moment of weakness'; she didn't want an abortion. She decided she was ready to be a mother, so we agreed that she'd quit taking the pill."

"Were you ready to be a father?"

"I was ready to do whatever she wanted, always. We both knew I wasn't likely to live long enough to wait until I was ready to be a father. She thought it was time, and I agreed. I would have agreed to anything for her, but that made sense."

"So you don't believe she tried to have an abortion. I understand that. Do you think her parents knew she was pregnant?"

"I don't know. She told me she was going to tell her mother first, but I don't know for sure that she ever did. You have to help me, man. I can barely stand to live without her; I have to know what really happened."

"I'll find out Freak, I promise." I'm not usually big on making promises I don't know I can keep, but I am big on justice being served. "I don't know how, but I'll find out."

He got up and headed for the door. As he left, he turned to me, "Thank you, for everything."

He was gone before I could reply, and Larry Joe came back into the room. We had very little to say at that point and took very little time to say it. Emily had an early morning meeting scheduled for Wednesday, so date night was an early movie. When I got home, I went back to figuring out how to live up to the promise I had made to Freak.

I wanted to find a way to talk to Mrs. Hightower alone about Katherine Elizabeth. I figured a mother would know more about how her daughter might react to an unexpected pregnancy than anybody. She'd especially know who her daughter might go to for help.

Talking to her was easy, but her husband gave all the answers. I needed a plan to talk to her away from him. Knowing I needed a plan was easy, coming up with a plan much less so.

I went to bed that night hoping to dream up a plan in my sleep. It didn't seem likely, but I wasn't having any luck coming up with anything helpful while I was awake. I even took a Tylenol P.M. to make sure I slept soundly. I figure if Barry Bonds can use performance enhancing drugs, I could, too.

Remarkably, it worked. The next morning I woke up with a plan. Not only did I wake up with a plan, I woke up with a plan that might work. I wasn't sure how Emily was going to like it when she found out that my dream and my plan included April and a motel room, but the plan just might work, and that is the important thing.

The plan was the reason I was standing outside Walt Garrison's Rodeo Bar when it opened that morning at eleven. Before that, I had called Blake for some information that I needed. Blake was his usual helpful self, after answering in his usual manner.

"What do you want this time?"

"Nothing much, just wondering if in the department's investigation, any pattern emerged about the mayor's habits. I'm looking for some place other than home or city hall for a little conversation."

"I'm sure the mayor of Dallas is at City Hall right now; you could cross the street and say hello to Ms. Miller." Blake can joke in any situation. That's something else we have in common.

"I'm talking about Mayor Hightower, Blake."

"You do realize that the investigation has concluded, don't you?"

"The official investigation may have concluded, but the case still needs to be solved."

"And the great detective has decided to go ahead and solve it. Why have you zeroed in on the mayor as suspect number one?"

"I didn't say I had, but 'the great detective' is a name I'll let my friends call me any time. And if you'll quit clowning around and help me out, I'll keep you on my friend's list. Don't make me invoke the Freedom of Information act."

"Sure, hold on while I check the files." I was fairly sure I heard him sigh before he put me on hold.

When he came back on the line he had good news, "It seems the Mayor is even more a creature of habit than Emily. His lunch ritual seldom varies, and he never leaves Mesquite: Monday at Steak and Ale; Tuesday at Salt Grass Steakhouse; Wednesday at Texas Roadhouse; Thursday at Outback Steakhouse and Friday at Hooters."

"Gee, which of these pictures is not like the others?" I laughed.

"Maybe after four straight days of having lunch at a steakhouse, money's a little tight. You know public servants don't make all that much money."

"Maybe you don't, but I've seen the mayor's house, or mansion, I should say. Besides from what I'm hearing, he may not fit the literal definition of public servant. My guess is that he'd be going to Hooters every day if it wouldn't hurt his image."

"You're probably right, but at least he's contributing to the Mesquite economy. I'd ask you what you're up to, but I know you wouldn't tell me and that might strain our friendship. Besides, you've already proven you'd rather sleep in a jail cell than fully cooperate with the Sheriff's department."

We left it at that, and I walked over to the Rodeo Bar. Even if the plan didn't work, it felt good to have a plan. Now if I could only get April to go along with it. She usually loved playing detective, so I was cautiously optimistic.

I sat down at the usual corner table and when April brought my iced tea, I asked, "Do you have a minute to sit and talk? I think I could use your help on my case."

The way her eyes lit up did nothing to hurt my confidence. Neither did the eagerness in her voice, "Sure, let me take care of a couple other tables, and I'll be right back."

Like most restaurants and bars, The Rodeo Bar prohibits its staff from sitting at the table with its customers. Also, like most restaurants and bars, that particular rule is treated much like the health code is treated in Deep Ellum. This is to say, it is broken with regularity and without repercussions.

___

When April sat down, I got right to my plan, "How'd you like to go on a date with a married man?"

"You're not married, honey, but I like the way you get right to the point."

"Not me, a rich married man,"

She laughed and her eyes lit up again, "I see why you thought of me."

The way her eyes looked when they lit up made me sure the mayor was going to fall for my plan. It also made me feel a little dirty for having dreamt it up. I was definitely going to have to take Emily someplace very nice for date night.

"So, are you just going to sit there daydreaming about Emily, or are you going to tell me how I can help you solve that girl's murder?"

"What makes you think I was daydreaming about Emily?"

"Other than the fact that it's pretty much all you ever do when you aren't with her; it's a fact that you always get the same look on your face when you do it. I've seen it a thousand times before, and I just saw it again."

It seemed pointless to argue with her, since she was obviously right, so I didn't bother. "I need you to seduce the mayor into meeting you somewhere. I don't think he's very committed to his marriage vows, so I think you can do it."

"He's a man, honey; of course he's not committed to his wedding vows, as you so quaintly state it. That's a given."

"So you'll help?" I asked.

"Always glad to help my favorite down on his luck detective, even when he's temporarily not down on his luck."

"How do you know I'm not currently down on my luck?"

"Well, Blake didn't pay last time you were here, and you actually let me bring you iced tea this morning. When you are down on your luck, you drink water."

She was right again, but I didn't like discussing it. "Want to hear the plan on how you can help out, or just chat about my lack of a career and my lack of success?"

"Let me check my other tables, then I'll come back, and you can tell me how I can help. But Baby, you are a success, you may not be a financial success, but you make your living helping people, and you have Emily. Most of the people who stay in this hotel aren't that successful, and this is the best hotel in Dallas."

When she came back, I told her about my desire to speak to the mayor's wife alone. I also told her about the way I saw him look at Adriana and his consistent lunch schedule.

"Hooters, you say? This may be even easier than I expected. How far astray do you need me to lead his honor?"

"I don't actually need you to lead him, or you, astray, as you so quaintly put it. I just need you to get him to go some place far enough away from his home that I'll have time to question his wife, without it being someplace he lets his wife know about."

"Sounds easy enough, but you're going to owe me big time anyway."

As things turned out, she was right again on both counts.

33   Two Dates

I called Emily as soon as I got home. I felt a little better as soon as I heard her answer, "Hello, Darling." Caller I.D. is such a wonderful invention.

"I was thinking, if you don't already have a plan for tonight, let's spend some of Freak's money at Nick and Sam's."

She replied in her Gracie Allen voice, "Nick and Sam's on a weekday? Wow! Gee Georgie; who are you having an affair with this time?" Since she had slipped into our George Burns and Gracie Allen routine, I presumed she was kidding. At least, I hoped she was.

"Oh just April from the Rodeo Bar, but it's nothing serious." I said it like a George Burns' straight line. At least I tried to say it like a George Burns straight line.

"April, huh? No wonder you feel like celebrating. Nick and Sam's, it is. I'll run by The Rodeo Bar, kill April around six. Then, I'll pick you up about 6:30."

That didn't sound very much like a Gracie Allen punch line, so I told her the truth, "Actually, it's not an affair. She's going to do some detective work for me, so we need to let her live."

"Thank goodness, I've always liked April. I like her even though she is far too beautiful to be real, and a serious threat to the continued happiness of every couple in Dallas County."

"Well, I've never noticed that about her," I lied, "but I hope you're right. That's how she's going to help me solve the case. But, 6:30 sounds about right. I'll make the reservations."

Dinner at Nick and Sam's is always a treat. It isn't something we can afford to do often, so we made sure we enjoyed the total experience. That included the tour of the wine cellar with its expensive wines, many of which were autographed by local athletes and other celebrities.

The date went absolutely perfectly, but it did nothing to help my investigation. April had seemed confident she would tempt the mayor by the weekend. That left me with three days to investigate thoroughly before I talked to Bunny Hightower again. I only expected one chance at it; I'd need to be ready.

Thursday, I bought Blake lunch again. He gave me copies of the coroner's report and police file. Since, the case was now officially closed, he didn't even have to risk his job for this favor.

I spent the afternoon calling Katherine Elizabeth's classmates at Ursuline. The file contained phone numbers for 183 girls. I learned that Ursuline is a great school that costs almost $10,000 a year to attend. I also learned that Justin Timberlake is dreamy, and Kelly Clarkson has a voice to die for. I learned absolutely nothing about Katherine Elizabeth.

In the evening, I went back to Deep Ellum and talked to some friends of Katherine Elizabeth's at various bars. I spent about four hours down there, but learned nothing, except that she had been very well liked.

If Deep Ellum was a high school, Freak and Katherine Elizabeth would have been a shoo-in for homecoming king and queen. Of course, Deep Ellum is not a high school even though it is more educational than most.

In all, I asked about 400 people about 4,000 questions about Katherine Elizabeth Hightower. The one I most wanted answered is the one I got answered the least. I asked it of everybody. If Katherine Elizabeth wanted to get an abortion in secret, to whom would she turn?

At Ursuline, nobody wanted to even speculate. Most said they didn't know her well enough to know. However, two girls who lived in Mesquite suggested that her brother knew enough shady characters that he might be able to help. Neither thought it likely that she would go to him, however.

In Deep Ellum, the consensus was that she wouldn't for religious reasons, but if she did, she would go to Freak. Of course, I had to presume that she hadn't turned to Freak, so that didn't help me much.

Friday morning, I called Ms. Phillips at the North Texas Food Bank. It only took a few minutes to establish that Katherine's relationship with her fellow volunteers was as non-existent as her relationship with her fellow students. That didn't surprise me.

Next, I took the drive to Mineral Wells to look at the lake house. As Jack Cannelly had described it, the house was small compared to the mayor's mansion in Mesquite. What Jack failed to mention was how secluded it was.

Sitting on about two hundred acres of land right against the lake, the nearest house to it was at least a quarter mile away. Apparently, Mayor Hightower had purchased the place with privacy in mind, as well as access to a mythical fountain of youth.

I got back to my office about noon. Two days of real detective work and I still didn't know anything I didn't know when Emily and I were at Nick and Sam's. I really wanted to talk to Bunny Hightower soon.

At two o'clock, the phone rang. I'm sure I wasn't the first guy to be happy to hear April's voice, but nobody's ever been happier. At least, nobody's ever been happier for the reason I was happy.

"Who's your hero, Cowboy?" she asked sounding very pleased with herself.

My friends don't call me Cowboy, either, but if her news was as happy as she sounded, she could pretty much call me anything she wanted. "I think you are. Tell me about it."

"It was a snap. I took off from the bar today. I got an old friend of mine to let me work the lunch shift at Hooters. The mayor showed up as expected, and I took his table. By the way, you forgot to mention what a jerk he is."

"I didn't forget, April. I just didn't want to scare you off. So what happened?" I probably sounded impatient, but that's only because I felt impatient.

"He tried to flirt with me, even though he's terrible at it. I flirted back, and he asked me what time my shift ended. I sat down with him and told him I'd end my shift any time he wanted. He suggested that I meet him at the AmeriSuites Hotel by Six Flags tonight at 6:30."

Six Flags is an amusement park in Arlington, at least thirty minutes from the Mayor's house even with no traffic. I couldn't have hoped for better, "That settles it. You are officially my hero. How much do I owe you?"

"Actually, you don't owe me anything. Counting the hundred dollar tip the mayor left me, I made more than I normally make at the Rodeo Bar. Do you want me to keep the date with the loser?"

I only had to think about that a few seconds. "No, there's no reason to keep the date. I don't trust him to understand that 'no' means 'no'. I don't want to put you at risk. Did he give you a room number?"

"No, I gave him my Blackberry® number; he's supposed to text me with the room number when he gets there."

"I think I have a plan. Can you come by my office and then head over there to make sure he actually shows? I'd hate to get to his house expecting him to be gone, only to discover that he's all talk, and didn't go to the hotel."

She agreed easily. Like I said earlier, April thinks she should be a detective, and she might be right. I called Jesse at the courier company. Jesse often leaves pretty early on Fridays, so I was pleasantly surprised when he answered, "Right on Time Delivery. What can we deliver for you?"

"Hey Jesse, I need a favor."

"As long as you don't want money, name it."

"No money, I just want to borrow a couple of your Nextel® radios tonight."

"Let's see, I've got twenty radios, and two couriers on call tonight. As long as you don't need more than eighteen, that's no problem. I assume you're on a case. Do you want me to come along as back up?"

"Actually, I don't need any back up this time, but thanks. I just have to ask a woman in Mesquite a couple of questions while my associate checks on some things in Arlington. Can I come get the radios now, or should I wait until after five."

"Actually, I was just about to leave when you called. I'll just drop them by your place?"

"Sounds great, I owe you."

"Not really, are you sure you just need two?"

I assured him I only needed two phones. After we hung up, I picked up the list of questions I wanted to ask Bunny Hightower and started reviewing it. Jesse came into my office about ten minutes to three, and he was positively beaming.

"Check these out, Ace. I hold in my hands a true miracle of modern technology."

"Jesse, it's a cell phone with a walkie-talkie feature. We've been using them for years. Sure, it's an improvement on the pagers we used to use back in the day, but I wouldn't call it a miracle of modern technology."

"You have no idea. These babies make those look like two tin cans and a string."

He obviously wanted to brag about his latest radios, and I figured since he was letting me borrow two of them, I at least owed it to him to act interested. "Okay, Jesse. What makes them so special?"

"These bad boys are built to military specifications for durability and have Bluetooth, GPS and LBS capabilities built in. You could drag one of these puppies behind a Jeep to the middle of nowhere and drive over it if you wanted. Not only would it still work, I could locate it from my laptop and go get it."

"That's impressive. I'm hoping to get in and out of Mesquite without getting dragged to the middle of nowhere behind a Jeep, but it's good to know you'll be able to get your phones back if I do."

"I always thought you would eventually learn to appreciate modern technology, but I'm starting to doubt it. Anyway, let me know if you need any backup; my number is programmed into both phones."

I pretended to be impressed, thanked him for his help and promised to get them back to him on Saturday. He wished me luck and left. I was glad I got him out before April showed up. I suspected he'd have wanted to hang around otherwise.

April arrived about ten minutes after Jesse left. The radios were sitting on the desk, and April was every bit as impressed by them as I hadn't been.

"Wow! The new 7050! I didn't even think these were out yet. They don't just give these away when you sign up. Since when have you been Mr. Technology? What's the plan, and are those a part of it?"

"I borrowed them, and yes, they're a part of the plan. All I need is for you to let me know when the mayor shows up at the hotel and when he leaves. Even if he only stays a few minutes, that will give me a half hour or better to talk to his wife."

"Oh, I'll be able to keep him there longer than a few minutes. When he texts me the room number, I'll text back that I'm running late. I promise he'll wait awhile."

"That will work. If I finish talking to his wife before the mayor leaves, I'll let you know. Whatever you do, don't take any chances. I'm not paying hazard pay on this case."

She promised to be careful, and we set the plan in motion. She went to Arlington, and I got my van and went to Mesquite. She called me before I was even out of the parking garage, and I spent the entire drive to

Mesquite listening to her talking about what great phones Jesse had loaned us.

At 5:58, I was parked about a block from the mayor's house waiting for the call from April. He'd sent her the room number at 5:46, but she hadn't seen him go in, yet. I would have thought 12 minutes would be enough time to get from a hotel's office to a room, but I guess not.

Finally, at 6:16, I heard April's voice over the radio again. "He's here. I just saw him go in. He also left me another text message telling me how much he's looking forward to making the earth move for me tonight. He sure is confident for a man his age. Viagra must really work."

I let that comment go untouched. Mayor Hightower's not that much older than me. I again reminded April to be careful, and I was ringing the doorbell within five minutes. I had my list of questions memorized, but conversation is often more revealing than a question and answer session. Tonight would prove to be one of those times.

34   Painted Lady

Bunny Hightower answered the door slightly less timidly than she had the last time I was here, "Yes?"

"Hello, Mrs. Hightower, I was hoping to speak to your husband. Is he here?"

"No he's not here. Perhaps you should make an appointment to see him at his office tomorrow."

"I guess I could do that, but I have already made the trip out here. I'd rather wait for him. Surely, he'll be home soon, won't he? Or did he have an appointment?"

Of course I knew he had an appointment, but I doubted if she did. She certainly wouldn't know the nature of the appointment if she did. Her hesitation made it clear that she didn't know.

"My husband does not always keep to a schedule. In his position, he must often work late hours."

I doubted that, but I was certain she believed it. She almost sounded proud that he worked late often. "Of course," I said, "Still, since I'm here, may I come in and wait for him? I promise if he doesn't arrive soon, you won't have to kick me out. I'll go peacefully."

It worked. She closed the door gently to remove the chain, and then opened the door slowly. I stepped in quickly before she could change her mind.

"Thank you. I'll try not to be a bother. Feel free to continue whatever you were doing. I'll just try to stay out of your way."

"That's all right; I was just watching the news. I try to watch it every night in case something happens that my husband needs to know. It's already to the sports and weather, so I guess nothing happened today of importance to him."

"That's very interesting." I lied again. "I guess there's more to being a politician's wife than kissing babies, and smiling prettily."

She laughed politely, something I'm sure she'd practiced many times. "Of course there is, which is fortunate for me. I hate kissing babies, and obviously smiling prettily is not one of my talents."

Since we were being so polite, I felt obligated to object. "I think you have a very pretty smile. My girlfriend showed me one of the Mayor's campaign flyers, and we were both struck by how nice your smile looked."

"You're very kind, but I'm not that naive. I know my husband's campaign spends a fortune airbrushing those flyers. I was an unattractive girl, and now I'm an unattractive woman. I understand that, and it doesn't hurt the way it once did. Do you have any idea how hard it is to be the only unattractive girl in a high school full of nothing but rich, beautiful children? Most children can be cruel; the rich and the beautiful have only perfected the art."

She stared at me, daring me to answer, so I did, "No, but children, rich or poor, have no monopoly on cruelty. In my line of work, I've seen plenty of cruel adults."

"That's true, but adults are cruel in different ways and for different reasons. Have you ever asked yourself why my husband and I got married?"

"No." The question shocked me, but I was happy to have her talking about anything. "I presumed that the two of you met somewhere and fell in love."

"Hardly, he fell in love with my money and was willing to accept me as part of the package. Me, I noticed that both his mother and sister were even more gorgeous than he was handsome. I was determined to give my daughter the best chance to not have to grow up ugly that I could. His genes provided that opportunity, and it worked. Katherine Elizabeth was as pretty as a girl could hope to be. She inherited all of her father's family looks."

"If you don't mind me asking, were you ever jealous of her?"

She laughed again, this time not as politely. "Oh, you've heard those rumors, too. You must be a better investigator than my husband thinks you are. They aren't true. I loved my daughter, and her beauty brought me nothing but joy. I somehow felt that her beauty made up for my lack of it."

She started crying, and I remembered that whatever had happened, and whatever the family might be hiding, she had lost a child. Every loss is painful, but losing a child is the greatest loss of all.

I went over to her and put my arm around her. She put her face to my shoulder and continued crying. I had come to Mesquite to interrogate her, but I was quickly losing interest in that.

When she eventually composed herself, she was apologetic, "I'm sorry. I've tried so hard not to break down, but I guess I'm not a strong as I hoped."

"Please don't apologize; I know the pain you're feeling is unbearable. You should feel free to break down whenever you must. My shoulders have been cried on before, and will be again."

"Thank you, and you have strong shoulders to cry on, but I can't afford to be weak. We have an election to win in the fall, and this scandal is going to make it harder. It would have been better if a murderer had been caught, but she wasn't murdered."

"That's what the police decided, but not everybody is convinced."

"Exactly, and many of the people who aren't convinced are voters. It's kind of ironic when you think about it. Our beautiful children have been instrumental in helping my husband achieve his dream, and now, it's possible that the death of one of them is going to take it away from him."

It looked like she might break down again, but she didn't. She pulled herself together and continued, "I assume by your presence here, that you are also one of the people who aren't convinced it wasn't murder."

"I don't know." I answered honestly. "But, I have a client who is, so I'm trying to earn my fee."

"Your client is that weirdo who claims to have been seeing my daughter, isn't he?"

"Yes ma'am. I hope I don't have to apologize for trying to earn a living. In my business, we don't get to choose our clients."

"No, I guess not. You don't believe him, do you?"

"Excuse me; I'm not sure I understand the question." It slowly dawned on me that Mrs. Hightower really didn't believe that Katherine Elizabeth and Freak had been an item.

"You know he went to high school here, don't you?"

"Yes, I know that."

"He was a terribly violent child. He used to pick on my son for no reason. He was arrested several times for assaulting other students. I never understood how he stayed out of jail. Of course, we only learned recently who his lawyer is, so now we understand. Anyway, there's no way Katherine Elizabeth would have been in a relationship with somebody who had been that mean to her brother."

"If you say so, but according to the police, she was with child when she died. My client thinks the child was his."

"If it was, then he raped her. That would explain why she tried to abort it. I've accepted that he didn't murder her, but I still think your client was responsible for her death."

"I understand your son has had a few scrapes with the law himself. Are you sure your daughter felt strongly enough for him to have it influence who she would date?"

"Who told you that lie, and why would you believe it? Maybe my husband was right about you, after all. Bobby Junior may not be as pretty as Katherine Elizabeth was, but he has a heart of gold, and he's never been in trouble with the law. I'm just as proud of him as I was of her."

So Mrs. Hightower knew that Freak had been in trouble with the law, but not that her son had. Maybe she wasn't hiding anything, maybe everything was hiding from her or being hidden.

Perhaps, I could take her to Freak's place and show her all the pictures of the two of them together to prove there had been a relationship. She probably still wouldn't believe it, and I didn't think it mattered.

"Are you sure Bobby's never been in trouble. Maybe, he's had issues that haven't come to your attention?"

"Everything comes to my attention. In this family, we don't keep secrets. There are too many people with agendas searching for skeletons in our closets for us to keep secrets from each other."

I thought about the mayor and his trip to Arlington, Katherine Elizabeth's popularity in Deep Ellum, and wondered how she could even make such an assertion. Then I realized; she believed it. She didn't keep any secrets from her family, so she didn't think they kept any from her.

"Speaking of Bobby, is he here? I've got a couple of questions for him, too." That wasn't really a lie, even though I'd only realized it while talking to his mother.

"No. he's at football practice over at the stadium."

"Really? I didn't even know he was on the team."

"Well, he's not a starter, but he is on the team. He hardly played at all last year, but he's hoping to play more now that he's starting to fill out. His dad is really proud about it, but I just worry that he might get hurt."

The expensive phone I was wearing vibrated then with a text message from April. I checked it as surreptitiously as I could. The message read, 'he left ftl - cm rsn".

Fortunately, I had learned enough text slang working as a bike courier that I understood that the Mayor had left the hotel in a hurry, and April wanted me to call her real soon now.

If the mayor was really driving faster than light, I had less time to get out of there than originally anticipated. I'd already learned more than I'd hoped to learn. Plus, I had a football practice to find, so I exited as gracefully as I could, implying that I would call the mayor's office tomorrow morning for an appointment.

As soon as I was back in my van, I called April. "You did great," I told her, "What do I need to know?"

"He sent me four messages while he waited. The last two weren't nice. He was obviously mad. I gave him excuses each time, but he obviously has anger control issues."

"Maybe," I interjected. "But in his defense, he was expecting to have sex with a beautiful girl, and it wasn't happening. No man takes that well."

"You're missing the point. I didn't know if you might need me to entice him again, so all of my messages to him were sexual. I wanted him to think I wanted to be with him as bad as he wanted me to be there. Also, right after his last message, which was downright hateful, he came out of the room, slammed the door and went to the parking lot without even checking out. I was going to try to follow him, but he was driving way too fast."

"You did the right thing, it's probably safe to assume he's heading home, and I'm not there, so that won't be an issue. I'm glad you didn't take any foolish chances. Thanks for your help. I'll pick up Jesse's radio tomorrow morning."

She accepted that, but it was clear that she would have preferred to keep the radio as long as possible. She offered several suggestions about how she could contribute to the investigation if she could keep it. A couple of them even made sense, but I'd already promised Jesse I'd return the phones the next day.

As soon as I finished talking to April, I called Jesse. He answered on the first ring, "Hello, Ace, how did it go tonight?"

"Good, so far, can you get on the internet?"

"I can always get on the internet, especially when two of my expensive phones are in the field. Why do you ask?"

"Just wondering if you could do a search and find out where the Mesquite Poteet High School football team practices."

"Sure, I'll get right on it. By the way your associate has left Arlington, and is about a block from your office right now."

I knew the radios had GPS capability, but I was impressed anyway. "Sure, she lives downtown. She's probably home by now."

"She? Your associate isn't the hottie I saw going to your office about ten minutes after I left is she? No wonder you were trying to get rid of me so quickly. Does Emily know about this associate?"

"Yes, to both questions. Is there any chance you could quit talking to me about my associate and find the location of that practice field while it could still do me some good?"

"Already on it, buddy. It's just off the freeway. From where you are, you need to make a u-turn and take the second exit. Even you can't miss the field from there."

I followed his directions and was watching a high school football practice within fifteen minutes. I was beginning to understand why Jesse and April were so impressed by these new phones. I wasn't yet as impressed as they were, but I eventually would be.

35   Football Player

It's been said that in Texas, football isn't a religion, it's more important than that. If the fact that high school football teams practice nearly year round doesn't prove it, the fact that about five hundred spectators attend a summer practice does. I grabbed a gimme cap and a clipboard from the van and tried to look like a scout or assistant coach from a Division II or Division III college team.

Actually D-two and D-three scouts and assistant coaches don't look much different than those from the major colleges, but every high school coach and most of the players already know everybody from the major colleges. The players were all wearing practice jerseys which have their number, but not their names.

I remembered from the campaign flyers I'd seen that Bobby is a slightly built kid about six foot tall, so I drifted over to where the wide receivers and defensive backs were working on footwork drills. I stood beside a guy wearing a Texas Tech cap and polo shirt and carrying a stop watch.

I waited until he finished writing something in his notebook then I asked, "You know which one is Hightower? I left my notes in the truck."

"Hightower?" The way he asked it didn't bode well for the boy's chance of being a Red Raider one day. But the man checked his notes and came up with it. "Number 50, it looks like they're moving him to linebacker this year."

I thanked him and pretended to make some notes on my clipboard. I walked toward midfield to watch the seven on seven drills. I found number 50, and he seemed to be holding his own. He also weighed about sixty pounds more than he did on any of the campaign flyers.

Some kids naturally gain weight at that age and hard work in a gym can pay dividends for someone who wants to play football. On the other hand, a kid with money and connections to shady characters can also find other ways to put on weight.

The team practiced for another hour, then headed for the locker room. I didn't see anything from the kid that looked dominant, so it didn't surprise me that the scouts who were crowding around a few of the players weren't crowding around him.

I followed the throng until I was close enough to yell out, "Bobby Hightower! Got a minute?"

He looked surprised when he turned toward me, but managed to turn it into a nonchalant walk as he headed my way. He didn't want to lose face by letting his teammates notice that he'd been surprised.

He had his father's dark hair and blue eyes, but the eyes lacked the piercing quality that worked so well for his father. He also walked with less confidence. He shook my hand when he got to me and asked, "Who you with?"

I'd been in his position many years ago, although in a different sport. I just couldn't answer that question with a lie. I made sure nobody else could hear us before I told him, "I'm not with a college, Bobby, but nobody has to know that but us when you hit the showers."

"Sure, whatever. So what are you doing here? Some kind of reporter doing an article on my dad?"

"No, I'm an investigator looking into your sister's death. Your mom told me I could find you here."

"Bullshit! That bitch doesn't even know what shape a football is, let alone where we practice. Besides, I thought the case was closed; accidental death resulting from being a slut and trying to avoid the consequences."

Blake had told me the boy had an attitude, but still it surprised me. "I take it your folks don't come to many of your games?"

"Hell no, they don't even know what position I play."

216

"She didn't have to tell me where the field was, she just told me you were at practice. One of the scouts from Texas Tech told me you were moving to linebacker. You looked pretty good in the drills today."

"Really, a Big Twelve scout told you I looked good out there? Wow, I wasn't sure about changing positions, but maybe the coaches are right."

I didn't see any advantage in mentioning that I hadn't actually said that, so I didn't. Instead I asked him, "Any thoughts on why your sister didn't just go to a clinic to have the procedure?"

"Procedure; it may be a procedure in the big city, but out here in 'Skeet', it's an issue. Daddy Dearest couldn't get elected dog-catcher if it got out that his precious little girl had to get that procedure." He said procedure in the exact tone of voice pro-lifers use when calling it an abortion.

"Do you have any idea who might have botched the abortion or how she might have connected with whoever it was?"

"How the Hell should I know? It's not like we're the Olsen Twins. She lived her life; I live mine."

"Sibling rivalry, huh?"

"Not really, there was never any rivalry. Sibling rivalry is based on a battle for parental affection. Our parents never showed any affection to either of us."

The attitude wasn't showing now. I realized that he was talking about things he'd discussed before, most likely with a counselor or therapist. I decided to keep it at that level, "So, didn't the two of you find common ground against a mutual enemy?"

"Shrink talk, huh? Did they teach you that at the academy, or did you grow up in a dysfunctional family, too?"

"All families are dysfunctional to some degree, Bobby." I told him without mentioning that I wasn't actually a cop and had never been to the academy.

"I guess you're right, but Kitty and I didn't really have a mutual enemy. I don't think she ever even noticed that the folks were distant. If she did, I never heard her comment on it. It's not like we were abused or anything like that."

"I've heard she kept her distance from her classmates at Ursuline. Do you think that was a result of her parents being emotionally distant?"

He laughed, but not rudely. "No, I think that's because they were girls. Look, we're talking about my sister, here. I don't want to be rude about her, especially now. But, the girl did discover boys pretty young, and she liked them, a lot. That's why they made her go to Ursuline in the first place."

I started to ask him if she discovered boys, or one boy, but I realized immediately that I didn't particularly want to hear his opinion on the subject.

"Hypothetically, if she had come to you when she got in trouble, would you have helped her?"

"I probably would have tried, but I don't know what I could have done. It's not like the girls flock to me like the guys flocked to her. I've never had a reason to look into that kind of thing."

For a Texas high school boy to make a statement like that while wearing a football uniform, he had to be thinking he was on a therapist's couch. I couldn't press the issue without hating myself later. Besides, I only had one more question to ask him, and this wasn't the time to ask it.

I thanked him for his cooperation and shook his hand again. Before he headed for the showers, he asked me a favor, "Hey, if anybody asks on your way out, could you tell them you're with the Longhorns?"

I promised him I would, even though I knew nobody would believe me if it came to that. Nobody asked me anything on my way out, so whatever stories he was telling in the locker room at least had a chance.

I didn't like the boy, but I knew first hand what a tough place a locker room can be for a mediocre athlete, so I hoped it worked. If being a private detective didn't work out for me, maybe I could develop a business pretending to be a scout to help average players with money boost their stock in the locker room.

I felt pretty good about my trip to Mesquite as I drove home. I hadn't solved anything, but I had a much better idea why a pretty and reasonably popular young girl in a public school had become an isolated girl at an exclusive private girl's school.

That reminded me that I wanted to know more about why a pretty young lady had left a paying gig in Las Vegas for her father's birthday in Dallas. Some families are that close-knit, but if I'd learned nothing else tonight, I'd learned that some aren't.

That night I dreamt about high school sports and how much money I'd have made in the NBA if I'd been talented, instead of just being tall. It wasn't a pleasant dream, but at least it wasn't a nightmare about spiders

Not dreaming about spiders counted as a victory since my next order of business was to investigate Bobbie Jo Nottingham. Saturday, I collected Jesse's phone from April and dropped them both at his office. When I gave them to him he asked me, "So, are you impressed, yet?"

"I'm starting to be. If I need to borrow radios on this case again, I definitely want these."

"Well, that's a start. Maybe, we'll move you into this century yet. Let me know if you need more help. Much as I appreciate your work on the bike, I'd rather see you succeed as a detective."

"Thanks. I'll let you know if I need anything."

I didn't think I was as far behind the tech curve as he did, but he might have a point. Maybe if I got a few more clients who left me the retainer after the case was closed, then rehired me before I could even start spending it, I could start buying this century's technology.

In the meantime, I needed to use the computer I already owned to find Bobbie Jo's parents. I easily found a phone number for Quinton and Muriel Nottingham with an address in an older section of Garland.

A male voice answered my call on the second ring, "Hello." He sounded unhappy to be answering a phone. I'd felt the same way myself on many occasions.

"May I speak to Quinton Nottingham?"

"Who is this?" The voice shifted from unhappy to angry.

"I'm a friend of Bobbie Jo's," I told him wondering if that was a total lie or not. "I'm just hoping to have a word with Mr. Nottingham."

"Bullshit! I don't know what kind of a joke you're playing, Mister. But it isn't funny." He slammed down the phone, and I set mine down and stared at it.

I went to the file cabinet to double check that Bobbie Jo's parents were named Quinton and Muriel. Having done that, I considered the odds that there was more than one couple with that name in the Dallas area. It seemed unlikely.

It also seemed unlikely that a wrong number would be that angry. That left me in the all too familiar position of knowing that there was more that I needed to know and not knowing what it was. It also left me in the familiar position of not really having a plan to figure it out.

I thought about driving out to Garland to talk to whoever answered the phone. I decided not to because he wasn't likely to be any happier to talk to me in person than he had been on the phone.

As I considered my other options, the phone rang. I answered with my professional greeting, "Pegasus Investigations."

"Did you just call my parents' house?" It was Bobbie Jo, and she wasn't happy, either.

"Yes, I did. Is there some reason I shouldn't have called? If there is, you never mentioned it."

"I didn't know you were planning to investigate me. Or were you calling just to say 'hi'?"

"I'm on a case, Bobbie Jo; I have to investigate everybody involved. That's how it works. You know enough about what I do to understand that."

"You're right. I just thought this might be different. I thought maybe since…." Her voice drifted, and I heard her sobbing. This case was suddenly overflowing with crying women, and this time I didn't know why.

When the sobbing slowed, I tried to reason with her, "Look, I appreciate all your help in Vegas. And I really appreciate your sacrifice in leaving your pets home to help me. I'm sure Freak does, too. But I still have to conduct the investigation."

"Damn. You really don't know. Charlie Ray thought you were just being an ass, but you really don't know, do you?"

"Know what?"

"My father's been in a coma at Parkland since a car wreck in February. Mom spends most of her time there hoping he'll wake up, and my brother's been house-sitting. That's why he hasn't been using his tour bus. He's basically put his career on hold so my mom can stay with my dad. When you told him you were my friend, he thought…oh, never mind. It's not important what he thought."

36　Intensive Care

I suspected that what Bobbie Jo's brother thought might actually be important, but I couldn't bring myself to press her on the issue now. Instead I just told her honestly, "I'm sorry, Bobbie Jo. I didn't know about your dad."

"I'll believe that for now. I guess your job sucks worse than I realized. But, you shouldn't call yourself my friend, since you're obviously investigating me."

Everybody loves to help investigate, but nobody likes to be investigated. I got used to that a long time ago. I promised her I wouldn't tell anybody else I was her friend.

Since we weren't friends, it didn't matter much what she called me. All that mattered to me was learning about her return from Vegas during the show's run. I was grateful for her help in Vegas, I felt bad about her father, and I didn't want to think of her as a suspect. However, I was conducting an investigation, and she was a suspect.

In fact, she had a plausible motive and no real alibi. Since she had already admitted she was willing to lie about the facts of the case, she had to be a prime suspect. I didn't have to like it, but I had to check it out. That meant I had to go to Parkland to talk to her mother. I didn't want to do it, but I was used to doing things I didn't want to do.

The first thing I needed to do that I didn't want to do was to call the Nottingham house again and apologize to Bobbie Jo's brother. I wasn't surprised or disappointed when he hung up without giving me a chance to do so. I decided Sunday would be a better day to go to Parkland than Saturday. Fridays and Saturdays are busy days at all hospitals, but even more so at Parkland.

I stood outside Mr. Nottingham's room for several hours Sunday afternoon before Muriel came out. She had gray hair and tired brown eyes;

she looked a little older than I'd expected Bobbie Jo's mom to be, but she'd been under stress for months, so that wasn't surprising.

Using the kindest voice I could manage, I spoke to her. "Excuse me, Mrs. Nottingham, may I speak to you for a minute?"

She looked frightened as she asked, "Who are you? Is it about my husband?"

I handed her my card, "No ma'am, it's about Bobbie Jo. I just want to ask you a couple of questions about her."

"Is she in trouble? What's she done this time?" Her voice was harsh, and she clipped her words sharply.

"Probably nothing, I'm just investigating something regarding one of her associates, and I'm trying to be thorough." Her fright was quickly becoming panic, and I hoped to keep her calm. I couldn't help but wonder what Bobbie Jo had done in the past that had her mother on edge.

"When you say 'associate', I assume you mean somebody in that grotesque revue she's in?"

"Yes, ma'am." I hadn't planned to bring it up since I wasn't sure if Mrs. Nottingham knew how her daughter made a living. But, since she knew, I could open up a little.

"I understand she left her troupe's performances in Las Vegas to visit her father. Was it common for her to drop everything for his birthday? Or was there a reason that you know about?"

"No, it was not common, but it also isn't common for him to be in a coma. She may have come back because she knew he couldn't kick her out or call her names in his current condition."

I noticed that she spoke of her husband in the present tense. I was careful to do the same. "They don't get along? She never mentioned that to me."

"Young man, my daughter does not share her family business with just anybody. Somehow, I doubt that you are a close confidant of hers."

"No, I'm certainly not. But she did accompany me to Las Vegas working on this case. It seems like it might have come up in conversation. What is the source of the animosity?"

"Oh! You're that detective? I didn't realize." Her voice softened as she continued. "I'm sorry if I sounded rude. My daughter has few friends, and almost no male friends. The source of the animosity, as you so delicately state it, is that my husband can be a jerk. My daughter has always been a handful. She has loved to shock people since she was a small child. As she grew up, she got very good at it. If you've seen her stage act, you realize how good she has become."

I acknowledged that I had seen it and agreed with her assessment and encouraged her to continue.

"When she told us she was gay, we both assumed it was just another attempt to shock us. She was in high school then and was already training spiders. We had gotten used to her enough that we didn't shock easily; neither of us reacted. However, the first time she brought home a girlfriend, her father did react."

I asked, "How did he react?"

"He started calling her names and kicked her out of the house. I tried to reason with him, but he can be very hard-headed. It's only recently he started to soften on the issue. Last year, he agreed to eat Christmas dinner as a family, if she agreed not to bring a girlfriend. Bobbie Jo, being just as stubborn as he is, declined the invitation, even though she wasn't seeing anybody at the time."

"Is she seeing anybody right now?" I asked. If she was, she hadn't mentioned missing her while we were in Vegas.

"No. In fact when she went with you to Vegas, she joked that she only agreed to go in the hopes that you would 'cure' her. I knew she was kidding, but I did allow myself to hope."

"It bothers you, also? The way you were talking, I got the impression that it was only your husband who had a problem."

"It bothers me only because it is causing problems for her and for my family. My husband is far too stubborn to not wake up. When he does, I have an intense desire for us to be a family again. I'm going to..."

I don't know what she was going to do, but what she did was start sobbing. Since her husband was in a coma down the hall, I knew why she was crying. I had no choice but to hold her softly and quietly for as long as it took.

When she stopped crying, I let go and we were quiet. There was no way I was going to keep asking her questions, and I didn't know what else to say.

She broke the silence eventually, "You're strong, but you have gentle arms like my husband. I think I miss his arms more than anything. I know he's going to recover, but sometimes I cry for all the wrong reasons. I'm sorry you had to see me break down."

"Please don't apologize, we all cry sometimes. Thank you for your time, you've been most helpful. I hope things work out for your family. By the way, I tried to talk to Charlie earlier, and he refused. Can you ask him to speak to me?"

"I'll ask, but it won't do any good. He's even more stubborn than his father. Before you go, can I ask you a question?"

This obviously wasn't the time for my old joke about how she just asked me one. Instead, I said simply, "Sure, ask me anything."

"Did you try to seduce Bobbie Jo while you were in Vegas?"

I tried to sound noble but not pious as I answered her. "No ma'am."

"Why not? Are you also gay, or did you already know about her orientation?"

"Neither. It was a business trip, not a junket. Besides, I'm in a relationship."

"Bobbie Jo told me you're a good man. I usually don't trust her judgment, but I think she's right this time. Did you learn what you came here to ask me?"

"You might be wiser not to trust her judgment, but I think I learned what I needed to learn," I told her honestly.

"Is my daughter in trouble? Do you suspect she's involved in that girl's death?"

I'm getting pretty good at lying to strangers, but not to those who just told me they think I'm a good man. I managed to get away without giving her a definitive answer or an outright lie.

After leaving the hospital, I went back to Deep Ellum to see if I could learn anything about Bobbie Jo's brother, but came up empty. Apparently, he's the only musician in town who doesn't hang out there.

By the time I got home, it was too late to be calling anybody at home. Instead, I sent Blake an email offering to buy him lunch Monday at The Rodeo Bar. While I was at the computer, I sent Emily one reminding her that I love her.

Then I went back to thinking about the case. Since I'd been back on it, I'd asked many questions, and I'd gotten many answers. However, I still had no idea how I was going to solve a case that wasn't even a case in the opinion of anybody except my client and me.

I definitely needed a plan, and I didn't have one. So far on this case, I was one for one on dreaming up a plan after taking a Tylenol P.M. If it worked once, it might work again, so I decided to try it again.

37   Usual Suspects

When I woke up the next morning at 9:36, I was one for two on dreaming up plans. At least I was well rested. I checked email as I ate a couple slices of toast.

I deleted most of the email, including two from wealthy foreigners wanting me to help them move their cash to the U.S. Most of the rest that I deleted were from companies promising they could increase the size of my manhood or improve my sexual stamina.

I replied to the one from Emily offering her own comments about my manhood and sexual stamina. I didn't need to answer Blake's saying he would meet me at Walt's at 12:30. Instead, I spent hours reviewing all my notes and then headed over to The Rodeo Bar.

At 12:24, I was sitting in a booth looking out on Commerce Street, with a glass of iced tea and a menu in front of me. The menu wasn't needed, since I already knew chicken fried steak was on it, but the iced tea was delicious and cold. I enjoyed it and the view of Dallas while I waited for Blake.

The view I was enjoying when Blake arrived was a young lady crossing Commerce Street wearing a short navy blue dress and matching pumps. He sat down across from me and enjoyed the view until she was out of sight. "So, is she your new suspect in the closed case? Or are you investigating her for some new client?"

"She's as much a suspect as anybody else at this point."

"Maybe you can't find suspects because they were right to close the case. Windmills are hard to defeat, Quixote."

"True, but I've got a paying client who doesn't believe the case should have been closed. He also has a dead fiancée and child. Windmills weren't responsible for their deaths. He knows that, and I know that. Do you doubt it?"

"No, I guess I don't. I'm just playing the devil's advocate for you."

April came over with two glasses of iced tea. She took our orders and picked up the glass I'd finished. She promised the food would be up quickly.

Blake took a sip of his tea, then looked at me. "I don't think I've seen you this disconsolate since you realized Isaac Moss was going to score on you at will in the hoop-it-up quarter-finals back in the day."

"Actually, I could have lived with him scoring, if I could have just kept him from dunking once in awhile. But you're right, I'm not happy. Freak deserves to know what really happened, and I'm not making any progress."

"How sure are you that that your client's not involved? I'm not suggesting he murdered her, but maybe they really didn't want the baby, so he tried the abortion himself."

"Aside from the fact that he's my client, I have two problems with that. First, I don't see why he would risk going to Uptown to dump the body. There are places all around Deep Ellum he could have put it where it still might not have turned up. Second, why keep me on the case at this point? The cops have dropped the case. If he hired me only to divert suspicion, it worked. Nobody officially suspects him of anything."

April delivered two chicken fried steaks and two fresh glasses of iced tea. Blake shares my dislike of talking business while eating, so we ate mostly in silence.

Blake finished before I did and immediately returned to his role as devil's advocate. "Maybe he dropped the body Uptown to frame somebody. It didn't work, so now he wants you to finish the job for him."

"Maybe," I admitted. "More likely I have an innocent client with a case I should keep trying to solve."

"Or better yet, a case you should actually solve," he pointed out accurately. "Let's assume a crime was committed, and your client wasn't involved. Who does that leave?"

"I guess it's down to Katherine's family, Bobbie Jo Nottingham or her brother."

"The spider bitch? How did she and her brother become suspects?"

"Don't let her hear you call her that, Blake. She doesn't take kindly to being called names, and she does train spiders for a living."

"I'll keep that in mind, but why would she be involved?"

"Honestly, I don't know. I thought maybe she had a crush on Freak and wanted to eliminate competition. But, I've learned she prefers women, so now I'm not sure. I do know she was willing to lie to give Freak an alibi, which would also have given her an alibi."

"Bobbie Jo's a lesbian? Are you sure?" I nodded and he continued, "Some guys downtown are going to hate that. She's been a big topic of conversation down there. Maybe she had something going with Katherine Elizabeth, and the pregnancy proved her lover wasn't faithful."

I considered that theory for a minute. "Have either of us seen or heard anything to suggest the victim swung that way?"

"No, I guess not. But we weren't exactly looking for that. What about her brother? What's his name, and why is he a suspect?"

"Her brother is Charlie Nothing, and apparently he knew Freak might be thinking about ending the revue. Bobbie Jo told me he would do anything for her. I know he loaned them his tour bus. Maybe he figured taking out Katherine might cause Freak to keep the show going, thus ensuring his sister's continued employment."

"His name is Charlie Nothing, as in Charlie Nothing and the Nothing Special Band? Jade's got all their records; they're pretty good. Did you talk to him?"

"I tried, but he's not talking. If I find a better reason to suspect him, I'll try again, but honestly, I think I suspect him mostly because he hung up on me."

"Hell, lots of people hang up on you, they can't all be suspects. You're grasping at straws. What about the family? Tell me what you've learned about them."

"All three have an alibi for when the body was dumped. I don't think they get along well enough to lie about that. However, all three have plausible individual motives, although those motives seem pretty thin, too."

Blake prompted, "Tell me about them."

"Daddy Dearest, as his son calls him, might have thought an out of wedlock grandchild would hurt his Christian values political career. I just don't see why he would talk her into an abortion outside a clinic or how he could have."

If Blake had a thought about that he didn't share it, so I continued, "Her mother could also have been concerned about the political impact of the child. She admitted that she married her husband only to insure that her children would be more attractive than her. She might not have wanted Freak's genes affecting her grandchild."

"What about the brother, he's the only one known for causing trouble."

"He says there was no sibling rivalry, but I doubt that. He also admitted that he was less popular with the girls than she was with the guys. He might have been jealous, or he might not have wanted her to produce the first grandchild."

Blake didn't look impressed with that theory, and I didn't blame him. I wasn't impressed with it either. I tried a different one.

"It's also possible that she went to him for help when she found out she was pregnant. I've been told he had shady contacts who might have attempted an abortion, without knowing how to do it safely."

Having finished reviewing the case, I realized I had a good reason to be feeling down. I hoped Blake might have a helpful suggestion.

He didn't. "So, you have a case that doesn't exist, with a crime nobody will want to prosecute, and suspects who didn't do it? Maybe you need to find some new suspects."

"Sure, how hard can it be? I've got my choice of everybody who's ever been to Deep Ellum, attended Ursuline Academy or Mesquite High School. Let's see, where else has she ever been? Oh yeah, let's not forget everybody who volunteered at the food bank. Maybe I should start by interrogating Emily."

Blake laughed courteously again, "I think you can rule her out as a suspect."

April brought the check and two more glasses of iced tea. I thanked her for her help on the case, left a reasonably generous tip, and Blake and I left. I had a full stomach and no idea what to do next.

On the walk home, I decided that calling Emily would be my next move. I didn't plan to interrogate her, but talking to her always makes me feel better, and it sometimes helps me solve a case. Feeling the way I did, I'd have settled for either one.

I planned to call Emily after she got home from work, so I had a few hours to kill. I walked past my office and turned right on Pearl Street. I almost never buy anything at the Farmer's Market, but it's a great place to walk around and think.

I got back to the office about four o'clock still without a plan. At six, I called Emily and asked her about her day. She mentioned that she was almost certain she was going to get the promotion, and then asked me about my case. I brought her up to date and asked her, "Do you have any suggestions?"

"No, but I do have one question. What was the question you decided not to ask the boy after football practice and why?"

"I'd like to know why his mother doesn't know about his legal trouble, but I know he won't tell me unless I have a way to force him."

"Maybe, you should try to find a way to force him, then."

"That's easier said than done, my dear. I've been trying to think of something that will do that since my trip to Mesquite."

She was encouraging, as always. "Keep trying, I'm sure you'll come up with something."

We discussed possible ideas for tomorrow's date night for a little while; then we discussed how much we love each other. After we hung up, I considered her advice.

Maybe I didn't need to force the boy to answer one specific question; maybe what I needed was just to force somebody to do something. So far, trying to learn what happened in the past wasn't working. I needed to make something happen.

Once I decided that, a plan came to mind quickly. I needed to force the action, and I knew the perfect actress to help me force it. I was sure she could play the role I had in mind. I just wasn't sure if she'd be willing.

The plan also had the potential to be an expensive plan, so I needed to talk to my client before I set it in motion. I had a plan that I needed my client to agree to finance and a near stranger to agree to implement, but at least I had a plan.

For some reason, I was certain both would agree. I again set my alarm for an early start in the morning. But for a change, I wasn't hoping to dream up a plan in my sleep. Instead, I was hoping to seriously disrupt somebody else's sleep.

38   Strange Bedfellows

Since my client doesn't have a phone, and I didn't want to wait, I walked over to his place at nine. I thought it might be too early to find him awake, but I couldn't start on the plan without first talking to him.

As I walked to Freak's front door, I noticed a beat up Kia Sephia parked in front of his house. It looked out of place in front of his house, but would have blended nicely in some parts of the neighborhood. I didn't give it much thought as I knocked on the door.

I was pleasantly surprised when he opened the door almost immediately. He was carrying a half full glass of orange juice and invited me to enter. I was surprised, but not pleasantly, when I saw Bobbie Jo and her co-stars sitting at his kitchen table.

Actually, only Bobbie Jo was sitting; her spiders were crawling on the table like toddlers in a nursery, only quieter and even more frightening. An almost empty bowl of cereal sat on the other end of the table. The spiders weren't crawling anywhere near the bowl, but I still shivered at the prospect of sharing a breakfast table with them.

"Sorry, Freak, I didn't expect you to have company this early. I would have called, but… well, you know."

"I know. I don't have a phone; I'm thinking about changing that. Anyway, I can tell from your expression you're here with more bad news. Hit me with it; I can take it."

While I was still trying to understand what he meant, he realized the true reason for my distraught look. He turned to Bobbie Jo. "B.J., can you, uh, y'all, give us a minute to talk alone, please?"

She had anticipated the request and had her little lovelies in their purple carrying case. Her high heels clicked on the hardwood flooring as she crossed the living area to the stairs. As she started up the stairs, she spoke, "We'll wait upstairs in the game room. If he has the cops with him to arrest me, please take care of Skipper and Skippette for me while I'm in jail."

Freak watched her disappear up the stairs; then turned to me, "What was that all about? She doesn't really expect you to have her arrested, does she?"

"If she does, she knows something I don't, which is always a possibility. I think she's just mad because I checked up on her trip back to Dallas during your Vegas run. As you know first hand, people sometimes get touchy about being investigated."

"Okay, I get it. What does bring you here?"

"I've got a plan for the investigation, but it could get expensive, and it could be a waste of my time and your money. I wanted to discuss it with you before proceeding, since the expenses will be yours."

Freak said, "Aight!" which translates from youth slang to English as 'All Right!' Obviously, he was happy that I had a plan, so I started to talk about my plan.

He stopped me before I even began, "Bobbie Jo's going to drive me out to the cemetery, and we need to get going. Spend whatever and I'll pay it; I don't care. If the expenses are more than I can pull from the trust fund, I'll make Larry Joe loan it to me. I'll stop by your office this afternoon, and you can tell me about the plan."

I had forgotten that Freak didn't drive. That did explain why Bobbie Jo was at his place. I kicked myself for not volunteering to take him to the cemetery myself. "Don't worry; I don't expect it to be that expensive. I'll start making arrangements. Call me around noon, and we'll set up the time."

Freak agreed to call me, and I left. One thing about investigators is that we always investigate. Instead of going straight back to the office, I found a concealed area and waited to see Bobbie Jo and Freak leave.

Less than ten minutes later they walked out his door and down to the Kia. He was wearing black jeans and a black tee shirt, carrying a single rose and what appeared to be a Bible. She was not carrying a purple box of spiders and was also dressed in black. If they weren't on their way to a cemetery, they had me fooled.

I may not be the world's greatest detective, but I'm not that easy to fool. Besides, by virtue of being a man, Freak isn't Bobbie Jo's type. Her mother may keep hoping some man will change her mind, but she shouldn't get her hopes up.

On the other hand, I was getting my hopes up. My client had agreed to finance my plan without even hearing about it. All I had to do now was make it work. As soon as I got back to my office, I called Jack Cannelly.

I gave his secretary my name and told her I needed to speak to the city manager. She suggested I leave a number, but I told her it was important and that I'd hold while she let him know. She sounded doubtful, but she put me on hold.

I don't normally have the patience to hold for very long. However, I was currently inclined to wait as long as it took. My plan didn't completely depend on the Cannellys' help, but without their help, it would have more risks.

Specifically, without their help, the plan would risk my investigator's license and Blake's continued employment. Thus, I was more than willing to hold as long as it took. I held for five minutes before the secretary came back on the line.

"Mr. Cannelly says he'll be right with you. Can you hold just a little longer?"

I assured her that I could, and she put me back on hold. While I waited, I wondered what 'a little longer' would mean. It turned out to mean eight more minutes.

The music stopped and I heard Jack's amused voice, "I thought I made it clear that I didn't want to buy that property downtown. You real estate people are more relentless than politicians."

By the time he finished, I heard him chuckling softly, so I decided to play along, "Actually, I realized there's no excitement in real estate, so I've decided to solve Katherine Elizabeth Hightower's murder instead."

Jack reacted as I'd hoped, "Wow! Murder? Seriously? I thought the case was closed. I thought the police ruled her death accidental."

"My client and I think the police closed the case too soon. We're going to do something about it, and we hope you and Bethany will help us."

"We'll do what we can. Well, I shouldn't speak for Bethany, but I'm sure she'll agree. What do you want us to do?"

"Actually, I need her help more than yours. Can you arrange for me to meet with her as soon as possible to discuss it?"

"Sure, I'll page her. She loves it when I page her when she's at a function. It lets everybody know how important she is."

"Thanks. Just call me and let me know when and where to meet her. I'll be at my office until I hear from you. You have my number?"

He assured me that he did and that he would call me back soon. I reminded myself that my plan wasn't guaranteed to succeed to keep from getting overly optimistic. It didn't work; I was truly optimistic for the first time since I'd found Freak waiting for me in my office.

With optimism comes impatience. Now that I felt like I had a plan, I wanted to start on it immediately. Since I couldn't, I paced instead. I'm a world class pacer, but it's hard for a tall person to pace in a small office. Fortunately, Jack's phone call came quickly.

"Pegasus Investigations," I answered in what I hoped was a professional as opposed to an eager voice.

Jack got right to the point. "Bethany will be at my office at 1:30. I can clear my schedule so I can sit in, if that's okay. I want to know about your plan, too. How long do you expect the meeting to take?"

"Of course, you're welcome to sit in. I value your input. It shouldn't take more than thirty minutes to an hour. Can you spare that?"

"If you're right that she was murdered, and I suspect you are, what kind of jerk would I have to be not to spare an hour to help you solve it?"

He had a valid point, and I saw no reason to mention that it was actually his wife who was going to help me solve it. Instead, I thanked him and promised to be at his office at 1:30.

I thought about walking down to Tootsie's for an early lunch, but decided against it. If Freak called right at noon, I'd have time to go to Mesquite for lunch at Mama's Daughters' Diner before meeting with Bethany and Jack. Either restaurant would be delicious and affordable, but I can walk to Tootsie's any day I happen to have cash money.

Instead of going to lunch, I went ahead and called Jesse. Since it was still morning, I wasn't at all surprised when he answered on the first ring.

"Right On Time Delivery; what can we deliver for you?"

"I'm hoping to borrow several of your high-tech phones this weekend."

"So Ace Ventura is still on a case?" Jesse sounded happier about me still being on a case than I was. Maybe, I wasn't as good as a bike courier as I thought I was.

"Yes, I'm still on a case. I'm planning a stakeout, and I was really impressed by the phones you loaned us before."

"Well, we don't do much on weekends. I only have four of the new ones, but I can probably spare eight to twelve compatible ones if needed. I'll need them all back by Monday morning, though. "

"I should only need four, plus one for you if you're interested in helping."

"Hell, yes! I'm interested. What do you need me to do?"

"Just need you to monitor the location of the phones, and keep me apprised."

"Easy enough, you'll owe me though if it cuts into my sleep too much."

"Actually, I'll be able to pay you this time. You'll be an expense."

Jesse wasn't used to me having that type of client, so he made several comments before we hung up. I let most of them slide. As I had hoped, Freak's call was punctual. The phone rang at 11:38.

"Pegasus Investigations," I answered.

"Sorry about this morning, I needed to go out there, and it was nice of Bobbie Jo to take me. I didn't want to keep her waiting any longer."

"Don't worry about it; I understand. Also, if you ever need somebody to take you, just let me know. As you know, my schedule is very flexible. Can you meet me at my office around four today?"

He thanked me for the offer and agreed to be at my office at four. He wanted me to tell him about the plan, but I convinced him it would be better to wait. Since he hates phones so much he doesn't own one, it wasn't hard to convince him.

I finished a chicken fried steak lunch and was sitting in Jack Cannelly's office at 1:33. Bethany was with him, and they were both as excited as school children on a field trip to be helping with an investigation.

I explained the plan. "Basically, I've given up turning up a hidden clue that might tell us what happened to Katherine Elizabeth. Instead, I want to force somebody to make a mistake. If we can scare the right person, he or she might panic and lead us to a clue."

Bethany asked, "How do we make that happen?"

"I want you to call Bunny Friday evening and convince her that the police have reopened the case and are getting search warrants for every place anybody in her family might hide something. Don't say it that way, though. I want you to mention as many as you can think of specifically. That will make it more believable. She knows you have friends everywhere. Even if she doesn't believe it, she won't be able to completely dismiss it, right?"

Bethany thought about it for a minute before replying. "I think so. She doesn't like me, and she thinks I'm an airhead because I'm prettier than she is. But she would have to wonder. What makes her the suspect?"

"Oh, there are plenty of other suspects. It just makes sense to start by trying to flush out three at once. From what I know of Bunny, even if she's completely innocent, she'll tell her husband and son about the call."

Jack confirmed my thinking. "Sure, she would. She can't stand to know anything without sharing it with everybody, especially her family."

Bethany nodded her agreement and we spent the next thirty minutes working on the exact script for the call, and deciding on which places she should mention specifically. We decided on the house, the mayor's office, the lake house, the boy's locker at school and the gym where Bunny works out.

I got their home number and told them I would call them Friday evening when I had everything else in place. As I got up, Jack asked one more question. "What do you do if this doesn't work?"

"I move on to the next suspect. Anybody can be frightened, especially if they're carrying around a dangerous secret."

I'm sure I sounded more confident than I felt, but they both looked convinced as I left the city manager's office and headed back to mine. I got back to my office a little before three and called Larry Joe. I told Adriana it was important, and she put me right through to him.

"What's so important now, Pardner?"

"I thought you weren't going to call me that any more, but I'll ignore it this time. I need several good investigators to assist me this weekend, and you have more experience hiring them than I do."

"I reckon I do. What's the job, and how much are you plannin' on paying?"

"I'll pay whatever Freak can afford; I need good help. He said if it gets too expensive for his trust fund, you'll cover it."

Larry Joe laughed. "That whippersnapper sure has his Daddy's confidence. I hope his trust in you is justified. How many sidekicks do you reckon you need?"

"However many it takes to have three, make that four, on a stake out 24/7 from Friday evening until early Monday morning."

"I'll take care of the hiring; you'll need to explain the program to them. I'll call you tomorrow morning and let you know the arrangements. Are you sure you know what you're doing?"

"As sure as I've ever been, Larry Joe."

If that didn't satisfy him, he had the decency not to mention it. After I hung up, I thought about my confident young client and his trust in me. I don't know that I'd done anything to earn that trust, but I was definitely planning to start.

Freak was going to be here soon. I spent some time going over my notes before he arrived. I wanted to make sure I had the details worked out before I shared them. Not surprisingly, he insisted on one change. As expected, my client is every bit as stubborn as he is confident and trusting. If he wasn't, I would not have lived to the conclusion of the case.

"Freak, you don't even drive. How in the world do you plan to help?"

He'd been in my office for about thirty minutes. It took about ten minutes to explain the plan to him. He liked the plan, but he wanted to be a part of it. The last twenty minutes had been spent arguing about his role.

"I could ride with you or one of the other investigators."

"I don't think you understand what we're doing here. We're investigating a crime. That has to be done by professionals, with licenses. I'm not saying you couldn't do it. But if we do find any evidence, we hope it will lead to a trial. If it does, our goal is to get a conviction."

"How does that affect me?"

"Having an amateur, particularly a former suspect, helping on the stakeout would give the defense team a way to create 'reasonable doubt'. Do you really want to find out what happened only to have the person who killed her found not guilty because you were there?"

"Them; we're looking for the person who killed them, not just her." He had a look on his face I hadn't seen since he took that swing at me in Deep Ellum. I wondered briefly if we had the same plan for whatever evidence we uncovered.

The look slowly faded and he continued. "You're right though. My daddy used to say, 'Hire good people; then get out of their way.' What about that Jesse guy, though? He's not a licensed investigator, is he?"

"No, but he won't be doing any investigating. He's just monitoring the radios."

"Then I'll hang out with him during the stakeout. Maybe he can show me how all that stuff works, and I can relieve him if he needs a nap or something."

I knew Jesse could easily work thirty-six to forty-eight hours without sleep. I knew that, but Freak didn't. "That's not a bad idea. Let me check with Jesse, but I'm sure he won't mind having you around."

Freak insisted that I call Jesse right then. Jesse agreed easily, so we left it at that. I gave Jesse's number to Freak and left it to them to make their own arrangements.

After Freak left, I called Larry Joe about the investigators. He told me the first shift would be at my office at three o'clock Friday afternoon for briefing. They'd work a twelve hour shift; then each would be responsible for briefing his replacement. That included me. The two teams would then alternate every twelve hours as needed. One extra person would be on call for the entire weekend.

Friday morning, I walked over to the Enterprise rental car place in the tunnels under Elm Street. My van had already been parked in front of the Mayor's house, so it seemed like a good idea to rent a less recognizable car for tonight's task.

Since this was an expense account item, I paid the extra few bucks for what they call shoebox insurance. I didn't expect to return the car in a shoebox, but you never know. I didn't expect to need a gun either, but I drove the rental to the garage to get my good handgun from the van, anyway.

Almost nothing I own can be described as top of the line, but that pistol comes pretty close. It's a High Standard Victor TX9317 twenty-two caliber with a competition-ready Tasco ProPoint red dot sight. The magazine holds ten rounds.

A former client offered it instead of paying me the two hundred dollars he owed me. Since it's worth over a thousand dollars even without the scope, I gladly accepted. Thanks to the scope, I'm accurate with it even though I'm not a great marksman.

Also, the whole assembly only weighs about three pounds and is small enough to fit in the van's console. I also grabbed the shoulder holster and my concealed carry permit. Remarkably, I've only had to pawn it once.

At three o'clock, three investigators, each of whom probably makes more in an average week than I make in a good month were sitting in my office waiting for instructions. I gave them the address in Mesquite and told them what we were looking to find.

Larry Joe had briefed them on the case when he hired them, so they didn't need much background. All I had to do was explain what we were going to do tonight.

"I've arranged for a phone call that we hope will cause someone in that house to react. Our plan is to follow whoever leaves and see where they lead us. We don't have to find the evidence, just learn who knows about it. If we find it, or learn what it is, that's great, but all we have to do is figure out who knows where it is and follow them to learn where they move it or get rid of it. It's a criminal case, but our role is strictly surveillance and tailing. Once we know something, we can turn it over to the police. Anybody have questions?"

They asked a few logistical questions regarding the house and the surrounding areas. Nobody asked why the client had hired me, instead of their high-tone agency. Also, nobody called me by any name other than my own. It can be a pleasure to work with professionals, occasionally.

By 3:45, the team understood the assignment and was ready to roll. Everybody had a phone with GPS capability, and we all had all the numbers. Whoever left that house would be followed, and Jesse would be able to track the path.

With high tech equipment and a professional team assembled, Pegasus actually resembled a real detective agency for a change. It had been many years since that had been the case, and I liked how it felt. Actually, it surprised me somewhat how much I liked how it felt.

At 5:43, I parked the rented sedan on a side street with a view of the mayor's garage, ready to follow the first car to leave. By 6:15, the others had checked in to say they had their positions and were ready.

I called Jack and Bethany's house, and she answered on the first ring. "Hello. Is it time?" she asked.

"Yes, are you ready?"

"Yes I'm ready. Actually, I'm a nervous wreck, but I can do this. It's important. I always do what's important. Anyway, that's what Jack's been reminding me for the last hour."

It was important, so I encouraged her, "He should know. I trust him, and I trust you. You'll be great, I know it."

Fifteen minutes later, she called me back. "I did it. It went exactly like we planned it. She bought it; I just know she bought it. Do I need to do anything else? I could really use a drink."

"No, you did great. Have a drink for me while you're at it. Give my best to Jack."

She promised she would, and we exchanged goodbyes. I called the rest of the team to let them know the game was afoot. I say things like that sometimes when I'm feeling like a real detective.

With everything in place, the hardest part of any stakeout began: the waiting. Anybody who thinks they have a boring job should try a stakeout just once to gain a little perspective on how boring a job can be.

Most boring tasks have a start time and an end time, so if nothing else you can count down the minutes until it ends. A stakeout can last a few minutes, a few hours or a few weeks. This one wasn't going to last weeks, but it might last days.

I settled into the waiting, with the toys I had brought to entertain myself. The first was the recording sunglasses Freak had given me earlier. I was amazed by how comfortable they were to wear and how securely the earpieces wrapped around my ears.

I couldn't imagine a reason to wear them on a basketball court, but I suspected they'd stay in place at least as well as Kareem's always had if I did. They were incredibly easy to use, and I started experimenting with different places to stash the recording unit.

I had just slipped it in my boot like a flask at Willie Nelson's picnic when it became obvious that this wasn't going to be one of those long stakeouts. A black Mercedes Benz came out of the Mayor's garage and paused in the driveway just long enough to hit the garage door button.

The windows were tinted like a limousine, so I couldn't see who was driving. It didn't matter, though. As the Mercedes backed into the street, and then screeched forward like somebody was auditioning for a part in the next sequel to The Fast and the Furious, I was sure somebody had taken our bait.

I eased the rental behind the Mercedes, and followed it out of the neighborhood onto LBJ Freeway. As soon as I was sure I had the tail, I called Jesse to tell him I was moving and to get the next guy into place by the garage.

"I already took care of it. As soon as your phone started moving, I got your backup in place. There's no chance we missed anything. So, who are you following?"

"I don't know yet, but whoever I'm following is in a hurry. We're going about seventy-five."

"You're also heading toward the intersection of I-635 and I-20. That's a huge speed trap; try not to get pulled over and lose the tail."

I thanked him for the advice, but I didn't need it. Whichever suspect I was following obviously knew about the speed trap, too. We made the turn onto westbound I-20 at a safe and legal fifty-five miles an hour. Once we were on I-20, our speed increased dramatically.

As we flew west on the interstate, my mind flitted over three ideas. First, I was glad I'd rented the car, since my van isn't built for speed.

Second, I wondered if leaving Mesquite on I-20 led anywhere related to this case other than Mineral Wells.

The third thing that crossed my mind as we passed Duncanville and Arlington at almost ninety miles an hour was the text message April sent me four days ago. In text lingo, 'ftl' means faster than light. We might not be going faster than light now, but we were pretty close.

As we entered Grand Prairie, my phone rang. I was surprised that the caller's name didn't show up on caller I.D, but I thought I better answer it. I left the phone on speaker as I answered with a curt greeting.

Freak's voice was the last one I expected to hear, but he sounded as excited as a child with a new toy, which in fact, he was. "Guess what?" he asked.

"This isn't the time for games."

"I'm not playing games. I just thought you'd like to know I have a phone now. I bought one of those cool ones like the one Jesse loaned you. I'm on the way back to his place now."

"That's great Freak, glad to hear it, but I'm tailing a suspect now. This isn't the time to chat about toys."

"Fine, be that way!" Hearing Freak's petulant voice wasn't much different at ninety miles an hour than it was standing still, but he was the client. Instead of just hanging up on him, I assured him I was happy that he had a phone now and promised to call him on it when I got the chance.

As I followed the Mercedes past Benbrook, I lost any doubt that our destination was Mineral Wells. Every time we passed a state sign warning drivers about the zero tolerance policy for speeding, I wanted to slow down.

However, I was staying far enough back to keep from being spotted that I had reason to hope the highway patrol would pull over the Mercedes, not me. Neither of us got pulled over. By dusk, we were on 180 going through Weatherford on the way to Lake Mineral Wells.

——

When we got to the Hightowers' lake house, I didn't want to be close enough to be spotted. As soon as the Mercedes started down the street, I turned away. I decided to circle around and enter the property from the lake side.

I had observed on my earlier visit that the boathouse had a good view of the house and several good places to hide until the time seemed right to move in on the main house. I holstered the pistol as I got out of the rental and started toward the boathouse.

As I walked through the thick woods, I saw that much of the grass and shrubbery looked like it had been decorated with Christmas tinsel. I knew this was just the setting sun shining on spider webs. I tried not to think about what creates spider webs as I turned on the glasses' recording device. I knew they would record whatever I saw or heard, but I wasn't sure how much of the main house I'd be able to see or hear from the boat house.

As things turned out, it didn't matter much. Using the boathouse as an observation point might have been a good idea. However, it would only have been a good idea for me if I'd been the only one to think of it, or at least the first one to get there.

The closer I got to the boathouse, the harder it became to push my way through the trees, shrubs and tall grass. There was probably a trail somewhere, but it had become too dark to even bother looking for it. The glasses shielded my eyes and the boots protected my feet, so I just trudged through.

As I came to a clearing with a view of the boathouse, I laughed to myself at Jesse's earlier accusation that I would never embrace modern technology. I carried with me the latest in radio technology, built to military specifications with ready link technology and GPS capability.

I also had a top-notch pistol in a shoulder holster. My glasses were transmitting every thing I saw or heard to a digital recording device in my left boot. I was as high tech as any Texas redneck could ever hope to get.

As I thought about it, it occurred to me that the gun might prove more useful in my hand than in my holster. As I reached for the gun, I heard a noise behind me. Before I had time to wonder what it was, something hit the back of my head, and everything went black.

I don't know how long it was before I woke up, but somebody had moved me from the clearing. I don't weigh enough to be an NBA power forward, but I weigh enough to be hard to move. That narrowed down the list of suspects a little.

As my brain started working again in spite of the throbbing headache, I realized my suspect list might not matter. My hands were wrapped behind my back cuffed around a pretty thick tree. The glasses were still on, but the way I was bound my only view was the moonlit lake.

I'm sure a great outdoorsman could have figured out what time it was by the angle of the moonlight or something. As a city boy, I had no chance. Obviously, it wasn't morning, yet. That was about all I knew for sure.

I tried to turn my aching head to look toward the house or boathouse, but all I could see in any direction were trees and several rows of what appeared to be bales of dried hay. Mineral Wells is more famous for heat than hay, so I presumed it was grass that someone was wisely waiting until summer ended to burn.

I was groggy, but not so groggy I didn't realize the trouble I was in. There was no way I could free myself, and very little chance whoever put me here was going to release me. That left me in need of being rescued, but I didn't see that happening, either.

Sure, Jesse knew where I was headed, but he had no way of knowing I was handcuffed to a tree. I was weighing the odds of being rescued when I heard Mayor Hightower's voice, "So, the great detective is awake finally. I trust you find your accommodations confining enough."

I turned my head toward the voice and saw the mayor walking through two bales of grass carrying a portable blow torch. I briefly wondered why he was carrying it. I quickly surmised that he wasn't waiting for the end of summer to burn the dried grass, after all.

If I'd thought I was in trouble before, there was no doubt, now. I'd never spent much time thinking about the best ways to die, but I'm sure burning would be low on any list.

"Still trying the quiet trick, huh? I've heard that can be really effective. Somehow, it doesn't have much effect on me with you restrained like that. Surely, you have a few questions you're dying to ask."

If he meant the question to be ironic, he didn't show it. As much as I normally like irony, I wasn't in a position to enjoy it at the moment. I wasn't in a position to do much of anything, actually. Maybe asking a few questions wasn't a bad idea.

The first one that came to mind was 'Why the hell did you kill your own daughter?' However, asking that one didn't seem like a good idea given my current condition. I decided on a different one.

"You do realize the cops know I followed you out here, don't you?" Lying to somebody who is in the process of killing me painfully turned out to be remarkably easy. I just hoped I lived long enough to lie to somebody who wasn't again.

"Sure they do, Peeper. Do you know that dried grass burns instantly when exposed to a temperature of a thousand degrees or more? Or that a propane blow torch exudes a temperature far in excess of that? Every cop in North Texas could surround us right now, and it wouldn't do you any good."

"When I light a few of these bales, you'll be a dead man in a matter of minutes. The best you can hope for is that they'll find your charred remains from the rubble which that house and these woods are about to become and be able to identify you."

I didn't bother telling him that nobody had made a keyhole that could be peeped through for decades. I doubted if he would care. Instead, I started back in on our game of twenty questions.

"So what's in that lake house you don't want the police to find?"

"Probably nothing, but I'm not taking any chances. That's where it happened. I didn't think anybody would check it, but I guess I was wrong."

"Don't you think committing arson and another murder is taking a chance?"

"Not at all, if by chance they don't chalk this up as just another West Texas grass fire, I'll tell them that whelp of Satan has been threatening to burn down my house for years, but I assumed it was an idle threat."

"Then, I'll tell them I don't know how he found out about the lake house, but maybe my daughter told him. They'll try the bastard for arson and murder if they happen to find your body. With any luck, he'll die in the electric chair."

"You think my client is the devil's child just because he suffers from a rare medical condition?"

"It's not a medical condition; it's Satan's mark. His father had it, and he has it. The apple doesn't fall far from the tree."

Suddenly, things started making sense. Anybody silly enough to think a tiny lake in the middle of nowhere contains the fountain of youth would be silly enough to think Freak's condition is the devil's mark.

I was thinking about what a shame it was that I only figured things out in time to die, when the mayor continued, "Besides, even without the mark, evil is evil. That demon assaulted my son in high school along with a bunch of other innocent kids for no reason. Of course, he always got away with it because his evil parents hired an expensive lawyer for him. I should have killed him back then, but I didn't. A few years later, I find out he raped my daughter. I could not let my daughter bear a child that was destined to be evil incarnate, so I did what I had to do."

"You killed your own daughter? If it was rape, what had she done to deserve to die?" I probably wasn't going to live long enough to use it, but I was hoping the recorder would survive. It would be nice if a confession were on it.

He sounded pretty defensive for a man holding all the cards when he answered, "No, I didn't kill her. I simply aborted the incubus' bastard imp."

"And the abortion killed her. Did you have Katherine Elizabeth's permission? Or did you try to do it while she slept? Or did you put her to sleep?"

"I had to do it the way I did. He had cast some kind of black magic spell on her. I didn't want her to suffer, so I gave her something to help her sleep. I hoped once the imp was out of the picture, she might snap out of the trance. Instead, that devil's child ends up killing my daughter, and now you pretend I'm the bad guy. I don't think so."

He obviously didn't think he was the bad guy. Most psychopaths don't. I didn't have a plan, but I let him continue trying to justify himself.

"I couldn't kill the devil, but at least I could try to get him sent to jail by making it obvious to the police that he was the one really responsible for her death. But then, you had to butt in and provide him with a bogus alibi. I was too weak to kill him years ago when I should have, but I'm stronger now. You are going to die first for your part in this; then he is. Either the state will execute him for your murder, or I'll do what I should have done years ago."

It was obvious that the fire the mayor was planning to start wouldn't be the only fire raging. The mayor had obviously gone inferno a long time ago, and nobody had noticed. I suppose it's hard to recognize when somebody that nobody really likes snaps, since nobody really liked them anyway.

All I could do was keep looking at him and hope the glasses were recording his confession and that either I would live long enough to get them to somebody or the recorder would survive the fire. I'd heard stories of data recovery teams pulling data from computers that had been destroyed; maybe that was possible with this also.

The mayor reached up and ripped off my glasses. He did it so violently that the cable came loose and he threw them down without even looking at them. "I want to see your eyes when you beg me to kill you." As he was talking he went behind the tree.

Since I didn't have the glasses anymore, I didn't even bother trying to see where he went. I suspected he was going to start the fire that would end my life painfully. However a few seconds later he was standing in front of me again. This time he held my pistol and Jesse's cell phone, instead of a blow-torch.

"I don't know how a low-rent shamus can afford this kind of technology, but it isn't going to help you any."

He then threw the phone down in the grass and aimed the pistol at it. The phone bounced, and he waited for it to land before he fired again.

The phone bounced again, and I suspected that any chance I had of being rescued because of its GPS locater was gone.

He fired a few more shots at the defenseless phone, then turned back to me. "So, who you gonna call, huh?"

Obviously, I wasn't going to call anybody. I also wasn't likely to be rescued by somebody tracking what was left of the phone. He pointed the gun at me. I tried not to look at the gun, but to look at him, instead.

He had a malevolent look on his face that is impossible to describe. However, it was obvious his hatred for Freak had grown to include me even before he spoke. "This would be a good time to beg me to shoot you. I hear burning is a painful way to die."

"Feel free to tell me if you think of a good way to die, but there's no way in Hell I'm begging you for anything. If you want to shoot me, go ahead, but don't expect me to give you the opportunity to pretend I begged for it."

For a while he looked like he might, but eventually he put the gun down and spoke, "I'd enjoy shooting you. I really would. But, anybody who is willing to work for Satan should expect to burn. It will prepare you for your eternity."

He started to walk away, but then he returned. "You know what? I may never have this chance again."

As he pointed my pistol at me, I was sure I was dead. He lowered it just before he fired, and the bullet ripped into my thigh. I wasn't dead, but I was in serious pain. I was also glad I'd brought the twenty-two and not my forty-five.

As the mayor walked away, I hoped he was walking toward the lake house. Unfortunately for me, he walked toward the bales of grass. I watched him start the fire and then walk toward the house and out of my field of vision. If I'd still been wearing the glasses, I might have tried to follow him.

Instead, I watched the flames dancing rapidly through the grass bales toward me. Obviously, the mayor had planned this well. Less than ten minutes after I saw the first flame, I was nearly surrounded by fire. I didn't have a priest around to render last rites, but I knew I was about to die.

When I heard the voice calling out my name, I first thought I was hallucinating. The voice was coming from behind the flames which almost surrounded me. Finally, I realized it was Freak, and that he had somehow gotten very close to me and was looking for me.

I screamed as loud as I could, "Freak, I'm over here."

He yelled back, "Where?"

"Toward the lake, can you get around the wall of fire? If you can't, it's about to be too late. "

He didn't answer, and I wondered if he'd become engulfed the way I was about to be. Suddenly, he burst through the wall of fire burning like chicken flambé. As he came out of the fire, he threw down the trench coat he'd held in front of him and did the tuck and roll until he wasn't burning and came over to me.

The coat had protected his upper body and face pretty well. However, most of his jeans had been lost to the flames. What remained was seared to his skin and he had severe burning on his forearms and legs. I knew he couldn't feel pain, but it hurt me just to look at him. It didn't help much knowing the same thing was about to happen to me.

"Dude, what the hell happened?"

"The mayor killed them, and he handcuffed me to this tree and set this whole area on fire. His confession may be on the recorder you gave me. Get it out of my left boot and get it to Blake. There's no way to save me now, unless you brought a hacksaw with you."

He bent down, lifted my jean leg and took the recorder. When he stood back up, I saw his nipple ring through a hole in his shirt. He realized just before I did what it might mean.

254

"Fuck the recorder! I'm getting you out of here."

If you've never seen a man with third degree burns rip out his own nipple ring, you'll never believe how horrible it looks. Blood started spewing as he did it. I wondered if even his revue's audience would be repulsed if he tried this on stage.

However, with the handcuff key he'd been wearing as a nipple ring since he'd promised Katherine Elizabeth he would, he was able to unlock the cuffs and free me. There wasn't time to do much about my leg, so I made a tourniquet out of my shirt, and we took off.

My wrists were sore as hell. My leg was almost numb, and I could barely breathe. Even so, as we headed toward the lake and away from the flames, all I could think about was Freak's burned and bloody body.

Freak couldn't feel physical pain, but he certainly could die. I wanted to make sure he lived long enough to see the mayor pay for killing his fiancée and unborn child. I hoped the glasses had recorded all the evidence needed to do that. Unfortunately, the glasses weren't built to the same military standard as Jesse's phones.

41   Extended Stays

When we were far enough from the woods that it wasn't likely for the flames to get to us, we both collapsed. We were both coughing badly. Freak was badly burned and clearly needed medical attention, and my head and leg were both throbbing.

On the other hand, we were both alive. When I finally had enough breath to speak without coughing, I asked, "How did you find me? For that matter, how did you get here?"

"Sam The Man drove me out here. Jesse tracked your phone to almost the exact spot. I know you told me not to come, but when you told me you were tailing a suspect, I had to be here. Plus, I realized I'm not really an amateur, at least not to the point it would jeopardize the case. When I did the ROTC thing, I was training to be an MP. Are you mad?"

"You just saved my life, and you look like you're about to die. Right now, I'm only mad at the mayor. Did your phone survive that run?"

"Shit! The phone's in my coat. It's gone. Even if it survived, Jesse will be tracing it to the fire, not to us. Maybe I am a damn amateur."

Looking at him, it was hard to believe that even he wasn't in pain. We had to get medical attention for him, and I still hadn't heard any sirens. I struggled to my feet. "Don't worry about it, now. Can you walk?"

He could and he did. We both stumbled a few times and took turns helping each other stand. We stayed close to the shore in case the fire continued to get out of control. We were both in bad shape, but I was the only one feeling any pain. That worried me.

I remembered from my earlier trip out here that there was a camp of rental cabins about half a mile from the lake house. I didn't know if we could make it that far. For that matter, I wasn't completely sure we were going in the right direction, but I didn't have any other plan.

Eventually, I heard sirens, and I wondered if we should turn back and hope for a rescue, but I decided against it. Freak was coughing more, and I didn't want to lead him back toward the flames. Just as the cabins came into sight, Freak passed out.

I couldn't wait there to be found, and I sure as Hell couldn't leave Freak laying there. I wouldn't have believed I had the strength, but somehow I picked him up in a fireman's carry and kept walking.

Finally, we got near enough to the cabins that somebody saw us. By then, I was barely more than crawling, and Freak was getting heavier by the minute, but a couple of guys approached us.

"Hey buddy, are you boys doing all right?" The question didn't speak highly for his intelligence, but at least we'd found a human.

"My friend is hurt. Do you have a phone? Can you call 911?"

If he answered, I passed out before hearing it. Fortunately though, he apparently called 911. When I regained consciousness, I was in a hospital bed, and Emily was sitting beside me holding my hand.

My head felt like somebody was pounding on it, and my ears were ringing. But, I was alive, my leg too numb to hurt much. The first words out my mouth should have been 'Here's looking at you, kid' or "I love you' or something else romantic. Instead I said, "Freak? Where is... is he..."

Emily answered before I managed to get the question into words. "He's okay, or rather, he's going to be okay. He's here too, but in ICU. They're doing some skin grafts, but they say he'll recover completely. Oh, and by the way, I love you."

"I love you, too. What time is it?"

"It's about noon, but what you really need to know is what day it is. It's Monday; you've been out of it for awhile. Blake wants to talk to you as soon as you're up to it. Should I call him?"

I tried to sit up, but couldn't quite make it. "Apparently, I'm still out of it. But I need to talk to him. I also need to talk to Freak. Is he awake? Is he allowed visitors?"

"I think so, but I don't know. Don't get too gung-ho, you got messed up pretty bad. I'll call Blake and see about Freak; you just stay in bed and relax." She kissed my forehead before leaving the room.

I stayed in bed, but I didn't relax. Instead, I went back over the case wondering if I should have figured out that the mayor was a killer without almost getting me and my client killed. I felt sure I'd missed something, but I had no idea what.

Emily came back in the room a half hour later. "Blake's going to be here at five. The hospital says we can see Freak then. You'll have to go up in a wheel chair, though. You're still a mess; you should sleep."

It was good advice, and I took it. As I drifted off, I felt her leaning down and resting her head on my chest. I suspected she'd been awake most of the time I'd been asleep, and it felt good to feel her there.

For the second time since I'd been on this case, I dreamt about April. This time, though, I also dreamt of a specific hotel room in Arlington. I didn't feel guilty at all about this dream; I only felt bad about needing to be asleep to realize what I had missed.

At five, two nurses helped me into a wheelchair. They wouldn't let Emily help with that process, but once I was in the chair they both left. Emily pushed me into the hall where Blake and Dougie were waiting.

Blake saw me and shook his head, "You hanging in there?"

I nodded, then looked at Dougie. Dougie glanced at Blake who explained, "Dougie asked to come out here. I reminded him that you might not want to see him. He promised to leave without saying a word if either of us says so. Since this hospital is in Tarrant County, he has no legal standing to be here. For that matter, neither do I. Emily says we should talk to Freak, but if he doesn't want to talk to us, we can't make him."

"It should be fine, did you get the recorder?"

"We did, and we got the statements you and Freak made to the Fort Worth Police. We know what you think, but we don't know if we can make any of it stick."

I only vaguely remembered making any statement, but that didn't surprise me, "Wait. Let's go see Freak and see if we can't work through this together."

Blake took over for Emily pushing my chair. She went back to holding my hand. Nobody said anything as we got in the elevator.

As the elevator door opened, Dougie spoke, "For what it's worth, I think you're a damn good detective." I wasn't sure I agreed, but I was alive, so there still might be time for me to prove him right.

Larry Joe and Daniel were waiting outside Freak's room when we arrived. We exchanged pleasantries; then Larry Joe said, "There's a nurse in there now. We can't go back in until she comes out."

The nurse came out shortly and ushered us into the room. Blake pushed my chair close to the bed so Freak and I could shake hands. After he shook my hand, Freak winked at Emily, looked around the room and fixed his gaze on Dougie.

Dougie averted his eyes, then spoke, "I have no legal authorization to be here, Freak. I'm only here because I want to see if we can make a case against the mayor. If you don't want me here, just say so."

Freak nodded at me, "Did you give him that same speech?"

Dougie smiled slightly, "Actually, Blake did it for me, but yes."

"If he didn't tell you to leave, I won't. You threw him in jail before you threw me in. What do you mean 'if'? Didn't that recorder have supporting evidence?"

Blake answered, "Yes and no. The recorder only has video. Our theory is that the blow to the head that knocked out the great detective also knocked loose the microphone connection. The video proves the mayor was there when it happened, and you can see him carrying the blow torch, which is suggestive. However, other than that, it will be his word against yours."

Dougie cleared his throat, "Unfortunately, due to the mistakes my office has already made on this case that makes it the word of two suspects against the word of the right honorable Mayor of Mesquite, whose daughter is the victim."

"What about the arson? That occurred in Palo Pinto County, what about that angle?" I wasn't too hopeful, but I had to ask.

Dougie shook his head, "They're not even treating it as arson. Don't underestimate the mayor's influence in that little town. Also, grass fires are too common out here. You'd never find twelve people to put on a jury who don't live in fear of their own place falling victim to one."

"Our only chance is to convict him of being responsible for the death of his daughter."

Freak screeched, "And his grandchild!"

"And your child, Freak. When we get him for one, we'll get him for both." I tried to sound reassuring by saying 'when' instead of 'if'. "Did anybody even question the mayor after the fire?"

Dougie shook his head, "If anybody did, it's not in the record. By the way, my boss wants me to drop this, but I'm not going to do it. If you can get me anything, I'll force it. If nothing else, maybe we can get him to cop a plea to something."

Whether it was a dream or a hunch or just wishful thinking, it was time to find out about that hotel. "Blake, do you have the phone number for the Rodeo Bar?"

"Excuse me?"

"We need to talk to April; she might be able to help."

"Even though you're almost certainly delirious, I'll trust you on this one." He pulled out his cell phone and made a call.

"Ana Marie, it's me. Can you get me the phone number for Walt's, I mean for The Rodeo Bar on Commerce?"

He held for a while then wrote down a number and thanked her. He dialed again immediately. "May I speak to April?" He looked at me suspiciously as he waited. Then she obviously picked up. "April, this is Blake; Carl needs to speak to you. Can you hold on a second?"

He handed me the phone. It hurt to hold it to my ear, but it had to be done. "April, do you remember the room number at that hotel in Arlington?"

"I don't remember it, but he sent it by text message, I'm sure I can get it. Hold on."

I held on, and she came back on shortly with the room number. I thanked her, and she told me to give her love to Emily. I promised I would. I handed the phone back to Blake and turned to Emily.

"April sends you her love." I then turned to Dougie, "How long would it take to get a warrant to search a hotel room in Arlington?"

"That's Tarrant County, so I'll need their cooperation, but I have friends over there. What's your reason?"

"The mayor recently arranged to meet a young lady there. He sent her the room number before he even got to the hotel and left without checking out. I think that might mean he keeps the place all the time for his affairs. It's probably not under his own name, but I'm sure his fingerprints will be on something, unless that hotel has the world's best maid."

Dougie nodded his head. "The mayor is keeping a hotel room as a stabbin' cabin? Don't that beat all? That's worth checking out. Let me go make some phone calls."

After he left, Blake looked at me. "I doubt if he has friends in Tarrant County, or anywhere else. On the other hand, I do. I'm going to make some calls, too. You should go to your room, you look terrible."

Emily agreed, "The nurse should be coming by with your pain medication soon." She looked at Freak and winked, "The hero here should probably sleep, also."

As Emily stood up to push me out, Freak stopped her, "Before he goes back, can we have a few minutes alone?"

When we were alone, he asked, "How likely are they to find something in that hotel?"

"That depends on how cocky the mayor is. He may be so sure nobody knows about the place that he has something hidden there, or he may not. If they don't, I'll keep at it."

"If nobody finds anything before I get out of here, I'm going to take care of it myself." His trademark petulance was missing. His voice was low, calm, and full of menace.

I knew exactly what he meant. I also knew nobody would be able to talk him out of it. As Emily pushed me back to my room, I wondered if I even wanted to talk Freak out of it. I very much hoped I wouldn't have to make that decision.

I don't remember much of the next few days. I drifted in and out of morphine induced slumber as Emily held my hand. I had several visitors, but I wasn't coherent during most of them. That changed at two o'clock Thursday afternoon when Emily woke me.

"Blake's on the phone. You'll want to hear this." She said as she handed me the receiver.

Blake sounded like he was about to explode with excitement, "You did it, Hotshot! We've got him nailed. Kenth's getting the arrest warrants now. You were right about that hotel room. He must have been certain nobody would ever connect him to it."

"Slow down, Blake. What did they find?"

"Well, they found your gun with his prints on it. It will certainly match the bullet they pulled out of your leg. But that's just the start. He also had several types of date rape drugs and sexual pictures of himself with at least twenty girls.

"Not all of the pictures appear to be consensual, either. His wife isn't going to be happy to see those, I'm sure. But here's the best part. He had a computer in there which he apparently used to surf for porn.

"But he also used it to download a few other documents. Included in those documents were instructions on how to perform an abortion. The boy is toast. Even Larry Joe couldn't get him out of this."

"Has Freak heard this?"

"No, Kenth just called me a second ago to tell me it was safe to start telling people. Of course, I called you first."

"Thanks, I'll go tell him."

Emily went and got the nurse. It took a little effort, but we finally convinced her that giving a burn victim good news could only help his recovery. Freak was awake when Emily rolled me in.

"We got him, Freak. He's going to jail for a long time, maybe forever. Even better, if he does ever get out, his life is ruined."

"I knew you could do it. Tell me about it."

"We did it, Freak. Without you, I'd be a charred corpse by now, and the mayor would be trying to find a way to blame you for that."

When I finished telling him about the hotel room and its contents, he asked, "Do you realize what this means?"

"It means he's going to jail."

"Not that, Dummy. It means you're about to be a wealthy man."

"How do you figure that, Freak?"

"The reward offer doesn't say anything about depending on who gets convicted. Larry Joe drafted it, and he made sure of that. He's not only going to jail, he owes you a half a million dollars for putting him there."

I had forgotten all about the reward. However, I liked the idea of collecting it. I especially liked the idea of collecting it from the perpetrator. Irony can be very ironic. I especially liked the irony of turning a nice profit from a case I didn't even want to take. At that point, I was pretty happy I'd accepted the Freak Show case.

42   Beautiful Friendship

On the Friday before Labor Day, Freak was transferred to Parkland's burn unit. For the next six weeks, he had a steady stream of visitors. My leg still hurt, but I could finally walk without assistance.

I checked in on him almost every day. Emily came with me when she could, but she got the promotion at work and was often too busy. Sometimes, there wasn't much to talk about, but we discovered he shared our love of old movies.

Emily and I continued to keep date night, so Blake and Jade always went to Parkland on Tuesday. Freak's morale was doing pretty well, considering his losses. Bobby Jo, April, Sam The Man, Larry Joe, and Daniel also made frequent visits. By October, April was spending more time with him than any of us.

The Cannellys and Dougie made occasional visits, and even Ezekiel flew in from Vegas to check on him. When it was just Freak and me, we often talked about old movies or entertained ourselves doing impressions. Sometimes, he asked questions about detective work. Blake told me police work was a frequent topic on his visits, as well.

Fittingly, it was on Friday the thirteenth that Freak told me he was being released the following Monday. He demanded a celebration, and he insisted that he pay for it. April arranged for the group to have the Rodeo Bar to ourselves the following Tuesday.

Tuesday evening, Emily and I walked from my place to the Rodeo Bar. When we got there, Blake and Jade were the only ones there. Daniel arrived next and sat down beside Emily. "My attendance at a celebratory occasion is atypical. However, it is patently manifest that tonight's soiree is obligatory."

Bobbie Jo came in next. I was pleased to note that she didn't have a purple box with her when she came in. Just in case though, I was happy she didn't take the open seat beside me. She sat beside Daniel, and he immediately started a conversation with her regarding 'the complexities of deliberation regarding the behavior of arachnoids.'

The others began drifting in fairly soon. Larry Joe had a big smile on his face when he came in. He walked directly to me and took the open seat. "Pardner, welcome to life at the top. Your reward check is locked up in my office as safe as an invisible harrow hawk."

I still don't know how safe an invisible harrow hawk might be, but I said nothing as Larry Joe continued. "That polecat is trying to wheedle out of most of the charges, but he's already offered a plea of involuntary manslaughter regarding his daughter's death. As soon as he did, I hit him with the request for the reward money. He tried to refute it. Hell, he even threatened to countersue me if I sued him for it. But when his wife got wind of all that, she just wrote out the check herself."

"I bet I know how she got wind of it, don't I?"

He actually blushed slightly, but he didn't reply.

"Thanks, Larry Joe. I'll be by to pick up the check when I get a chance. How much do I owe you? Is it a flat fee or a percentage?"

"All part of my work for my real client. You don't owe a thing. Of course, if y'all want to retain me for financial counseling or estate planning, I'm expensive, but I'm worth it."

Emily answered, "I think I'll be taking on those roles, Larry Joe. Thanks for the offer, though."

"Fair enough, little lady. I was just making an offer." He turned toward me, "Besides, I got a hunch me and you are gonna' be thicker'n grits and gravy pretty soon. I reckon it's better to have somebody else handling your money."

I had no idea what he was talking about, but that wasn't unusual. Larry Joe took the seat beside me and started a conversation with Blake who was on his other side.

Freak and April were the last to arrive, and Freak was positively beaming. I'm sure he wasn't the first guy to beam when escorted some place by April, but somehow I doubted if that was why he was beaming.

As they came in, Larry Joe and Daniel left the chairs beside Emily and me. Freak sat beside me and April sat by Emily. I could tell Freak had something planned and that Larry Joe and Daniel were co-conspirators.

I also realized that the table was arranged so everybody could look at the four of us. Freak ordered a coke for himself and a white wine for April. April's boss and one of her co-workers were handling the party, and they brought the drinks quickly.

When everybody had their drinks, Freak stood up. "Everybody, I propose a toast. Here's to new beginnings and happier endings!"

We all toasted; then everybody but Freak sat back down. I guess I should say, everybody sat down but Freak and me. He held my arm as I started to sit, and soon we were the only ones standing.

He raised his glass to mine again. "To new beginnings with new partners; I want to buy forty-nine percent of Pegasus Investigations. How much do you want for it?"

His friends and mine all applauded, and I began to suspect I'd been set up. "You want to invest in my agency? I guess Larry Joe's not that good a financial advisor after all."

"You don't understand, Dude. I don't just want to invest. I want to be your partner. We can make Pegasus Investigations what it used to be. Hell, we can make it more than that. We can make it the biggest, baddest agency in the southwest.

"You already told me you couldn't have solved this one without me, and look how much you made on it. With your experience and my unique gift, we'll reinvent the business. This is what I was born to do. Hell, even if we suck, it'll take years to burn through that reward money and the amount I can invest right now. By then, I'll be twenty-five and my trust fund will have vested. We can't fail."

266

I thought about what he was saying. It was the last thing I'd expected to hear, but it made sense. Heck, I'd been pretty much failing on my own for almost two decades. Freak had helped tremendously on the most profitable case I'd ever had. Maybe we could do it again.

I turned to Emily, "What do you think?"

"What do I think of you taking on a wealthy partner? I'm an accountant, what do you expect me to think?" She stood up and kissed me. "Go for it. Think how happy the old man will be to see Pegasus back on the map."

I turned back to Freak. "I guess we're going to be partners."

As I shook hands with my new partner, Emily and April hugged. I had most definitely been set up. I'd never seen Freak this excited, "Man, it's going to be great. We're gonna make Pegasus Investigations a legend."

"Sure, we will, Freak," I told him. Then I continued with my best Bogart impersonation… "the stuff that dreams are made of."

"You bet we will, but I don't think I want to be called Freak anymore. I'm sticking with the name my parents gave me. By the way, your Bogart impersonation still sucks."

"Well, if we're going to be partners, you might as well get used to not being called by your real name. It seems to go with the territory."

"I'm already used to it." He smiled, then used his Bogart voice to again call me by a name that isn't mine, "Louis, I think this is the beginning of a beautiful friendship."

"It just might be, Freak. It just might be."

"My friends don't call me Freak anymore."

ACKNOWLEGEMENTS

Brian and Lezlie would like to thank:

Our friends and family who supported us by being encouraging when we needed encouragement; being honest when we needed honesty and somehow knowing when to do which; but mostly, for always being there. Without y'all, this novel might not have been started.

And everybody; friends, family, strangers who became friends and strangers who remain strangers, who showed a little interest in the novel along the way and inspired us to include some part of you in a character or chapter. Without y'all, this novel might not have been as interesting.

Brian also thanks:

The waitresses who never complained when one guy with a laptop camped at a four-top for hours at a time, night after night, especially those who gently reminded me that social networking isn't the same as working on a novel. Without y'all, this novel might not be finished.

Lezlie also thanks:

My husband, Mark, who has never once threatened to have me committed, despite the fact that I sometimes talk aloud to the characters in my head. Without his patience and love this novel might have been partially written from a padded room.

www.ingramcontent.com/pod-product-compliance
Lightning Source LLC
Chambersburg PA
CBHW071129170626
46809CB00002B/545